This edition first published 2020 by Fahrenheit Press.

ISBN: 978-1-912526-96-3

10 9 8 7 6 5 4 3 2 1

www.Fahrenheit-Press.com

F 4 E

Deer Shoots Man

(then steals his cigarettes)

By

Tyler Knight

Fahrenheit Press

For William Goldman

Raymond Chandler once said, “Dead men are heavier than broken hearts.”

Bullshit.

"...fuck..."

"What's wrong?"

"You're slipping..."

"What do you mean, I'm slipping? Ain't you done this before?"

"Not really," I say, "Usually, I'm really trying to kill somebody."

"Ain't that some shit," Chauncey says, "Hanged by my ankles by the one assassin who's not tryna to kill me."

"Here... Take my hand."

"What's the point?"

"To pull you up!"

"No, the point of all this bullshit if you ain't tryna kill me?"

"Interrogation is more effective with a threat of death behind it. Saw it in a movie, I think."

"Amateur."

"Grab it!" I say, "...come on, try again!"

"I can't reach. Hold on to me with both hands! Don't let go!"

"Trying... Oh no," I say.

"Don't let me go!"

"I'm so sorry..."

"Oh, Lord Jesus, please don't let this motherfucker drop me!"

"Tell me where you hid the hPEG file..."

"It's in my iGlasses," he says, "You drop me and break them, your ass might as well jump, too."

"Cool, that was easy. Here we go."

I start to pull him up.

"Hold up, you was fakin'? You wasn't gonna drop me?"

"You kidding? Sal would shank me personally."

"Asshole!"

"Yeah, you know," I say, "the threat of death and all..."

"Shit, I got osteoporosis. At my age, fallin' asleep can kill me."

"Don't make me laugh!"

He laughs, and I join him.

"A'ight, now," he says, "Can we wait to give each other reach arounds 'til after you pull me up?"

I put my hips into the rail for leverage and lift.

I say, "You know how to use iGlasses?"

"Yeah, man. I had my optometrist fit 'em into my Gazelles frames. You think all us old heads still be stuck on hand-held phones?"

"You should at least upgrade to a Vaunt."

"Naw, man. They nerdy and you can't customize them."

I'm lifting Chauncey over the railing by his bunny slippers when his feet slide out of them and, just like that, I'm holding empty shoes. I catch his last words as he slips from my grasp and falls:

"You cocksuck--"

Thud.

Chauncey impacts with a bubble wrap tarp spread across the marble floor and red mist spritzes from his mouth like a blast of air freshener.

Spine - Knee – Bubble Wrap: Snap! CRACKLE! POP!

The puff hangs in the air before dissipating, raining down upon the tarp.

I sit down on the landing with my back against the railing and set the slippers down beside me, handling them like a pair of soufflés. Then I look at my hands... My ring finger looks like a mastiff chewed it off past the first knuckle on a tan line still new enough to be crisp, like some fucked-up "Maim Here!" mark. My pinky is straight-up gone. You take for granted how critical pinkies are for navigating everyday-life tasks like, say, holding onto an octogenarian gangsta rapper until you lose one... A pinky, not a rapper.

With Chauncey dead, even if I hand over the hPEG file to Sal I'm fucked...

I could pretend I never found him, but if I return empty-handed, I'm fucked...

If I leave the hPEG file and run... Yep. Fucked.

Good evening, sir, this is Life Alert. We've detected a fall. Would you require our assistance this evening?

Fuck!

This voice, posh and female, sounds hollow like a recording from a doll that speaks when you pull its cord.

I peer over the railing... Chauncey's corpse is splayed across the plastic. Knees bent the wrong way like a cricket's. Mouth twisted and tongue out. Face frozen into a rictus of shock reserved for stumbling upon your wife in the act of fellating the village idiot.

Fuck! Fuck! Fuck!

Hello? Mr. Trustfall. Are you well?

Yes, Trustfall. Under the circumstances the irony is as hilarious as a public hanging. His generation began this trend... reverting to a time when a surname reflected something meaningful about its owner: a trait like 'Esposito' (little husband), or an occupation like Miller or Smith which, because of machine automation, those names are as endangered as the professions they once described. Chauncey parlayed his fame as a gangsta rapper into a career as a motivational speaker.

Mr. Trustfall?

The voice is coming from Chauncey's body. The juxtaposition of the accent crashing against the visuals is jarring, like Samuel Jackson's performance in *Snakes on a*

Plane dubbed by Dame Judy Dench. Exquisite corpse is exquisite.

At the moment, this is the least of my concerns.

Okay, I'll just tell Sal that he jumped.

No, better... He tried to make a run for it but he slipped...

Dame Judy says,

Please don't fret, sir," "We've dispatched paramedic and LAPD assault drones to your GPS location. They shall arrive in—

Dame Judy finishes her sentence in a computerized voice:

—thirty seconds.

Fucking AGI surrogate.

I shout over the balcony, down to the corpse, "It's cool, I'm fine!"

Very well, sir. We shall cancel the dispatch--

"Thank you!"

--as soon as you recite your passcode.

Out of growing desperation, I try to imitate Chauncey as best I can.

"It's all good, playa! False alarm!"

Getting into character, I grab my dick for emphasis but feel stupid when I remember she can't see me.

Your password, please. Twenty seconds remaining.

I run down a flight of stairs, across the loggia, and down another flight.

Ten seconds.

I say, "I'm old as fuck and I don't remember things like I used to. Can you give me a hint?"

I'm terribly sorry, but I'm afraid that would be an egregious violation of protocol... Three seconds. Two...

I'm rifling through Chauncey's pockets, searching for his wallet when his lips move and he speaks:

"November eleventh, two thousand sixteen."

I stifle a scream and pee a little.

Thank you, sir. How may I conclude this call to your satisfaction?

"Go fuck yourself," Chauncey says.

Very good, Mr. Trustfall. Please enjoy the rest of your evening and, if you would, complete the email survey. Thank you for choosing Life Alert!

The birthday on my Wikipedia page, the one everyone sees when they Google me, is inaccurate. He recited it correctly... That, and his last name... A realization hits me like a punch to the gut. With a sledgehammer.

I say, "Where's your Life Alert? I can call the triage drones!"

"Nigga, I'm looking at the backa my knee. If I live, my life is over."

Matter oozes out of the hole where an eye should be, like yolk taking its time through a cracked egg.

I crouch next to his good eye so he can see me.

"When I was a kid," I say, "I never allowed myself to imagine what it'd be like to meet you."

"I been following your career. You was doing real good in your title fight 'til you started gettin' fancy and got knocked the fuck out."

"Happens."

"No, Oranjello. Shit happens, you done fucked up."

"There's a lot more to it than that... And, I go by DeShawn."

"Why your middle name? OJ makes more sense."

"An assassin named OJ," I say, "Yeah, that's much better."

Chauncey's inhalations come as wet sucking, like the last drops of a milkshake coming up the straw.

"Do you want a Vicodin—"

"No."

"—or a drink?"

"I'm in recovery. One sip, I'm dead at the base of a Motel 6 toilet by Monday."

His laugh is raspy. I nod.

I say, "I'm not a killer... I've never killed anyone before."

"No shit, boy. Stick around for a hot minute ... You gonna watch that change in real time."

"Why'd you give me a stupid name if you knew it would make my childhood hell."

"I read the name in *Freakanomics*. Thought it was an Iceberg Slim book... Be happy I didn't name your ass Chauncey Trustfall, Jr."

I smile.

Chauncey says, "Do me a solid."

"Sure."

"Reach in my pants and pull out what you find."

I stare at him.

"Go on now, boy. I ain't got time to fuck around."

I reach into his pants and my fingers brush against something solid.

"Pull it out, nigga!"

I sigh.

I liberate from his pants... a metal case the size and shape of a deck of playing cards... It's locked.

The case glows with warmth from being stashed next to

his balls, and it's way heavier than its size suggests it has any right to be... Embossed on its side, a symbol worn nearly smooth as though from heavy handling:

शवि

I run my thumb over the script... The symbol depresses like a button, followed by a prick on my finger. The case says, "DNA match: 100%."

It clicks unlocked.

I inspect my thumb where the case stuck me. A droplet of blood, already coagulating to a bead.

Inside the case, menthols with a piece of wrapper yellowed with age that reads: Pall Mall, 'In Hoc Signo Vinces'... and a windproof torch lighter.

Before I can ask Chauncey about the case, he says, "Fire up one of them smokes for me, would ya?"

"Cigarettes will kill you."

"Yeah. But it takes a long time."

"How are you going to smoke with your face all fucked up?"

He coughs.

"You gonna do it for me. Take a hit to get it going, and stick the filter in my neck hole."

I pull his turtleneck down. A gold-plated neck stoma glints in the light. A microprocessor whirs, and the valve which allows Chauncey to talk dilates. I light a Pall Mall, puff at it to get it going, and jam it into the stoma. Perfect fit. Chauncey closes his lips, and there's a wet sucking sound as the cigarette jammed into his throat glows orange and then greys over with ash. He holds his breath and a plume of smoke seeps out of his eye socket and then he exhales, blasting smoke out of his nostrils. I remove the cigarette to flick the ash, and smoke pours from the stoma like a smoking gun... I take a drag from it and stuff it back into his neck. We take turns, sharing the menthol. I grind it out on the tarp when it's done.

Strange... The cigarette case is still just as warm to the touch as it was when I took it out of his pants when any conduction of body heat from his skin to the case should have faded by now.

I try to stuff it back down inside his pants, but he says, "You hold it for me. Consider it your inheritance."

I heft it up and down in my palm.

I say, "You smoke menthols from a cigarette case made of lead you keep stashed against your nuts? No wonder I came out fucked up."

"Sheee-it, it ain't lead. I ain't tryna die of no lead poisoning!"

The metal's surface is tarnished like a spoon.

I say, "Long-term silver exposure is toxic too."

"Naw, nigga, it ain't no silver neither!"

"Good. I was beginning to question your sanity."

"It's plutonium... Wait, come back, you pussy! It's safe to touch! A'ight now, sit your ass down... Pick it back up... Alpha rays can't get past your skin..."

I sit.

"Don't be hidin' it up your asshole and you'll be cool... Keep that shit next to your junk, like a man do..."

I say, "Do you write greeting cards?"

"...And don't try and fuck it neither... I'm just saying... It be all toasty next to your dick... A man gets to thinking..."

"I think I'm good on that."

"In Pelican Bay we made fifi bags with sandwich baggies and Jell-O from the cafeteria... You wanna keep 'em between your thighs so they be nice and soft when you ready to f-"

"Amazing. You just fucked up my childhood retroactively."

"I'm just sayin'... The government be after my ass for my

secrets..."

"Right."

Time increases between each of his breaths. He's gathering the strength to speak again. I wait. When he speaks again, his words come in a series of gasps on and whispers out.

He says, "...the file's a recipe, too... but ain't the main ingredient Sal wants... stay away from Sal... no matter what."

"What's up with the James Bond bullshit for some stale-assed menthols?"

He says, "...it ain't about what you put in the case... it's what you put the case in..."

Chauncey's neck is no longer strong enough to keep his head upright. His head lolls to the side.

He says, "...you're a twin..."

"Who? Where's my twin?"

The muscles in his face slacken. Though his one remaining eye is aimed at me, he no longer tracks me nor anything else on this plane of existence.

"...with... your mother."

"But my mother's gone... Hey! Hey!"

A moment passes...

Then another...

And another.

A pink froth of bubbles spills from his lips.

"...no shit, boy..."

Those words come as a wheeze. I lean my face close to his to understand him better.

"...I killed her first."

Chauncey headbutts me in the eye and I recoil backward.

"Sonovabitch!"

My vision tears over. I rub my eye. When it clears, I look down upon Chauncey. He lays still, and foam no longer bubbling, clings inert on his lips.

I rifle under his turtleneck finding his Life Alert pendant

on a golden rope chain, blinged out and covered in diamonds. I let it slip from my fingers without me pressing the button... Nausea overwhelms me in back-arching fits that threaten to snap my spine. I stand and rest my hands upon my knees, but when I bend over and open my mouth, nothing comes up. After the dry heaving passes, I wipe the spittle from my lips and catch my breath. I study the man at my feet. A faint hint a brine on his clothes...

"Who were you?"

A hermit crab plushie scampers up to me: Jacquelin, my AGI-enabled plushieBot.

It says,

A vehicle is pulling into your driveway. A Los Angeles Police Department robbery-homicide cruiser!

The doorbell chimes.

I lift Chauncey's shoulders to move him but his bones crumble inside of his skin like pretzel sticks in the bottom of a lunch sack.

The doorbell chimes again.

Without thinking I wipe my hands onto my shorts, smearing them with blood and bone. I pocket his iGlasses and pivot to escape out the back door when an idea strikes me... I run into the laundry room and return with a laundry bag.

There's a beep from the security terminal next to my front door.

Jacquelin says,

Access Granted!

The door swings open as I'm dumping the last of the soiled training clothes on top of the corpse.

She lets herself in and assesses the columns of moving boxes, me, and the tarp, everything - all before the door has finished closing itself behind her.

I say, "You can't just barge in like that!"

She walks straight to the tarp, stopping with the toes of her Doc Martins at its edge. We stand face to face, with Chauncey stiffening under the clothes pile between us.

She says, "What's the point of trying to evade me when you know it's inevitable that I'll catch up to you?"

"If I'm inconsistent you'll think I'm up to something."

"You're always up to something."

Something at her feet catches her attention.

She squats down to her haunches and her leather motorcycle jacket falls open to expose a vintage Joy Division t-shirt and her detective's badge with gun rig. Without touching anything, she examines speckles of blood on the tarp that are no larger than the size of a pencil tip. Then she peruses me: My breathing; my language, both the spoken and body variety; my clothes, where her attention fixates on the bloody handprint smeared onto my shorts.

She stands, glaring at me with naked disgust. Her hands go to her hips so her arms are akimbo. One hand finds its way to the butt of her gun and rests there.

She says, "Go ahead. Start lying."

"I smothered my dad and left him for dead under the pile of laundry."

"No, smart ass," she points at the blood with a toe, "This is impact spatter. I'm sick of telling you to change at the gym on sparring days and dump your workout clothes in the washing machine. In. The fucking. Washing machine! What'd you do, strip your clothes and fling them from the top of the stairs?"

"You need a new argument, Shonda. You don't live here anymore."

"Yeah, and in three days neither will you. I'm done fighting... Come on. Let's get this over with so we can go back to being strangers."

She steps over the laundry to a pair of kitchen stools and

pulls one up to the tarp. The stool she didn't choose, caddy corner to hers, has a display case on its seat. Matted behind the glass, a Miss New Jersey sash and tiara.

I say, "You forgot these. Framed them for you."

She nods but makes no effort to reach for the case.

In a quick motion, I take the case off the stool and sit on top of the Valentine's Day card the case was covering. Shonda pretends not to notice, and I pretend not to notice her pretending. 2,266 days of marriage summed up in a single sentence.

She wears a black Penrose circle pinned to the lapel of her leather jacket. An urge to let out an audible sigh bubbles up in my chest, but I suppress it because, no... I won't repeat that mistake...

Shonda says, "Smoking again?"

"No... Yeah."

A trace of a smile across her lips. I could never outright lie to her, so I learned to hide my lies inside of the truth.

"DeShawn, you still have some time to get your shit together.

But not for much longer."

"Nice."

"If only you were less nice."

"What do you want from me?"

"Balls!"

I say, "Sure. Step into my time machine."

"Oh, please. Like you'd do anything differently."

"Like different would matter?"

"I'd have set them straight."

"How does standing up for myself mean letting my wife do it for me?"

"It's called teamwork."

"You don't bring a wife to a gunfight."

"You do if she packs a .45."

"I screwed up and they made their decision... I'm not meant to be an inspiration. I'm a reminder."

The way she's looking at me... Sadness? No... This is pity.

My hands shake. She reaches across the tarp and takes mine in hers and stills them... She's not wearing her ring. I guess I expected that, but...

I say, "We almost made it, right?"

She nods towards a stack of moving boxes. She says, "This is what a lifetime of 'almosts' looks like."

She gives my hand a squeeze before withdrawing hers to pull a stack of documents bound by paper clamps out of her messenger bag.

Divorce papers.

"Seriously? It's fucking Valentine's Day."

She hands them to me with a pen on top. The divorce papers are printed on a thicker stock with a slight gloss finish like her Valentine I'm sitting on... Fancy, like this is an occasion for celebration.

I say, "I've got some deals in the works."

"Christ. Forget marriage, we're not even in the same conversation."

"I'm ready for couples counseling."

"Now you're ready for therapy? You know, I should thank you. If you were supportive, I never would have found the Church of Galacticology."

"You "found" Galacticology like a lamb finds a wolf. They stole my wife."

"Excuse me!" she says, "I'm not an object, and I'm nobody's damn sheep."

I stare at the divorce papers and pretend to read them, but my eyes skim the same lines again and again.

Shonda breaks the silence by saying into her Vaunt, "Negative, dispatch. That's Beverly Hills and I'm 10-42 for the night."

With every part of the city outside of private property under surveillance down to the Planck length, you'd have to be desperate or stupid to rob or kill. Nevertheless, for Shonda business is good. She once told me the average person walks past 16 murderers within their lifetime, two of those being serial killers. At a sporting event of 80,000 attendees, your guaranteed to have three in attendance.

Shonda glares at me... She also told me that you're most likely to be murdered by the person you're closest to.

I use the display case on my lap as an ad hoc table, though the stack is thick enough that I probably don't need to. I put her pen to the first sheet's waxy surface to sign where indicated... But, her pen scratches dry and colorless grooves. I had her pen back to her and shrug.

She says, "I made flyers for my downline earlier, and forgot to switch out the paper tray before printing the docs. You got another pen?"

"Nope..."

She scrutinizes my face.

"Whatever, DeShawn. Leave the papers on the counter. I'll get them tomorrow."

I say, "You should take that call."

Shonda stands. For a while, she stares at my left hand long enough to be uncomfortable for both of us.

She says, "Where's the watch he bought for you?"

"Time stopped for me that day."

"God has forgiven us."

"God is bleeding. And, seriously? A God platitude from a member of the Church of Galacticology?"

"Religion aside, I'd make the same decision today. Some things are worse than-"

"Death is death. If there's a fate worse than death then people would compare fucked-up things to that fate instead of death."

"You don't need a time machine to visit the past. You're already trapped in it."

She stands and slings her bag over her shoulder and says into her Vaunt, "Copy that, dispatch. On my way. ETA 20 minutes."

I say, "Wait."

I hold the display case for her to take.

"You're forgetting this again."

Shonda says, "You think I forgot it the first time?"

She sighs, then levels me with a smile that floods my brain with all kinds of pleasure chemicals. There's a glimpse within her shift from when she decked a grabby host, live, on the Miss America show. An act which cost her the crown but earned her a tour of the talk show circuit and the title of America's Sweetheart.

She says, "Take off your shorts."

"I'm not feeling very sexy."

She tosses her handcuffs onto my lap. "I'll make you feel sexy... One last time."

I stand, then take her in my arms and kiss her on the forehead. "Be seeing you, baby girl."

She says, "Yeah, probably not a smart idea anyway."

"No."

"One more night, I'd shoot you in the face."

"One more night, I'd load your gun."

We laugh... Sort of.

She nods.

Watching a woman fall out of love with you within the space of a single conversation is to observe her shape-shift in real time to a three-dimensional memory of what you've had. The person you're observing now looks like her but it's not. She's gone. This is someone different.

Jacquelin says,

DeShawn. A friendly reminder that the medications in your cabinet are past their expiration date.

Shonda kisses my hand and says, "Goodbye, Dee."

Jacquelin says,

Happy Valentine's Day, Shonda!

Shonda opens the front door and punts Jacquelin out of it. She leaves, and the door clicks shut behind her.

I touch the seat of the stool she was sitting in... feeling her warmth fade as entropy steals it away... People... The shit we do in the private moments when nobody else is watching... What's wrong with me?

We met when I was bleeding on a stool in a cage and she was a Bellum ring girl. Between rounds she said hello, and that was that. In that instant I knew that my last time saying goodbye to a woman I'd love was behind me... Shows what I know, right?

Jacquelin re-enters the house through a pet-door flap.

I run to the bathroom and lean over the toilet and retch blood into it, punctuated by spitting bits of stomach lining into the basin. I put the fire blazing in my throat out by running my mouth under the faucet, swallowing, swishing a mouthful of water around then spitting it out into the sink. Above the sink, a reflective energy door.

"Jacquelin," I say, "Unlock medicine cabinet."

Yes, DeShawn.

The mirror fades away to reveal shelves full of inhalers. All of the medicines unopened, set to expire with their holographic seals intact.

I reach past the inhalers and grab a device from a shelf that resembles a meter a diabetic would use to test glucose levels.

Its readout from yesterday says, "96," in yellow numbers.

I hit RESET, and prick an index finger.

I wait...

The display skips numbers and chirps:

86.

Red numbers.

Swell.

I snap the meter in two and toss it into the trash can on the way out of the bathroom. I go back for an inhaler.

Back in the foyer, I uncover Chauncey, then flip one of his legs down and out of the way to its natural position and pull his iGlasses off his face. Cracked lenses. I put it on my face and it powers up right away. Although it's not fitted to my facial geometry, the fit is surprisingly close... But because my eyesight is superior to his, the VCSEL-projected imagery is way off and my eyes keep chasing a focal point that always seems to be disappearing around the next corner. But it works.

I use my date of birth for the password.

Open files...

And search for an encrypted hPEG folder, aaaand...

ROKO'S BASELISK SURVIVAL GUIDE (for Dummies)

"...da fuck?"

Whatever. Good to go. I message Sal about the entire situation from Chauncey's iGlasses.

This outdated tech hurts my eyes so I snatch it off. I sit with my back against the front door and wait.

Without turning around to look, I can tell you all about the horizontal hatch marks carved into the door jamb. That each mark has a corresponding date. That from my seated position, the lines start at a shoulder height and rise to eye level where the last mark terminates. And that the name, Miles is carved atop them all. I can describe for you all these things because I put them there. I reach behind me and run my fingers across scarred wood, reading it like Braille.

The iGlasses chirp and the reply to my message comes:

"Leave the body. Bring the file. Wear a cup."

Just then, a moan from under the laundry pile. I rush over

and uncover Chauncey's face... Still alive!

I press his Life Alert button. When the next dispatcher asks what the emergency is, I explain and request triage drones, leaving an open a window for them. I collect the laundry and the tarp from Chauncey's body and dump them in the laundry room where I change into clean clothes. A different pair of board shorts, and a hoodie from the Inosanto Academy of Martial Arts where, before I was excommunicated from the clan, I was a fifth-generation instructor of Bruce Lee's Jeet Kune Do, Indonesian Pentjak Silat, Filipino weapons art Escrima, and 10th Planet Jiujitsu.

"Jacquelin," I say, "What's the point of Valentine's Day?"

Valentine's Day commemorates the date when the martyr Valentine of Terni was stoned to death. He was executed at the behest of Emperor Aurelian for wedding lovers in secret against Roman law.

But I already knew that... One side effect for the brand of human I am (chill, you'll figure out what I mean by this soon enough!) is near total recall of useless trivia. (And if you think these hyperlinks are annoying then imagine how I feel!)

I dump Shonda's card into the recycling bin.

~

The garage door scrolls upward against the night sky with the foreboding of emergency broadcast text ascending a TV screen to reveal... Ashes drift down, smothering palm trees and burnt-out cars under a film of grey snow.

Christmas eve in reverse.

I pull my hoodie down to shield my head from the soot, and the surgical mask up over my face to minimize breathing particulates into my lungs that used to be other things: sofas, soiled diapers - God knows what. Flip flops slap at my heels, stirring up ashes as shuffle down my driveway.

The American dream thrived in this neighborhood until the Los Angeles Social Credit reforms looped a garrote around its neck and strangled all life from it one household at a time. Tonight, all the homes lay dark. It's silent except for a buzzing street-lamp wrapped with flyers of lost pets who will never find their ways back home.

A breeze as soft as a baby's sigh tickles my cheek. I catch the motion of something zipping out of peripheral vision and into my six o'clock, but I don't bother turning my head to track it. You'll never see a swarm of LAPD dragonFlies unless you're meant to see it and, had it determined that I was a threat, I'd be telling you my story through a Ouija board. If the swarm is patrolling out here, that means the surgical drones are inside tending to Chauncey.

A copy of the Los Angeles Sentinel sits on the curb, wrapped in its mylar bag. The fact that nobody read The Sentinel back when the average citizen was long-form literate beyond emojis and pictograms inoculated the newspaper to the decline of print media. When the Fourth Estate died, reading long form followed, going the way of writing cursive. I pick the paper up and sit on the newspaper-shaped nuclear shadow embossed within the ashes.

While I wait, I unwrap the paper from its mylar wrapping. the above-the-fold headline screams:

PRINCESS CHARLOTTE CAUGHT STEPPING OUT WITH VELOCIRAPTOR

...below the fold:

DEER SHOOTS MAN, THEN STEALS HIS CIGARETTES

... and, buried in a corner on page three:

FIRES, LOOTING RAVAGE SAN FERNANDO VALLEY

I hold a palm out to the flurries... Oily flakes the texture of shredded liquor store bags cling to my outstretched palm as though static charged.

The silence is shattered by a chiming within my skull only I can hear. An instant later, a heads-up display of blue text glows in my field of vision, always in the foreground at a perpetual arm's length.

My Vaunt chimes:

Friday, 2.14.2053 - 22:31:19 PST.
(1/1) Good Evening, DeShawn! Your Uber has canceled because your Social Credit is declined. Please raise your Q-SCore to the minimum acceptable level.
< archive |reply > | menu >>

I dismiss the message with a head motion you'd mistake for flicking bangs out of my face except for the fact that my 'fro is braided into cornrows.

I power up Chauncey's iGlasses and call another Uber using his celebrity-level Q-SCore.

My Vaunt chimes again:

Friday, 2.14.2053 - 22:31:48 PST.
(1/1) audio: Three-Day NOTICE OF SALE warning on your First United Credit Mortgage.
**Q-SCoreMoralityClause*
FUCM Bank, an equal housing lender!
< archive |PLAY > | menu >>

I don't play the message. Trust me, you do not want that

shit playing inside your head. megaCorps are notorious for encoding sub-frequencies within debt (to society) collection messages that cause erectile dysfunction in deadbeats until the Q-SCore balance is reconciled, in some fucked-up passive-aggressive eugenics.

Thank the Chinese for LA's Social Credit system. They implemented it in 2020, ostensibly as a means of measuring creditworthiness and behavior prediction of its citizens. The City of Los Angeles merged this concept with Q score, the celebrity's star power ranking system which determines who stars in movies or headlines at Coachella... Q-SCore was born.

Add to the list of consequences for low Social Credit, the government may revoke your social security; inability to qualify for healthcare; life insurance companies refusing to deal with you; and which neighborhood you are allowed to live in because you may only live in a neighborhood where an average residents' Q-SCore is equal to or lower than yours, but no matter how much money you have, you may not live in an area where you are outclassed. So, yeah... I've got until Monday to raise my score or the bank will exercise its Morality Clause and seize my home. The only place I can go is the San Fernando Ghetto.

A notification pops up, alerting me that my car is arriving. My knees ache at the thought of folding myself into a Prius.

A car approaches, washing me with its headlights and glides to a stop at the curb beside me... a Rolls Royce Phantom.

Well, shit. How you living, Chauncey?

I get in and the door slides shut behind me.

We exit the community's gates. The Phantom's energy shield, a wisp of blue light, travels a centimeter ahead of the car like colored smoke in a wind tunnel. It whisks away ashfall.

The Phantom's artificial general intelligence surmises

that I'm a classic hip hop kind of fellow and, without asking, changes from the sugary sweet NeoHipPop song to an audioCast of Gucci Mane's *Changed.* This happens to me every goddamn time. I mean, yeah... it's accurate... I love me some classic hip hop but what the fuck?

Whatever.

The Phantom says,

Welcome to Uber: Vaunted Service.
Would you care for a refreshment?

"No."

How about those Lakers—

"Shut the fuck up."

I put on my pre-AI era NIHL Headphones (no relation to noise-induced hearing loss syndrome) and drown song out with the only thing they play: white noise static traceable all the way back to the Big Bang.

I get funny looks whenever I wear my NIHLs in public. Nowadays headphones are as antiquated an affectation as wrist watches, drive-throughs and disco, but I keep a pair with me at all times. Walking down city streets. Ubers. Everywhere. It discourages the NLP-engineered small talk with the Uber's AI (or any human, for that matter). Bad enough being trapped in a car with another chatty passenger or a driver back when humans used to operate these things.

Who the fuck am I kidding? This is my jam! I stow my headphones in my hoodie's marsupial pocket.

The 2017 version of Mane, who today lives a Luddite existence as a neoZen cleric in the Alaskan tundra, laments about how hard it is to change.

A signal light flashes red. The bass thumps as we pull to a stop at the 405 freeway's onramp, awaiting our turn in the queue. To ease the burden of traffic, cars are released onto the freeway in groups of ten at intervals which are timed according to traffic demands.

The light flashes green and my back sinks into the seat as the onramp computer squirts my pod of cars onto the 405.

Rows of holoBoards arch over traffic like a herd of brachiosaurus grazing on neon palm fronds. Technicolor adverts scroll around their necks and up to the signage proper, creating an anamorphic illusion of continuity as our Uber drives past them like eyes following you in a painting. Each ad chases us from screen to screen, blending seamlessly in parallax to the city background until we've seen each newsVertisement play in its entirety.

Looming over the freeway, an elderly Dave Chappelle wrapped in a shawl sits in front of a crackling fireplace petting a kitten in his lap. Instead of a chyron crawl captioning him as he speaks, he holds up cue cards and flips through them for us to read:

Did you know that when you fall and hit your head, you can slip in and out consciousness several times in the first five minutes alone?

On the next holoBoard...

In fact, my neighbor laid on the ground for days only to have her kids discover her tabby, Ariana Fluffigton, eating her face...

Dave, following my car with his eyes as I drive underneath him, continues on the next holoBoard sign:

...It was Christmas time when H.R. FlufnStuf tripped me and sat on my chest waiting for me to pass away. And, to think my loved ones were in the very next room with no idea that I was all fucked up.

Dave holds up his Life Alert pendant wrapped in a crochet macaroon cozy hanging from a lanyard of yard around his neck. He continues on the next holoBoard:

Thank the Lord I had Life Alert! Don't fall victim to your cat. Get Life Alert before you need it. When kitty goes for the kill, it's already too late!

The next holoBoard airs a newsVertisement: A live feed of the riots and fires in the San Fernando Valley running split screen with Uncle Morte, the curmudgeonly grim reaper mascot for FallState Insurance, schlepping military junta coverage; followed by a newsVertisement blending a TMI update from the 127th Academy Awards hosted by the AIG sim Hope-RAH!, paired with a sales pitch for Fleeker, the new app for your in-ear Halo device so you can wear your HyperGram filters everywhere you go in real life!

The ad features motion-capture action star Andy Circus strutting down Farmer's Market using Fleeker to shapeshift into a panda on stilts... then into a dropped ice cream cone... then into ingenue Sévérine Falk, near-orgasmic from dopamine hits to her brain as she racks up hearts from strangers she passes and...

...back to a TMI report that Andy Circus has just died! Killed on set... his throat ripped out by a koala during a motion capture stunt gone wrong designed by special effects team, Dunning and Krueger, FX.

The Andy Circus Death Counter on the bottom of the screen clicks up like an analog odometer to 31, and a gong tolls.

But wait...

...the newsVertisement blends into a Life Alert ad showing Circus was saved again!

As the car drives under an overpass, a sensation vibrates throughout my body akin to a mild tingling if you sat on your hand. Sensors on its underside scan cars passing beneath it for life to ensure that all riders comply with mandatory carpool/rideshare law within LA. When the law designed to reduce Los Angeles traffic passed, human ride-share drivers went bye-bye overnight to optimize the extra seat space.

Traffic creeps into the Sepulveda Pass.

A cone-shaped funnel of glass balancing on its tip looms from a hillside. THE OTIUM. A football field wide at its base, radiating wider as our eyes travel up towards its 68th floor.

The Otium.

It's regarded as one of mankind greatest feats of engineering... because, earthquake country. The land it juts out of was previously home to the Skirball Cultural Center until they razed the museum to raise the hotel-casino/shopping center/office space.

The Otium's flickers from behind its energy field, rendering it with a distorted appearance as though you're observing it through a cascading waterfall.

Drones battle fires that lick at the hillsides on both sides of the freeway. The flames burn so near to the shoulders that when I lower the window to take pictures the heat bakes my cheeks as though I've opened an oven door.

My Uber crests the summit like a rollercoaster car at its apex, facing down.

Descending through the pass, I'm confronted by a panoramic view of lights into the Valley below. Dappling the landscape, lights from LAPD drones wink blue and National Guard drones a solid red as they cast down searchlights. LAFD HoverJets drop water, dousing intermittent stipples of fire glowing in the hills across the basin like a line of florescent crayon scumbled across black paper.

The car is supposed to take the 101 freeway but before we reach the interchange it makes a sudden shift into the exit lane for Mulholland Drive. The Phantom breaks into the music to tell me we've re-routed to pick up another passenger.

We slingshot down Benedict Canyon and coast into the pickup port in front of the Beverly Hills Hotel.

The door opens and a flash of red tumbles into the seat next to me. The audioCast changes its preference settings to 20th-century rock. The door slides itself shut and we pull away. Before the interior light cuts off, I notice the feet of the other passenger. White Chuck Taylors high-tops sodden with blood. A red and beaded ball gown slit to mid-thigh but torn the rest of the way to her pelvis, exposing livid claw marksF on her hip. Unrestrained by a seatbelt, she leans forward in the seat as though poised for something. Breasts exposed at the sides. The words, "*IN HOC SIGNO VINCES*," tattooed across her ribcage in all-caps Courier New font.

We turn onto Sunset Boulevard, passing under a nightclub marquis that splashes the car's interior with neon-flavored light. A sparkle snags my attention. Clutched in her hand... A decapitated Oscar statuette, flecked with blood... still moist.

My eyes jump to her face.

Peeking behind amber locks are eyes, money green, evaluating me. Gazing into the face of someone with perfect symmetry is unsettling, like locking eyes with a tiger at a zoo then discovering the glass between you is gone. A bruise on her cheek does nothing to diminish the harmony of all her features working in unison.

"Please, be funny."

"No pressure, right?"

"Life is pressure."

"You'll judge me for my off-color humor."

"I'm already judging you."

"And?"

She says, "You've got time for two more song changes to redeem yourself."

"What makes you think you're my type?"

"I'm young and blonde. I'm everybody's type. What happened to your eye?"

"My mouth."

"Care to elaborate?"

"I doubt it's as interesting as the story behind yours."

She smiles revealing teeth an unholy shade of white.

"I already know my story, DeShawn."

"How do you know who I am?"

She turns to her window and says to the glass, "You don't remember me. Shame."

"Who the hell doesn't know who you are? You're Sévérine Falk."

She turns to me, narrowing her eyes to slits. The gaze she focuses upon me evokes a sense of sinking exhilaration in my gut like the first time I skydived, stepping out of an airplane at 12,000 feet.

"I said, 'remember me,' not 'recognize me'."

Sévérine opens her mouth to speak, but lets her thought die without shaping it into words. Instead, she gives me a dismissive wave of her hand. She dumps her headless trophy on the seat cushion between us, dabs at her bruised cheek with a fingertip, then digs into a crocodile-skin bag large enough to stuff a grade schooler into.

Last year an insider leaked the value of the Oscar swag bags that each nominee in a major category received as worth $350,000. Included amongst the participation-trophy goodies, a stick of Chapstick that cures herpes (oral, not genital) on contact with next-gen CRISPR gene editing; a roll of toilet paper encoded to donate $1,000 to the World Food Programme each time you flush a square; a Halo (retail valued at $77,000) preloaded with apps that include one for a single-use GOD (Gyges Optical Diffuser) Mode, which is a civilian version of the military app developed by DARPA that renders you invisible(ish) for thirty seconds; Tragical Negro, a play on words of the magical negro character trope manifested as a holographic projection of a famous African American pop-culture character of your choice who acts as a sounding board to help you find solutions to problems; and a Rhett Kingly Vibrating Dildo that cures herpes (genital, not oral). This year, as if in an act of defiance to public outrage, the Academy doubled down and stuffed the same Shit-We-All-Get items into snake-skinned Hermes Birkin bags.

The song fades into Til Tuesday, *Voices Carry*.

Sévérine pulls an aspirin tin out of her bag, shakes some pills into her palm and returns all but one which isn't quite the same size as the others. She pops it into her mouth and swallows it dry.

I say, "Let me get one of those aspirins."

"You don't want these. They thicken the blood and cause headaches."

"In that case, give me two."

She hands me a couple and I eat them.

She says, "Let me help you out. Nine years ago. De Stijl."

"The Style?"

"De Stijl. As in, the Dutch art movement. It's the club in Stockholm decorated in primary colors."

"Like a Mondrian..."

"Correct," she says, "A painting... or that garish hotel up ahead."

I slouch in my seat and slide a hand down the front of my shorts.

"Hooray, mollies," I say.

The car turns onto Doheny, twisting through switchbacks and into the Bird streets above the city lights.

I take the inhaler out of my hoodie pocket. I twirl it between my fingers of my good hand, flipping it back and forth over my knuckles like you'd do a holoPen... I feel her watching me.

She says, "Where did you get that?"

"A Father's Day gift."

"Today is Valentine's Day."

"Come by for Thanksgivings. They're a riot."

"I'm certain you're alone Thanksgivings, too."

"Ironic humor."

"You're not funny, you're a dick. The irony is, you're clueless why."

"Enlighten me, Princess."

"No... No, I don't think I will."

"You think you're better than me because 15-year-olds like your CGI ass?"

"You've whored yourself out plenty... You've no idea the sacrifices I've made."

"At least I have my soul."

"We're both photons bouncing off a screen," she says. "Except your screen was a wee bit smaller, wasn't it?"

"Oh, mine's just right, Goldilocks."

"What's that saying about size versus motion?"

"When will you realize you could've had both?"

"When you took off your pants. By then it was too late."

"When you reach my age, I'll laugh in your face."

"When I reach your age, you'll already be dead... I didn't mean that."

"It's okay, I say, "This night can't end soon enough and it's just beginning."

"My stop is coming. Give me your Vaunt. Hurry up."

"Why?"

"Do you always talk your way out of getting laid?"

"Yes."

I hand her my Vaunt. The car passes a man with a tattoo-sleeved Latina in dolphin shorts beneath an umbrella... Walking a lion's-head rabbit.

"Hey," I say, "Was that Rhett Kingly? The holoPorn star?"

"He's a neighbor... But he introduced himself to me as Kent Light Yr., the screenwriter who wrote those space kola movies."

"Of course, he would... In Hollywood, the only thing lower than a screenwriter is a male porn star."

The Phantom stops in front of a mid-century Richard Neutra house.

She says, "Do you use WhatsApp? No. Figures."

She slides out of the Phantom.

"I have a Swedish number. This is easier."

Sévérine lobs my Vaunt back into the car. I make no attempt to catch it. It bounces off of my grinning face.

"Why don't I just come in?"

"I just tossed you a life preserver."

"Wouldn't I put the life vest on before I get wet?"

"I said preserver, not 'vest'. You're already drowning, baby."

"How's that?"

"Do you know what the greatest threat to a lifeguard's life is?"

I say, "Baywatch reruns?"

"That was funny. No, it's the drowning person they're rescuing. The victim holds on too tight dooming them both."

~

The Phantom stops in front of Jumbo's Clown Room. Despite the name, nothing about this establishment is funny.

Before the car door shuts itself behind me, I'm at a jog across the parking lot, peeling off my hoodie and stripping to the waist as I go. The club's door practically bursts off its hinges from the music banging on the other side of it. Next to the door, a plaque from the City of Los Angeles designating the Clown Room as a historical cultural landmark like the one at Sévérine's house. Next to that, a poster that says KARAOKE NIGHT.

The doorman wears his head shaved into a Lock of

Horus. An irradiated bandanna across his face filters the ash but exposes his glowing jawbone beneath it like an x-ray. A Heckler & Koch USP .45 tucked into his waistband. I toss him the inhaler I took from my medicine cabinet. He catches it and opens the door.

The boom, bap! of classic hip hop throttles my face the instant I enter. Across the space, a woman gyrates on a platform, shouting Lil' Kim's *Queen Bitch* into a microphone:

Lyrically, I dust em, off like Pledge
Hit hard like sledge-hammers,
bitch with that platinum grammar
I am a diamond cluster hustler
Queen bitch, supreme bitch
Kill a nigga for my nigga by any means bitch
Murder scene bitch
Clean bitch! Disease free bitch!
Check it...

Pushing through the sound waves to enter is like wading upstream in waist-high water.

At the far end, an MMA cage wedged between two pole dancer platforms, everything jammed within a space you'd have trouble u-turning a limousine within. A pole dancer spins an iron butterfly on one platform, but nobody pays attention to her. The crowd dances around the other platform where the music is coming from. Intermittent gaps in the crowd offer glimpses of the karaoke singer shaking her hips to the beat in Daisy Dukes, but even then, a ten-gallon hat hides her face. The song goes into a turntable solo and she thrashes about the stage, her Uggs boots kick the air as she leaps.

Bobby materializes from the crowd. We walk.

He hands me a tablet. His hands are Smurf blue.

I say, "FUCM Bank teller slip a dye pack in with the

cash?"

"Something like that..."

I skim the details on the tablet and hand it back to him.

I say, "This pay really isn't worth the risk."

"You want better risk? Rob a liquor store instead."

"That's a better idea except for one problem."

"What's that?"

I say, "No establishments in LA County carry cash anymore thanks to you."

"No, it's perfect, see? It's a felony even if you don't steal anything. I'll wait 'til you get away, then I'll turn your ass in... We'll split the reward."

Bobby always looks two sports bets gone wrong away from selling oranges under the freeway, but looks can be deceiving. The truth is, he's just one sports bet gone wrong from selling oranges under the freeway. He reeks of booze and there's a 90-proof sheen of sweat beading on his forehead that could power a funny car. He hasn't run a comb through his mullet in so long that the tail is starting to dred lock. When the light hits him just right, you'll catch a glimpse of lice and/or bed bugs playing Marco Polo in his beard... Chicks dig him.

He hands me a case which I open and take a mouthpiece out of and tuck behind my ear for safe keeping. I put my false teeth into the case and hand it back to him.

Bobby says, "You did it?"

I nod.

"How'd it go?"

"A man almost died because of you."

He nods.

"Now we're even."

A state athletic commission official appears and walks lockstep with us. He passes me a tablet... The name, "Bobby Money," is filled into the slot designated for my manager... I sign with a thumb scan and return it to the official without breaking stride.

I say, "You changed your last name."

Bobby says, "I come from a family of exterminators."

"So?"

"So, would you fuck a fight trainer named Bobby Roaches?"

"Freddie Roach did okay."

Bobby says, "He trained Pacquiao, and you ain't no champ. Besides, my name isn't Roach. It's Roaches. That's gotta be at least twice as fucked up."

"Why 'Money'?"

He shrugs.

"It's aspirational... And it gets me laid with all those Q-SCore celebutants... Bitches love irony."

I laugh.

"Nigga, please! A Vaunted girl risking her social credit to hook up with you? You look like you slept in a field."

"No, they're into that, bro. You have no idea how many I hook up with on the down low through the SlummR app. It's awesome."

The three of us stop at the stairs leading up to the cage.

A kid mad-dogs me from inside of it. Clint, the Cudgel. Son of the punk rocker, Chet Chernobyl. Clint paces back and forth, working himself into a pre-combat frenzy. He shouts at me, but his words are washed away in the karaoke blasting over the PA.

From a distance, Clint has what appears to be a series of sub-dermal horns implanted into his shaved head. Intimidating, until you get close enough. When Chet Chernobyl hired a CRISPR lab, Gemination Corporation, to gene hack his embryonic son's DNA, he thought, what could be more punk rock than if the scientists spliced in goat DNA so Clint would grow satanic horns?

They botched the job. Instead of horns, Clint was born with a crown of nipples which later developed into udders when he reached puberty.

Clint presented Bellum, the premier mixed martial arts

organization, with a dilemma: he was too good to ignore, great for the pay per view numbers, but nobody wanted to fight him. So, Bellum cut him from the fight roster, put him in a suit and moved him to the post-fight show commentator's desk. Until broadcast Standards and Practices complained. It was too impractical to cover Clint's udders with floating censor bars — he moved around too much when demonstrating moves in the post-fight analysis — so Bellum pixilated his entire head before eventually giving up and cutting him from the organization altogether.

I grab my mouthpiece from behind my ear and I jam it into my mouth. When I bite down, it snaps into place onto my remaining upper teeth with a satisfying pop.

Bobby digs into his backpack and gets started on his routine as an athletic commission official observes. Bobby loops some wraps around my hands, then helps me pull on a pair of MMA gloves. He wraps tape over the Velcro bindings and then tears the ends of the tape with his teeth.

I hold my hands out for the official to inspect my gloves. He signs my right glove, but his smartPen hovers frozen above my left hand. Expecting five fingers and seeing only three instead tends to do that. He checks my eight fingernails for length.

With a practiced motion, Bobby smears petroleum jelly onto my nose and lips and brow from a quiver of swabs which he always keeps at the ready, tucked behind his ear. I'm trying to remember when I've seen him without them behind his ear... Come to think of it, he showed up to serve a three-year stretch in LA County Jail with swabs of lube behind his ear. Not a good look.

The official taps my junk with his smartPen to make sure I'm wearing a cup, and I grin so that he can see my mouthpiece.

Done.

A holograph of Notorious B.I.G. materializes on the

platform next to the karaoke singer. He taps his foot, nodding his head as the woman continues:

Bet I wet cha like hurricanes and typhoons
Got buffoons eatin' my pussy while I watch cartoons
Sleep 'til noon, this rap Pam Grier's here
Baby drinkers beware, mostly Dolce wear...

We climb the steps of the cage.

I say, "Wait... 'Bobby Money'?"

"Yeah."

"You're Mexican..."

"El Salvadoran. What's your point?"

"Your new name in Spanish means... Roberto Dinero?"

"Famous sounding names are catchy... I was Rob Blow for a day, you know, on account of my cocaine side hustle? But the wrong people kept swiping my SlummR account... Make this quick, would ya? I got a threesome after this."

During the MC's introductions, Clint, the Cudgel circles laps around the cage as though marking his territory. I turn my back to the cage's center and face the corner support-bar cushion. He bumps my shoulder as he passes me, nearly knocking me down. I don't react. I keep my gaze on the face-height semi-circle of holes in the cushion that, if I still had them, would align perfectly with my front teeth.

The ref calls us out to the center of the cage to remind us of the rules of engagement. Clint, who hasn't stopped insulting me for being old and telling me what he's going to do to me since I climbed up the stairs, looms half a head taller than I am. He tilts his head down so his head breasts hang down over his eyes like bangs... His areolae are a livid pink... and, he's lactating.

So, yeah, check this shit out...

CRISPR babies are the designer children of the hyper-rich, conceived in a clean room and genetically modified to bespoke specifications. At first, CRISPR engineered babies were designed to edit out the less desirable traits from their parents, specifically any predispositions to disabilities or genetic diseases. Cancer and viruses were all but eradicated. Naturally, someone got the idea that while you're under the hood, why not select genes for the most desirable attributes?

Cosmetic alterations for height, hair, eye and skin color segued into manipulation for intellectual capacity... Want your kid to have the best chances of success in life? No problem.

Even certain personality traits like assertiveness can be selected for to give designer babies a competitive advantage. Eventually the competitive arms race got so perverted the predispositions for empathy were switched off entirely.

This gave rise to the class of sociopathic super babies each endowed with extreme advantages from birth. The class disparity gaped wide open within half a generation, rendering upward class mobility all but impossible, shattering the illusion once and for all of the Ameritocracy... I mean, so much for telling little Jimmy that if he studies hard and is a good person, he can be anything his heart desires in life.

So, earlier when I said viruses were all but eradicated, that only meant immunity in people who are conceived the old-fashioned way and then later had any genetic flaws edited out while they were a zygote... The irony is, this immunity doesn't apply to CRISPR babies conceived whole cloth in a lab from genomes.

It's estimated that 8% of the human genome originated from viruses. Viruses which lay dormant within the genetic code of every single human being alive. Viruses that would never surface and manifest but for human meddling. They became de novo mutations.

These afflictions manifest in different ways. Some diseases lurk in your DNA, popping up at any time like murderous stalkers hiding in the bushes. Then there are the few expressions with exploitable mutations which are like enemies with benefits. All labeled under the catchall synecdoche, PYRRHIC.

Factoring in PYRRHIC, the life expectancy for CRISPRs each year past age 36 resembles the odds of a 78-year-old American man living to see another year: Basically, a coin flip. It's worse for offspring of a first-generation CRISPR. They never see age ten...

The ref looks directly at me while reminding us to "protect yourself at all times", taking special care that I acknowledge him on this specific point.

I nod.

Upon conclusion of the instructions, I hold my hands out to touch gloves. Clint declines. We go back to our respective corners.

I say to Bobby, "What's my strategy, here?"

"That depends," he says, "You lactose intolerant?"

Both Bobby and my opponent's coach exit the cage. The door clangs shut and locks behind them. Someone behind me yells for me to retire. A loaded beer cup hits the mesh in front of me, splashing its contents into my face and some of it gets into my mouth... It's not beer.

The ref checks with each of the cage side judges and then the timekeeper to make sure they are ready, then he asks the same of us.

"FIGHT!"

The Cudgel charges across the canvas at me, arm cocked back, telegraphing his intention to throw a John Wayne haymaker. I change levels, lowering myself for a takedown which he reacts by dropping his hands to defend what he believes to be my takedown attempt with a sprawl.

Sold and bought.

I rise the instant he commits and my Muay Thai round kick finds his face. A slap crackles in the air as my instep crashes into his jaw. He drops in place, straight down like an elevator with its cable cut and I'm already turning to walk away before he thuds into the canvas like a goddamn highlight reel moment.

Except, when I place my weight on my foot to take a step, I drop to the canvas next to him... My ankle. Possibly sprained, probably broken.

Yay.

This, people, is why you land your Muay Thai kicks on your shin and not your foot. Easy enough in training on the Thai pads, but with a moving opponent's head it's like adjusting your baseball bat mid-swing to catch a slider with perfect placement.

The ref, mouth agape, hasn't called the contest to declare me the winner... He looks at me, and then at Clint who's splayed face down like a starfish, then back to me... As though he's considering whether he should call the outcome a double knockout.

Fuck that!

My opponent hasn't moved since the kick. He's so still, you could trace chalk around him. I drag myself over to my opponent to make this emphatic and clear. Choking an already unconscious man would be pointless... Unless I wake him up first, then choke him unconscious again?

Nah.

And, it's illegal to strike an opponent in the back of the head. Imagine getting disqualified from a fight you should have won by knock out because you're trying to prevent it ruled a draw...

I reach my opponent, and glare up at the ref.

"He's out," I say, "Call it!"

The other corner is screaming at the referee from their place outside of the cage. The ref is still caught in a decision loop.

Only one thing to do. This sickens me... Fuck it.

I roll Clint onto his back, straddle his chest, and rain a storm of elbows down into the face of a defenseless man.

The maximum amount of force an unarmed person can generate against another human being, more than any punch or kick from a standing striker, is ground and pound. If physics 101 tells us that impact force is mass times acceleration, then the larger the striker, the greater the potential for damage. Even so, much of the force any punch a standing striker generates is lost through energy transfer into the very ground the striker is standing on. This isn't the case when you're mounted on your target and striking downward because unlike when both parties are standing vertically, when you're mounted on top of a horizontal target, gravity leverages all your mass down into the other person beneath you.

My elbow clips his nose. It explodes. Blood drains down into his esophagus and he gurgles on his own blood.

I repeat, "Stop the fight!"

From the kid's perspective, this could not possibly be worse. At least when both you and the person who is punching you are standing, your head moves on impact which mitigates the force. This can't happen if your head is trapped in place by the ground. There's nowhere for your head to go, and the ground acts as a force multiplier.

The parchment-thin skin of the kid's brow line bursts and splits open like a ripe plum exposing blood-saturated flesh underneath.

"Stop the fight!"

The Cudgel's corner throws a towel into the cage, but it lands behind the ref and out of his line of sight. I continue my assault.

Each blow bounces the kid's head off the canvas. An elbow cracks across his eye socket, reviving him long enough for the next elbow to both knock him out and wake him up again.

I drop an elbow onto his crown. It skips off his forehead and bursts open an utter. Clint, the Cudgel's sweet, warm milk squirts into my open mouth. I spit it out and dry heave.

For fuck sake! I stop my assault and roll off of him.

He struggles up to one knee, then climbs to his feet. The Cudgel doesn't seem to know where he is until he sees me sitting on my ass. Then he's all, "Hell, yeah!" and lets his hands go on my tee'd up head.

I drop onto my back and the Cudgel follows, falling into my guard. I wrap my legs around his waist and snatch an arm pinning it to my chest, shutting his assault down to harmless one-handed pitter patter and I'm shifting my hips to sweep, strangle, or whatever the fuck I want to do to him at this point when the ref snaps out of his daze and dives between my opponent and me and waves the fight off.

A moment later I'm standing in the center of the cage leaning on Bobby's shoulder for support as the ref holds my wrist in one hand and Clint's wrist in his other. The ref raises his hand in victory.

Welcome to my motherfucking life.

~

I'm sitting on a stool at the bar with my foot propped up on Bobby's lap with a bag of frozen buffalo wings on my ankle while he cuts my hand wraps away.

Bobby says, "Your ankle is fucked."

"You should see the other guy."

"See 'em for yourself."

The "other guy" sits at a table with a go-go dancer squirming in his lap to a chic-this-week NeoSynthPop track. Laughing. Paramedics are entreating him to leave with them but he's not having it.

Bobby says, "Some stitches and a blowjob, he's fine tomorrow. You're proll'y fucked for a month."

A trio of girls with retro A Flock of Seagulls haircuts walks past our stools... snatches of conversation shouted between the music.

"—but the next day she tried to abort—"

"—kidding me?"

"—for that kind of money, they can—"

"—gross!"

"—more if you raise the baby—"

A fight promoter tosses cash onto the bar and then chases after the girls.

Bobby snatches my prize money and slaps some bills onto the bar.

Bobby says, "Barkeep! Three Crackles, neat!"

The barkeep pinches the bills between her thumb and forefinger like a soiled diaper. She says, "Cash? Really, dude?"

Bobby claps my back and nods to the VIP section.

He says, "See those heavy-bottomed lasses?"

He points to a booth in the VIP section where two women who look like a Patrick Nagel painting come to life sit. Koi and Coy Kalashnikov. You could mistake them for mother and daughter, but they're actually identical twins born a generation apart.

The Sisters Kalashnikov were conceived and edited in Gemination Corps' lab when the ballerina couple who ordered them was killed by an avalanche on K2, orphaning the twins before they were born. Coy was placed in the womb of a surrogate mother who could only afford one of them. Koi was frozen long enough for Coy to reach the ages of puberty and consent. That's when Coy leased her womb to Gemination Corporation and carried her sister to term. Coy named Koi with a homonym because, as their matching baby doll t-shirts (which are age appropriate for neither of them) say, "Fuck You If You Can't Tell Us Apart."

AK-47s with over-the-barrel sound suppressors slung across the Sisters K's chests. A swarm of selfie drones orbits them like the rings of Saturn.

"Yeah, of course," I say, "Augmented reality real-person shooter gamers. I watch their kill uploads on Twitch and

HyperGram."

Bobby says, "CRISPR baby mutants... Sorry. Psychically-conjoined twins. Their bond makes them unbeatable, but that's how PYRRHIC manifests in them: Rumor is, if they're separated greater than seven feet their heads explode, so they do everything together..."

Bobby fastens a Church of Galacticology pin to his shirt collar, except his looks like an updated design from Shonda's pin. This time I do sigh aloud.

I say, "For fuck sake, not you too!"

"You should look into this. I'm just saying. You're seriously obstructed. It got me through my stretch in LA County."

"Which time?"

Bobby says, "Andy Circus said on the Hope-RAH! show that the Purge Session technology changed his life... Said that going Lucent is better than being Vaunted."

"He comes back richer each time he dies, so I guess he would know... Galacticologists worship an alien named Mr. CtSulu."

Bobby says, "We replaced Mr. CtSulu, and we can't go by Galacticology anymore. We lost simultaneous lawsuits from Star Trek, Scientology, and the estate of HP Lovecraft... Infringement of intellectual property."

"What does the Church of Galacticology go by now?"

He says, "The Children of Tendu."

Bobby spreads his hands apart in the air as he says this as though the new name should materialize in sparkles between them.

"They optioned the IP rights from some screenwriter," Bobby says, "They're using one of his heroes as their new God. What's that writer's name? Ken, something or other..."

"You mean, Kent Light Yr.?"

"Yeah. That's the guy."

"Fuck off! So, now they worship an anal-retentive koala

from the Boötes Void named..."

"Schmeezus."

"That's just lazy writing!"

"It's a wombat actually, not a koala. They're both indigenous to Australia. With its accent, it's an easy mistake to make."

"It's from space!"

"You can tell by the poop. Wombats are the only animals with cube-shaped poop."

"Well, your boy Andy Circus got mauled to death by a wombat on set today... If they worship Schmeezus then who the fuck is Tendu?"

"Exactly. Mystery is sexy."

I shake my head. "A god, based on a movie, based on a comic book."

"Graphic novel."

"A children's book," I say. "Written by a holoPorn star whacked out on ayahuasca! Who does that?"

"Lewis Carrol" Bobby says, "Anyway, when the option expires, the IP rights revert back to the screenwriter and The Children of Tendu are back to square one. You see, Light Yr. also wrote their bible."

"Fucking Hollywood. Even gods hide their past in this town... And, how is that possible? Do wombats have square assholes?"

Bobby shrugs. "Yet another mystery... Solve it, you'll get a Nobel Prize."

Three glasses slide down the bar, fizzing as though spiked with pox.

I say, "I hate Crackle."

"Who the hell hates Crackle?"

"I like my caffeine and narcotics separate."

Bobby tosses a glass back and winks. He scoops my change off of the bar and pockets it.

Speaking with Crackle gliding down your throat has the exact opposite effect on your voice as talking after sucking on a helium balloon. In a satanic voice, he says:

"Fuck yeah, SlummR! Let's see if that rumor is true."

Bobby saunters off with the other two glasses towards the VIP section. The guard lifts a velvet rope for him, and he plops down in between the Sisters Kalashnikov.

Fuck it, there are two of them and only one of Bobby. I hobble over to the VIP section.

The guard holds up a hand.

He says, "Sorry sir. You can't enter the VIP section."

"Why not?"

"You're too important."

"What's that?"

"Your Q-SCore. You're not obscure or poor enough."

"But Wikipedia deleted my page, and I'm getting divorced and my house foreclosed, both on Monday!"

"Come back Tuesday. It's country-western night."

Bobby smiles and gives me the middle finger.

I limp over to the service door and smoke a menthol.

When I return, Bobby and the Sisters K are gone, but the doorman is there.

He's not wearing his x-ray bandanna indoors, but his jawbone still glows through his translucent skin like a phossy jaw-afflicted matchmaker from the 1800s.

Skull Face says, "Sal will see you now."

I nod.

I say, "Let's get this over with."

He says, "So, maybe you slip out the service door when I'm not looking..."

"Where would that leave you?"

"Better than where you're at."

I inspect the three fingernails of my left hand, then look across the bar to Sal's office door.

I say, "Where the fuck am I going to go? I gotta take a piss on the way."

He walks beside me as I limp through the Clown Room and towards the bathroom. Patrons jostle in and out of the bathroom. A man, leaving, holds the door open for me. His hands are Smurf blue. Skull face waits outside.

Inside, patrons using urinals, sinks, and sinks as urinals. I pick a stall and pee. At eye level, a sign:

Warning: Urinal Mints Protected by Anti-Theft Countermeasures!

I look down...

A black-and-white holographic-commercial flickers atop the urinal mint: a man and a woman kissing on a beach... Burt Lancaster and Deborah Kerr in *From Here to Eternity* ... Waves lap at their feet as music swells in a chorus of strings... and a voice over with a Mid-Atlantic twang says:

Are you dissatisfied with your penis? Would you like to be like Burt and get it on with a beautiful young woman like her all night long? Of course, you would! ... Columbia Pictures and MacroHard Corporation, incorporated, Inc. presents... the centennial anniversary of "From Here to Eternity" erectile dysfunction pills! Be like Burt! Make it last an Eternity!

The couple has stopped getting it on and are now staring up at me. Deborah Kerr pouts. Burt Lancaster says,

Hey, Mac, do you mind?

I finish my business and zip up.

Next to me, a man, on his knees and sleeves rolled up, fishes the mint from the urinal. An alarm trills!

My neighbor says, "Sonovabitch!"

The man yanks his hands from the basin. They're Smurf blue.

Skull Face is waiting for me when I exit the bathroom. We continue through the Clown Room to the office door. I go through the door alone and he closes it behind me.

A lock clicks.

Current events clippings thumbtacked to the wall connected to each other by strings of yarn... A poster of Tarkovsky's "The Mirror" hangs on the wood-paneled wall to the left of a desk that looks like it was salvaged from the same lonely roadside where a nut would go, "This is a perfect place to dump bodies!". The office looks like it was furnished by either an overworked TV showrunner or a freshly-pardoned serial killer starting over after a lifetime in solitary... In other words, no difference in psychological profile.

Hanging on the wall to the right of the desk, dual PhDs in Genetic Engineering and Game Theory from Cambridge, both awarded to Sal Ip-Tze Sum.

A stainless-steel door behind the desk.

Sitting on the desk with her legs dangling over its edge is the same woman who was singing karaoke on the platform.

The last snowflake to land on LA's Walk of Fame melted on contact nearly a century ago, folks. Even in the dead of winter, you'll waste an afternoon searching LA for a ski outfitter. Yet, she's bundled up inside of a parka with its tags still dangling from a sleeve as she takes her time pulling a pair of thigh-high wool socks up to the hems of her cut-offs one leg at a time. Uggs boots on her feet. She zips her parka up, covering her Taylor Swift t-shirt. At some point in everyone's adult life we settle into a style of dress that feels comfortable and, Diderot Effect notwithstanding, we begin to let the latest trends pass us by. She got off the fashion train at high school.

She's missing the same pinky and index fingers I am except, unlike my choice to live with my avulsions, she opted for robotic prostheses that almost pass for human digits.

Almost.

Visually they're perfect until you see them in motion. The movement of her prosthetic digits isn't quite in synch with the natural fingers next to them... It's not like they are herky-jerky per se, it's actually the opposite. They're too smooth, which makes the natural digits next to them appear stop motion.

Meet Dr. Sally Chen, boys and girls. Chen, a variant of the Cantonese surname, Sum, is Sal's ancestors' act of defiance to the Romanized surname change trend. Sal, of course, is diminutive for 'Sally,' but you'll want to forget this fun factoid. Never call her Sally.

Sal, while speaking orders to someone in Cantonese through her Halo, nods at me and gestures to the front of her desk where a pair of bean bags flank a spool repurposed as an ad hoc table. Her gesturing motion draws her attention to the tags dangling from her sleeve. She bites them between her teeth and slashes it off with an Emerson CQC-7 whose blade snaps to life as she pulls it from the pocket of her short shorts in one simultaneous motion.

I hop over to the beanbag. Instead of attempting to lower myself with a jacked-up ankle and poor balance, I aim my ass at it and fall backward. The bean bag lets out a sigh as I sink into it:

SHHHHHHH!

On the spool, a certified triple platinum award for the record, "Hand of the Machine" by artist MC Lecher. Its cover art features a strange-loop illustration of a skeletonized robot hand painting itself into a corner. MC Letcher remixed classic love songs into nihilistic ballads of death and destruction.

The breakout song, *My Boyfriend's Black (and you're gonna be trouble!)* earned him his first Grammy.

BZZZZZ!!!

Flies spazz to their deaths inside the light fixture... Dead roaches entombed long enough for the light bulb to bleach their husks white.

THOOK!

In a blink, Sal's knife quivers to a stop in the bean bag between my knees.

"Show me your dick."

Sal plops down into the other bean bag holding a six-pack of Crackle. She snaps a can open and foam seethes over its lip.

"What?" She says, "Girls talk."

She offers me a can but I wave it off.

I say, "What's with the British villain accent?"

"It's from Hong Kong."

"You're from Brooklyn."

"And you're from Inglewood, yet you talk like a white boy."

"I emigrated from England but was raised in Inglewood."

"Like Slick Rick."

"Yeah. Except his accent is from the Bronx."

"How's my accent?"

"Better than mine. Anything you want to tell me about the job I just did?"

"Congratulations, you didn't fuck up. What, you're expecting balloons and confetti to drop from the ceiling?"

"Why didn't you tell me MC Lecher was my father?"

She shrugs. "Because it's funny?"

"I might have killed him."

"Comes with the job."

"Is Bobby's debt squared?"

"For now."

"Good. I quit."

What I just said amuses her, but the way she laughs gives me the impression that it's a joke at my expense based on arcane knowledge I wouldn't get anyway. Sal evaluates me as though deciding on something, takes a pull from her can and sets it on the spool.

She says, "Did you know that my grandfather was an economist?"

I nod "No".

"Keith Chen," She says, "He specialized in American

Behavior. He was the head of economic research for Uber, pre-Singularity. He's the guy who foisted game theory onto the Internet economy by inventing surge pricing based on the price people are willing to pay in any given situation... But what he's known for is the economics of whoring."

"The economics are self-explanatory. It's the oldest profession, after all."

"You'd think, right?

So, my grandfather wondered if it was possible to teach monkeys the concept of money, so he designed an experiment.

There were two enclosures: a big one where the monkeys were contained as a group, and a smaller one where the monkeys could enter for one-on-one interaction with human handlers. The handlers gave monkeys coins and, as predicted, if they couldn't eat or fuck them—"

"Sal, is this shaggy dog story going anywhere, because-"

"Yeah, chill!"

I settle into my bean bag for the story, making a mental note to fact check it later on Wikipedia.

Sal continues, "... So, when the first monkey gave what it thought was a useless coin back to its human handler, the handler gave it a treat. This taught the monkeys that the coins had value. You could trade them for something good.

Once the animals learned this, Dr. Chen furthered the experiment by introducing the concept of prices... Trading one coin would get a monkey a small cube of Jell-O, but trading three coins would get them an apple slice. The monkey preferred the apple slices over the Jell-O and would stop spending one coin to buy Jell-O, and instead would save up three coins so they could buy the apple slices. This was proof that monkeys could plan for the future, and they would start saving their money accordingly just like any human being would! Well, except you... You let Bobby handle your money and now you have to work doing shit jobs for me, hahaha...

One of the most powerful motivators of human behavior is risk aversion. Chen was curious: Could the monkeys grasp the concept of loss?

He instructed the handlers to introduce the concept of gambling...

All monkey and human interaction were divided between two handlers, handler "A" and handler "B". Handler A would show the monkeys a grape and then would flip a coin. If the coin landed on heads, the handler would give the monkey two grapes. However, handler B showed the monkeys two grapes first before flipping a coin. If the coin which handler B flipped landed on heads, then handler B would take one grape away and give the monkeys only one grape. Even though the odds of a coin landing on heads or tails are for all intents and purposes the same, the monkeys began to ignore handler B's take away game and preferred handler A's reward game... Remember, the odds are the same. This established that monkeys suffer from the same irrational fear of loss that humans do.

One day, a monkey accidentally spilled his savings of coins in the large enclosure containing all of the other monkeys. The other monkeys went into a money-grabbing frenzy!

Instead of intervening, Chen just observed what happened. In one corner of the enclosure, he witnessed a male monkey carrying a coin as he approached a female monkey. He offered her a coin. She took the coin, and she presented herself to him. This transaction was the first observed case of prostitution among monkeys..."

Sal takes a pull of her Crackle. When she takes the can away from her mouth, she stops just short of lowering it all the way. She holds the can in front of her face as though reading its label, but it's obvious that the can only happens to be there and she's staring through it.

"Hello? Sal?"

It's only when Sal's eyes refocus and she smiles that it

occurs to me that she was texting with her Halo.

The office door bursts open and Skull Face trundles in carrying a pair of crutches. Sal grunts as she fights her way out of her bean bag's grasp. Skull Face helps me out of mine and hands me the crutches.

Sal says, "Are you circumcised?"

"For fuck sake. Do you really need another hostile work environment claim filed against you?"

"Chill, Rasputin. You quit so your ass is fair game. C'mon, I wanna show you something."

She walks and I follow her on my crutches. When my foot lands there's a hissing sound and something moves underfoot. I barely keep my balance as I shift my weight back onto the crutches. I look down. A pair of pastel-green marbles slashed down the middle tracks me from above a mouth yawning open like a laptop. Four teeth spring forward.

"God damn! What the fuck!"

"There you are, baby! Aww... Magic is saying hi to you. DeShawn, say hello to Magic Johnson."

"You let an anaconda roam loose in your office?"

"He's a reticulated python."

The snake's spring-loaded body that's five times longer than I am tall tenses. Its skin, iridescent black and green, shimmers like the surface of a bubble.

I say, "Whatever! Get it away from me!"

"It's not 'whatever'. You'd appreciate the difference if you were his prey. Pythons can snatch a sleeping orangutan from a tree in total darkness by tracking its body heat."

I want to back away but those eyes lock me into place like a fawn with a flashlight shined into its face.

Sal says, "Magic finds cages disagreeable. You of all people should be able to empathize."

"What if it turns on you?"

"Never! He loves his mama, don't you baby?"

Magic Johnson says, "Sssssss!"

"He's just cranky because I haven't fed him in a few days."

It hasn't blinked since engaging me in a stare down. I back away and it rears up to knee level and bares its fangs, so I freeze again.

Sal gives Magic a boop! on his nose. It slithers away but twists its head back to give me an "I wish you would, motherfucker!" glare before vanishing under her desk.

"Adorable. Wish I had another just like him."

I say, "I don't care if you gave it a last name, it's a wild animal!"

Sal stops at her desk and pulls out an inhaler.

"Aren't we all?" She says. "Don't fool yourself, the veneer of human civility is condom-thin."

She shakes the inhaler, then pumps a blast into her mouth.

I say, "Shonda and I tried those."

"How's your boy? Miles, right?"

"You can cut the show for my benefit. We both know those inhalers are useless."

"They serve the exact purpose I designed them for," she says.

"What purpose is that, false hope?"

"You're welcome."

I say, "How far has yours progressed?"

Sal returns the inhaler to the drawer.

She says, "I won't be needing my naughty Easter bunny costume this year."

I nod.

I say, "Are you in pain?"

"Oh, fuck yes."

"Good."

She smiles.

I say, "I'm sorry."

"Liar. C'mon, I wanna show you something."

Sal walks. Skull Face makes an 'after you' gesture with a

pistol in his hand.

Sal pauses to dig a knit ski cap out of a parka pocket. It's pink with a Wu Tang 'Ws'-and-crossbones pattern resembling eight-bit video game graphics, with a pom pom on top as big as a cantaloupe. She wears it back on her head for her bangs to peek out in front like a Keebler elf. The pom pom bounces as she walks.

I laugh.

She says, "You wouldn't be laughing if a pom pom saved your life. They were invented to protect tall people from banging their heads in confined spaces or low ceilings."

"You're as tall as a 4th grader."

"It works just as well for falling objects, too."

The three of us go through the stainless-steel door behind Sal's desk. Sal, me, then Skull Face, who makes a point to stay behind me. Cold air rips my breath out of my lungs and my fingertips immediately begin to sting. We've entered a deep freezer. My eyes adjust to the dark...

A pair of goons wearing leather jackets and gloves stand facing me. Light from the door behind me reflects off of the pistols they both brandish in their hands. One of them looks like Tom Hanks if he never made it as an actor and squandered his life directing holoPorn in Tarzana. The doe-eyed one wears a perpetually startled expression. She looks like she just stepped off the plane when the Galacticologists stalking LAX for new recruits turned her out and put her on the corner of Sunset and Vermont with holoPamphlets to solicit their ideology to tourists.

At their feet, a tarp... My bubble-wrap tarp. With three men stripped to the waist kneeling in a triangle on it. Among these men is the kid whom I just fought, and Bobby, both of them convulsing with violent waves of shivers.

And laying on the tarp in the middle of the group, Chauncey. Alive. A patch on one eye, a cast on his arm, and a giant Flava Flav clock around his neck.

Behind everyone, a stainless-steel toolbox and life-sized ice sculptures of Snow White and the Seven Dwarfs.

Hanks pats me down while Bambi and Skull Face keep their guns trained on me. He taps the case inside my shorts and, assuming it's my cup like the ref did, passes over it without further inspection.

"He's clean."

Sal walks over to Bashful and kneels.

I say, "Be careful going down on those Dwarves. Your tongue could freeze to a circle of dicks."

"Hey!" Bobby says, "Don't poke the bear!"

"This bear's been poked many times."

Sal says, "That's not funny."

"Sure, it is. Because you see, there are seven of them and you can't get dick inside your mouth fast enough-"

Sal picks a plastic freezer bag of steaks off of a bottom shelf, unzips it, and dumps the meat onto the floor.

She says, "No... Okay, first of all, explaining a joke kills it. But it still wouldn't make any sense because you mixed metaphors. Now, if the sculptures were Goldilocks and the Three Bears and you made a bear-bang joke, then it could be funny."

"Uh huh."

"Plus," she says, "jokes ending with a hard-consonant sound in the punchline, like 'k', subconsciously trigger laughs."

"Like, three carnivores tag teaming Goldilocks?"

"Exactly, yeah."

I nod like I'm considering this. "Nah, it doesn't work 'cause, you see, one of the Three Bears is a girl and the other is just a baby--"

Bobby says, "Shut the fuck up!"

"Thank you!" Sal says.

I sigh. "Have some dignity, Bobby. She's going to kill us anyway. Isn't that right?"

Sal straddles Chauncey and pulls on a pair of fur-lined

gloves.

She says, "Yeah, pretty much..."

Bobby says, "Why kill me?"

"Loose ends are a bitch," Sal says.

Sal pulls the freezer bag over Chauncey's head, grasps an end in each hand, then places a knee on Chauncey's chest and pulls the slack taught, smothering him to death. Chauncey's good eye goes wide like it's on the verge of popping out of his head.

"Haha," Sal says, "That's the same WTF! look on his face the first time he saw me after all these years."

Sal steps on Chauncey's face with the knee that's not digging into his chest and pulls harder.

She says, "The thing that would surprise most people is just how difficult it is to strangle somebody by hand. It certainly surprised me the first time..."

She squeezes. Chauncey gurgles. His feet thrash and he paws absently at the plastic bag around his head.

"It's nothing like the movies... Even if someone is mortally wounded it can take a really long time..."

When Chauncey stops moving Sal releases the bag, and his head topples to the side and settles like a dropped sack of oranges.

Sal stands up and stamps her feet on the tarp.

"Haha, my foot fell asleep..."

She sighs.

"...Killing with gloves on is worse than fucking with a condom."

Sal bites off her left glove and a henchman slaps a pistol in her outstretched palm with the efficiency of a surgical tech passing a scalpel. She pulls a sound suppressor from her coat pocket and screws it onto her gun.

Sal kicks Chauncey's arm out of her way like a pair of jeans on a dorm room floor as she steps over him on her way to The Cudgel kneeling next to Bobby. She presses the barrel of her gun to the kid's forehead between the horns and a...

BANG!

...from the freezer door as it slams shut, snuffing out any light and warmth from the freezer like blowing out a candelabra.

The sound of people mouth breathing...

Then...

A click, like someone slamming down on a stapler and a flash strobes across the kneeling kid's surprised expression - the light flees his eyes before darkness reclaims his face.

Thud.

Feet rustling across plastic...

Heavy breathing...

Click - flash!

Thud.

Within that flash a glimpse of a face in terror, and something hot and viscous splashes onto my cheek.

Heavy breathing...

Feet treading plastic...

Whimpering...

The freezer door opens, baptizing corpses in a sliver of cool light. Blood spray like a Rorschach inkblot on the tarp. At my feet, blood oozes out of the ears and mouth of Clint, the Cudgel, mingling with shards of skull. Blood trickling down my legs that I never even felt get on me. I shiver so hard that I clench my jaw in fear of biting through my tongue. Bobby sits in place, still... an occasional ghost of mist seeps from his bluing lips.

Sal says, "If you let that door shut again, you'll be kneeling on the tarp next."

Skull Face says, "I'm sorry, Sally."

"Do we have something to prop the door open with?"

His eyes sweep across the contents of the freezer.

He says, "I don't think so... Nothing is heavy enough, but I'll hold it open."

Sal chuckles. "Now, there's an idea. Are you familiar with

Occam's Razor?"

He says, "Razor, what?"

"Would you take a teeny tiny step back, please?"

He takes a half step back into the doorway, and Sal loosens a volley of bullets into his face. His hand slides off the door handle and he falls straight down in place and the door swings closed, slamming to a stop on what's left of his head.

Sal says, "Problem solved... Oh, don't look at me like that. That wasn't because he called me Sally. Haha, okay, yeah. Yeah, totally it was."

She stops in front of Bobby and presses her pistol to his temple. Bobby, listless, doesn't react.

I drop my crutches and make what in my mind is a leap toward Sal, but with my body half frozen my effort must seem risible. The Porno Hanks kicks my good ankle out from underneath me and I fall onto my face. From my vantage with my cheek on the concrete, I see underneath the racks to the next row over... Bodies, a score of them, shrink-wrapped in clear plastic. The red toe tags designate them as clones.

Sal rambles on about r/K Theory and self-sacrifice vs. self-preservation which I couldn't follow even if I wasn't clinging to consciousness by a filament. She stuffs her pistol in her waistband and blows warm air onto her hands and rubs them together.

"Fuck!" Sal says, "Hypothermia could kill you in here!"

She unfurls her knit cap down over her face... Her hat is a ski mask. She takes a second to align her eyes and mouth with their corresponding holes, then says, "Don't worry, sweetie. This will be over soon..."

She hands her gun to Bambi and says, "Shoot them both, but do it on the tarp. Make sure to vacuum seal DeShawn's corpse and leave it in the freezer. Dispose of the other bodies however you want, but do not fuck that part up with DeShawn's corpse."

She steps over Skull Face on her way out of the freezer without pausing to look back.

Damn. Even Magic Johnson looked back.

Porno Hanks tucks his gun into the pocket of his leather jacket and tries to drag me onto the tarp, but struggles. It's a vintage leather café racer jacket like Shonda's... I always wanted one of those... It's funny how your mind drifts to inconsequential things under stress... Hanks has a hard time dragging me, so Bambi, sighing, stows her weapon and helps him. If there's a window of opportunity to overpower them and get out of here with my life, it's right now. Overcome with drowsiness, I'm a passive observer as they dump me onto the plastic.

Powerless to even hold my head up, my chin lolls down to my chest. Hanks pulls my head up by the tails of my cornrows, and Bambi presses Sal's gun to my temple... The muzzle is still warm, wet with gore, and it reeks from just being fired.

With my peripheral vision, I see her finger travel in the trigger well to squeeze the trigger, and...

Nothing happens.

She removes the gun from my cranium to inspect it...

Disengages the safety, then presses it to my temple again...

I flinch as it CLICKS, but Hanks holds me steady.

Bambi racks the slide to chamber a round and presses the gun to my head again...

CLICK.

A long exhalation bursts free from my lungs, I realize I've been holding my breath the entire time.

Bambi releases the clip from the butt and says, "I'm out. Give me two rounds."

"Can't," Hanks says, "That's a nine, and I've got a .45."

"Well, give me your gun!"

"We're in an enclosed space. You fire a gun without a suppressor and we'll all go deaf. Besides, they'll hear us in the club and Sal will shank us where we stand."

Bambi says, "Whatever, man."

Pop! Pop! Pop!

Hanks says, "Stop playing with the bubble wrap and go to the tool case. We're going old school."

Bambi leaves me with Hanks to rummage around inside the metal case...

Pulls out a long-handled hammer/axe...

Hanks says, "Now that's cool. Let's not waste it on these losers. Save it for the final kill."

Bambi exchanges the multi-tool in favor of a plasma torch, and...

Hanks frowns and nods.

She looks disappointed and pouts. She swaps the torch out for an ice-carving chainsaw with a blade half as long as she is tall.

Hanks gives a thumbs down.

Bambi scoffs. "Oh my gosh, look who's a mister smarty pants! I'll bet you've been saving that reference forever."

"Haha, yeah. I've always wanted to do that."

Bambi returns to me and Hanks with the chainsaw. Hanks yanks my head upright to expose my neck.

Hanks says, "Okay, look. I'm standing right here so if you go wide, you'll get me, too."

"That's tempting."

"I need you to take a few practice swings before you turn that thing on."

Bambi sighs. She says, "Yeah, yeah... Safety first."

She chokes up on the grip and takes a practice swing which terminates as a tap below my ear as gentle as a kiss.

Hanks says, "That's too high."

"No shit..."

"You really don't want a live blade bouncing off his skull."

"I know!"

"And, you have to follow through... No, don't aim at his

neck. Visualize a point on the <u>other side</u> of his neck, and swing to that."

"Stop mansplaining!"

"I'm just saying..."

"You want to do this?"

Hanks grins. He says, "Yeah, fuckin' A! Gimmie!"

Bambi hands Hanks the chainsaw and they swap places.

Hanks says, "You can do the homeless one next."

Hanks relaxes his grip and widens his stance. He takes a practice swing which ends with one of the blade's shark teeth nicking my neck just above the clavicle. Satisfied, he powers up the saw. The motor whines to life and the blade spins into a blur.

"Okay, now watch... Hold his neck straight up and down, I'm not a vampire! That's it... Now, watch how it's done..."

Hanks arcs the blade into a backswing and begins to bring it forward to consummate my neck with steel and...

The hairs on the back of my neck stand up and there's a crackle and pop like lightning with a sizzling sound of fatty bacon dropped into a frying pan.

Hanks screams.

His swing arcs wide and he buries the saw blade into Bambi's bowels. The spinning blade tosses intestines out of her body cavity like spring-loaded snakes bursting free from a gag can of potato chips. The saw is a beaver hopped up on speed munching through her spine and, Bambi, a felled sequoia, topples over. Hanks, moaning, drops the saw and sits down in place. The saw continues its wrath inside of Bambi like an electric toothbrush chattering and skipping around inside a sink before its grip safety engages and it powers itself down.

Chauncey is sitting behind the plasma torch which he's propped up on its case to hold steady.

The freezer reeks of ozone and waste like a port-a-john blasted by lightning...

Porno Hanks' degloved face slides down his skull like

boiled meat sloughing off a drumstick, and it dangles from his chin by a flap of skin...

Bambi's innards decorate the dwarves like Christmas garland.

Shane Black would be proud.

Hanks says, "This sucks."

He's holding his still-smiling face in one hand like an actor with a Greek comedy mask. He's attempting to cover the tragedy by flipping it back onto his skull.

Hanks turns to Chauncey and says, "You've ruined my SlummR date. My profile picture won't match."

Except, without lips, it sounds like, "Goo goo-gin guy ginguh gay..."

At that instant, Hanks' head flares up like a struck match and there's a jagged line burnt into my vision like I've stared at a flash of purple lightning, tracing all the way back to Chauncey.

"Fuck!" I say, "You could have warned me you were going to zap him again. I was looking right at him and now I'm night blind!"

"I was aiming for you," he says.

His words come as a lisp, whistling between a bloody hole where teeth used to be. Both lips busted open. Sal's goons worked him over well.

I stand up. This takes a while because the cold has seeped into my bones and my entire body feels dull like my hand after I slept on it all night. I hop my way over to Chauncey, passing Bobby on his way out of the freezer, dragging himself over Skull Face's body. One good thing about the cold is that it has numbed my ankle to the pain. By the time I drag Chauncey out of the freezer, Bobby has gone. My night blindness has faded enough for me to search under Sal's desk and around her office... No sign of the python.

Exhausted, I collapse onto the floor next to Chauncey. He's passed out and fading fast. I search under his shirt for his Life Alert pendant before I realize that it's the big-assed clock around his neck. I spin the minute hand around until the time strikes 11:59:59, and... An animatronic mini Flava Flav busts out of the clock's face like a cuckoo and raps the chorus from Public Enemy's, *911 is a Joke.*

This Life Alert emergency and surgical response service is an indulgence only the top one-tenth of one percent of the population, the Social Credit Vaunted, can afford. Personalizing it for their clients is the least they can do.

I'm wondering how the hell Sal didn't smother him to death until I remember his stoma.

"We're on our way, sir," from the Life Alert pendant.

I take my surgeon's mask from my hoodie pocket and pull it down over my face and pull my hoodie up over my head just in time to duck as the Life Alert drones fly past me and attend to Chauncey.

After treating Chauncey, a drone circles back to me and scans me, starting with my ankle and working its way up my body.

Thanks, Dad.

When it gets to my chest cavity its siren scream, projecting a hologram diagnosis of my ankle (sprained, not broken), and then a 3D image of what it saw in my chest that I'm well aware of. The machine shoots my ankle up with a painkiller and anti-inflammatory cocktail then flies out the room without any advice or treatment for the later affliction because there aren't any of either to give.

I consider waking him to interrogate him about the plutonium case while he's drugged up, but the ambulance and LAPD are never far behind the Life Alert drones. I gotta split.

I take a menthol from the case and then stuff it back down the front of my pants again, think the better of it and pull the case out and return the cigarette.

Back in the freezer...

I take Porno Hanks' jacket off of his corpse and put the case in the inside breast pocket. The jacket fits a little snug over my hoodie, and with the case taking up space inside its inside pocket but fuck it, it's free and kids today wear their asymmetric jackets unzipped and open anyway. The case tingles warm against my heart.

I check the jacket pockets as one would when going through a dead man's shit... Matchboxes from the bar, a princess-cut engagement ring with a receipt of purchase from a pawn shop... a key for a storage unit at All Valley Public Storage... and a shitty love poem written to a "Marci" on the back of a pawn ticket for a 1967 Omega Constellation from the same pawn shop as the engagement ring.

Hank's Vaunt powers up to the last thing he was looking at. An invoice to Sal and a holoCard. I project the card:

An alive version of dead Porno Hanks and Bambi come to life before me. Both in tuxedos, standing back to back with their hands clasped together and fingers interlaced forming imaginary pistols in front of their faces like James Bond.

Bambi says, "Hi, I'm Marci Kruger with an "I"!
Hanks says, "And I'm Rupert Dunning with a capital "D"!"
Dunning and Kruger do Kung Fu kicks into the air. Together, they say, "Thanks for choosing Dunning and Kruger FX, LLC."
Marci says, "Experts in movie stunts, special effects, and private investigation!"
Rupert drops into a downward-facing dog pose, presenting himself to Marci who grabs his hips and mounts him.
He says, "And master yogis, Pilates, and tantric sex instructors, too!"
Marci says, "And script consulting feedback—"

I swipe the card away.

In Marci's pockets... A photograph of a young Marci dressed like a princess sitting on a sofa between an elderly couple she more than casually resembles... and an uncashed cashier's check issued three years ago from a law firm for the sum of $811,014. I flip the photo over... There's a hand-written note on the back in large, loopy cursive letters. I don't read it. I return everything to her pocket.

On the way out of the freezer I grab the plasma torch, because it's a motherfucking plasma torch. It looks exactly like a soda gun that a bartender would squirt a fountain drink or beer into your mug, right down to the 8.4-ounce reservoir at its butt. I wonder...

I pick up Sal's can of Crackle and try to peel the label off. It tears and peels unevenly like stubborn masking tape sticking to itself on its spool... My third try with a can in the six-pack, the label peels off clean. Sticking my tongue out of my mouth while I concentrate... I line the label up with the torch reservoir... It's not a perfect fit, but it's pretty damn good.

The torch and reservoir, no longer than two fists stacked on top of each other and as thin as a flashlight, slip into my jacket.

Jumbo's Clown Room is dark and empty. I draw the hoodie strings tight so the hole opening is no bigger than a sleeve's before exiting the club through the service exit.

Hollywood smells like a garbage fire.

A worker, hosing chunks of food from rubber kitchen mats in the alley, doesn't give me as much as a glance. Falling ash collects on the mats as fast as he can wash them. I limp away from Jumbo's a few blocks before calling an Uber with the Vaunt I snatched off Porno Hanks, not at all expecting his Social Credit to be good enough for an Uber to actually show up...

What if this guy has warrants? Shit, I could be calling my ride straight to jail! I scan up and down the streets for patrol cars then the sky for drones. Ashes drift down onto my cheeks from a black sky.

Nothing...

Not one to take chances, I take the glasses off and set

them on a bus bench at Hollywood and Western and step back into the crowd and wait...

A kid rolls by on a skateboard carrying a dozen roses. Red pops against the background of the colorless wasteland. In front of him, a holoVid projected from his skateboard: MC Letcher in concert, sitting at a piano and performing his hit, *I Do You* sampled from Stevie Wonder's love ballad, *Do I Do.*

"When I see you in the street
Imma blast your ass up off your feet
My prison shotgun shoots through doors
I shoot it sideways 'cuz the bullets hurt more.

Wikipedia says MC Letcher's *Hand of the Machine* is an autobiographical album...

And he was on the gifted and talented fast track in high school, but never followed it up with college...

He grew up privileged in Oyster Bay but spent a stretch in Pelican Bay for... cutting the tags off of mattresses. His gang was in a pitched battle in a strip mall, and soon he was the last man in his set standing... and he was out of ammunition. The enemy gang had Uzis. All Chauncey had was sharp teeth and a sharp mind. He ran into a mattress store and bit the plastic tags off of some mattresses. While the enemy gang stalked up and down the aisles for him, he used his lighter to fuse the tags into square-shaped laminates and rubbed their edges against the concrete floor until the squares were sharpened to keen-edged ninja stars. The rival gang didn't stand a chance.

No mention of me, my mom, nor, if he's to be believed, a twin on his Wikipedia.

A Children of Tendu street recruiter approaches me with a fake smile and a pamphlet outstretched but spots the blood on my Speedos. Thinking the better of talking to me, he targets another mark instead and heads toward him. The recruiter pauses at the bus bench to inspect Dunning's Vaunt. As he reaches for it, an epoxyNet drops from the sky, both tasing and binding him to the sidewalk, and LAPD patrol cars screech to a halt and officers pour out with their guns drawn.

As the police cart the recruiter away, a Prius pulls up next to me, flashing its rooftop Uber holo-sign. I open the door and the intro to Beethoven's 9th symphony, 1st movement blasts out. The Prius is stuffed with ravers, their clothes covers in holographic kaleidoscopes that pulse and swirl to the music.

I squeeze into the car and pulls my Vaunt from my hoodie... Cracked. Because, of course it is.

A laser pops out of the head rest in front of me. I scan my Vaunt into it.

The Prius AI says, "Destination, Mr. Trustfall?"

I shout over the blaring trumpets: "Home!"

The Prius lurches forward. A zombied-out girl next to me wearing a *FREE OJ!* T-shirt yacks up Skittles-colored pills onto my Speedos... She plucks the pills from my lap and re-swallows them... Fuckin' white kids...

"Hey, Uber! Stop by a Target! I need pants!"

The car spins into a sharp turn, and zombie girl kicks my ankle, making me wince in pain... I pick up a half-digested and heart-shaped pill... and pop it into my mouth.

"Chew it!" the girl says, "works faster that way!"

As we zip onto the 101 Freeway, I come down from the adrenaline high and crash hard. The car wakes me up as it turns the corner onto my street. The TMI holoFeed plays the end of a story about MC Letcher surviving a gang-style execution in a local club of il'repute, and segues into a story about the canceled title fight at Bellum.

My flip flops kick up ashes as I make my way up the driveway. Jacquelin senses my arrival and opens the door for me.

Good morning, DeShawn. Can I do anything for you?

"Yeah. Arm the alarm and turn on the shower."

Just a reminder: the medications in the medicine cabinet have expired.

"Go fuck yourself."

~

The Uber drops me off at the curb in front of the Neutra house. In the daylight, you can now see that the home, all glass and concrete, is perched on the hillside.

I make my way up the driveway, singing and whistling Chauncey's song, *I Do You* that's been stuck in my head all day...

When I see you in the street
Imma blast your ass up off your feet
My prison shotgun shoots through doors
I shoot it sideways 'cuz the bullets hurt more...

I see motion through the frosted-glass panels flanking the front door.

I ring the doorbell. The door opens and a beam of light blasts out. Behind the light, a cherub under a tangle of curls stands inside the doorway, gazing up at me from eyes not much higher than the knob... The boy swipes his wristPhone and the flashlight app terminates.

The boy says, "Hello, mister."

"Uh...Hi."

I scan the homes in the neighborhood... I've got the right house.

"Hey, little man," I say, "Is Sévérine here?"

"Yes."

He stares up at me, offering no further explanation.

I say, "I'm here to see her. Go let her know I'm here."

"No. I will not."

"Why not?"

"You can't tell me what to do."

"Your right," I say, "I'm sorry. Please?"

The boy leaves the door ajar but doesn't invite me in. He skips down a hallway on a floor made of glass. Curls bounce up and down like Slinkies. He stops and turns.

He says, "What's your name, mister?"

"DeShawn. My name is DeShawn."

"DeShawn, who?"

"She knows more than one DeShawn?"

"Obviously."

"Alright. I'm DeShawn Trustfall."

"You're not DeShawn Trustfall."

"Haha... Okay, why not?"

The boy chews his lower lip. He seems to come to a decision.

He says, "Wait here, please."

He climbs a spiral staircase and disappears.

I step into the threshold.

The glass floor exposes a view down to the pylons the cliffside house is poised upon...

Glass walls. Nothingness on the other side...

I creep inside as though walking a plank at sword point. I light a cigarette and—

—a flash of purple zips down the stairs! It neighs and gallops to a stop at my feet. Googly eyes spinning... A Lance, the Unicorn plushieBot.

The unicorn says,

Kibosh the smoke, dickhead.

I flick the cigarette outside.

Lance guards me. It paces back and forth like George

Carlin on stage mid-rant.

I hold Chauncey's cigarette case in front of the plushieBot.

"This symbol on the case..." I say, "What's this mean?"

Unicorn plushieBot sighs.

Seriously? It's Sanskrit for Shiv, ...
You know? Shiva? Destroyer of Worlds?

"Got it."

Read a fucking book, you degenerate.

I hear the boy from the top of the stairs.

"Mamma," he says, "there's a man at the door for you! He's got my name and is pretending to be me!"

~

Sévérine, the boy and I sit at a dinner table next to a floor-to-ceiling window. Glass beneath us. Unobstructed views of LA unfurl in all directions.

Sévérine and I sit across from each other. The boy sits in a booster seat at the head of the table. He grips his fork the way you would a hammer, attacking chocolate cakes in his bowl. A pastry box of the treats on the table says in Swedish:

"NEGERBOL"

I haven't stop staring at the kid since we sat down for dinner. He's got epicanthic folds to his eyelids. A slight cleft in his chin, both like mine... The odds of both features appearing in the same person...

Sévérine watches me stare.

She says, "He's a miniature you."

I smile at the boy.

"Hey," I say, "We're going to be buddies, okay?"

"We'll see."

"What do you mean?"

He says, "Guys always say that to me. I think it's just because Mamma is famous and really pretty. But they never stick around."

I say, "But, this is different... Hey, I know what it's like because I never knew my mom or my dad. I'm not going anywhere."

The boy releases his fork midair and it clangs to his bowl. He props himself up onto his elbow.

"You were like Oliver Twist?"

"You mean, was I an orphan? Yeah..."

"Did you sing songs?"

"Haha, no. It's not like the movie. Hey, do you like movies...Let's go to the movies. After it ends, we'll get in line and see another."

"Mamma never has to wait in lines. What movie are we going to see?"

"Whatever you want. Something with your mom in it? The Red Geisha?"

"That's not really my momma. Plus, she's a terrible actress. The girl in the Boötes Void movie should have won."

Sévérine smiles. "That was more like a commercial for Galacticology than a movie."

Both the boy and I reach for the carafe of glögg at the same time. I let him take it.

I say, "Hey, Dee—"

"DeShawn," says the boy. "My name is DeShawn."

"Sorry... Hey, DeShawn. Do you like sports?"

"Mamma, is this man going to keep asking me stupid questions forever?"

"Probably. At least until you too get to know each other better, but yes, probably. Be nice."

I watch them interact with each other. I try to remember my mother's face... I can't.

I say, "Why do you have to go back to Stockholm next week?"

"He's got school. Also, I'm prepping for a film I'm directing in Denmark. Preproduction is everything."

"Football," DeShawn says, "My favorite sport is football. I like Arsenal. They're my favorite team. I also like e-sports like real-person shooter games."

"Isn't Arsenal in London?"

"Yes, but Mamma thinks their new center is cute. He's Welsh."

"I see."

"He gave me his jersey."

I glance at Sévérine, she shrugs.

I say, "So, how long will you be in Scandinavia... I mean, when are you and DeShawn coming back to the States?"

The boy continues, "But Mamma's favorite friend is the race car driver. He talks funny like Speedy Gonzales. When we were in Monte Carlo, he let me sit in his car. All the women kept trying to get his attention, but Mamma always wins."

Sévérine says, "Okay, baby, I'm sure he doesn't care."

"And, he taught me to count in Portuguese and he had really nice hair like Mamma... He takes a lot of selfies... I don't think he has any shirts, though. He never wore any."

I say, "Really? Does your Mamma have a lot of friends?"

She says, "That's none of your business!"

"You're right. I'm sorry. Would you pass the wine, please?"

The boy picks up his fork.

"Mamma, what are Negerbols made of?"

Sévérine says, "I don't know... 90% chocolate?"

He stares at the chocolate cake.

He says, "So, this is ten percent negros?"

The more I try not to laugh, the worse it gets.

"What's funny, Mamma?"

"Nothing, he has a lot of growing up to do. Let's get

those jammies on, min älskling. He'll tuck you in, right, Dee?"

I say, "Yeah!"

The boy slides off his chair and walks over to me. He raises his arms and opens and closes his hands. I lift him up. His arms wrap around my neck. Without much space separating our faces, our eyes have to travel to take the entirety of each other in.

"Hey, you can call me Dad, okay?"

"Too soon," he says.

The boy squirms. I ignore the cue for a beat before letting the boy go.

He says, "Good talk, mister."

The boy and his mother walk hand and hand up the stairs. I walk to a bathroom. I shut the door... and I lose it.

A rap on the door... I splash water on my face to mask the tears before opening it.

Sévérine is there.

"Hi."

"Hi."

I try to squeeze past her but she blocks my way. She steps inside the bathroom and pulls the door shut behind her.

She shakes her head.

"Uh-uh. No."

"But you said I can tuck him in. I want to tuck in my boy."

"You can cry," she says, "but you have to get it all out in here. Tonight, he's forming his first memory of you. The memory he'll carry with him for the rest of his life. So, when you walk out of this bathroom, you better have a smile on your face."

"Okay."

She says, "Let's get one thing out of the way. We are never going to end up together."

"How can you say that? We're just—"

"Shut up. Don't interrupt me. If you still want to get to

know him, great. There's no chance with me. Never. You're here for him. If that's not okay with you, go away forever."

I nod.

She says, "I'm giving you a chance here. One chance."

"Okay."

"But if you break my kid's heart, I will fucking kill you. Do you understand me?"

"I would never—"

"Good."

She glares at my ash-encrusted flip flops.

"In order for you to be in his life, you need some stability in yours. I need you to get your shit together. Has your suspension ended?"

"Yeah."

"When was your last Bellum fight?"

I say, "Fuck Bellum."

"That's not helping your cause, here."

"They fucked me."

SLAP!

"Grow up!" she says. "I'll see what I can do."

I nod.

She searches my face.

"Are we good?"

"Yeah..." I say, "I think so."

"Alright, then," Sévérine says, "Wipe your face. Now, let's go say goodnight to our baby. Time to be a daddy."

She speaks a command to her homes AI, and the mirror obscuring her medicine cabinet dissolves away to reveal its contents... The same schedule of medications that are inside my cabinet. The name on the inhalers' labels: Nils DeShawn Trustfall-Falk.

~

The Uber stops in front of my house. There's a man sitting on my steps... It's Bobby, wearing red Speedos, running shoes and my bathrobe stands up when he sees me. He splashes through my koi fish moat and, trampling my lawn, he sprints toward me with a crazed look in his eyes. His arms are Smurf blue...

"Keep the car! Keep the car! We gotta go!"

He's got my bathroom scale in one hand and garbage bag slung over his other shoulder like a ghetto Santa.

"Are you burglarizing my neighbors again?"

I move over, but instead of diving into the seat next to me, he drops the scale onto the sidewalk.

"Strip down to your underwear and get on the scale!"

I stare, blinking at him.

"Fuck, dude. C'mon!" he says, "I've been calling you for an hour! Bellum booked you for a fight!"

I take off my uniform: leather jacket, hoodie, board shorts.

"Never thought that'd ever happen... Hey, I'm only a few pounds over fight weight since yesterday, so why are you stressing out?"

"You're fighting two weight classes down at Lightweight. The challenger dropped out and you're the replacement at 155 lbs."

I step onto the scale: 173 pounds.

"This is gonna be sketchy, but it's doable," Bobby says.

He tosses the scale into the car and dumps the garbage bag's contents onto the seat:

my mouthpiece and cup...

bags of Epsom salts...

my good towels...

bottles of rubbing alcohol...

a garbage bags box from my kitchen...

a roll of duct tape...

...castor oil...

...a coffee mug with a bag of chewing tobacco stuffed inside.

And a shopping bag from the corner drug store.

He tosses me the garbage bag.

I know what time it is: I bite a hole in the bottom, and two on each side, and pull it over my head like a tunic. Bobby duct tapes the bottom around my waist and then tapes a bag around each of my arms for sleeves.

He dives into the car and slides over to make room for me, and the playlist shifts to his settings and plays Atlanta Rhythm Section's, *So Into You.*

I hesitate, standing outside of the car with my hand on the door.

I say, "What time is the weigh in?"

Bobby pokes his head through the doorway.

"We got a half hour, no... make that 27 minutes to make it to the Otium to check in. Then 2 hours and 27 minutes to get your ass onto the scale to make weight for the official weigh in. Not just be in the room, be on the scale."

"Room?" I say, "What are you talking about?"

"You're weighing in twice. The first is official, and the second is for the Pay per view. The official weigh-in is going to be behind closed doors inside the boardroom. That's the one that counts. The pay-per-view weigh in afterwards is just for show. Once you make weight for the official way in behind closed doors, you're golden."

"What's the point of that?"

Bobby says, "They already had one opponent drop out. It's to save Bellum the embarrassment of you showing up and missing weight on live paper view. If you can't make weight, it's better for them if you miss weight behind closed doors where they can explain it away. But this is the spectator sport, and the fans want to see you square off under the lights. No more jaw flapping! Let's go!"

I don't like this. Weight cuts are hell even when you have an entire training camp to deal with them. In a perfect world, weight loss happens weeks before you step foot on a scale mostly through fat loss.

Fat loss is the first component to making weight for a fight. The second component, loss of water weight.

Okay, check it out... Say you walk around naturally at 190 pounds, and you compete as a welterweight at 170. You get booked for a fight that's, say, eight weeks away, so step away from the pizza and you get your ass in training camp. You burn fat naturally during workouts in training camp, combined with manipulating your diet and nutrition over this eight-week time span. You get yourself close to the goal weight the days before the fight, but leave yourself a few pounds overweight... Say, 178 pounds, the day before weigh-ins. That night before weigh in day and throughout weigh in day you, you purge the remaining eight pounds of weight through water. In combat sports with weight classes, the larger combatant has an advantage. The saying goes, a decent big man will usually beat a great little man, so the entire point of weight classes to eliminate the size advantage.

The logic of leaving the eight pounds to cut in water weight is that after you officially weigh in at 155, you can start rehydrating the instant you step off the scale and have a full day before the fight to gain all that water weight back...

Most times, when you step into the cage to fight the next day, not only would you have regained all that water weight back, often times, you'll have gained even more. It's not unusual for a fight contested at the welterweight class limit of 155 pounds have both combatants step into the cage close to 180 pounds when the fight starts. Legally, the only thing that matters is your official weight when you step onto the scale the day before.

Done correctly, the more weight you lose through fat loss during the weeks leading up to the event, the less weight you have to lose through water the day before. If you're lucky, you get the full eight weeks, but often times, fights get offered on short notice and you'll struggle to burn as much fat as possible in maybe as few as two or three weeks, then make up the difference by purging your body of water... Our bodies are about 70 percent water. You lose more than about five percent of that water and you're compromising your health. Ten percent water loss in a short time period and you're in the danger zone. Lose too much water to fast or fail to rehydrate properly and you can suffer from all kinds of wonderful maladies including stroke, kidney failure and/or heart failure, thickened blood the consistency of sludge. In short, you drop dead.

Even if you manage all of this carefully, your brain, in its dehydrated state, if far more susceptible to damage from head trauma, like a kick to the head, and you're willingly stepping into the one situation where that is a guaranteed occurrence. So, maybe you take a beating but rally to win your fight. Your brain starts to swell inside your skull and pressure builds up, and you've got a wicked ringing in your ears... The promotor gives your belt or crown or pimp chalice – whatever - while the color commentator hands you the mic to walk the viewers through the playback and as you search for the right words to reply to a question and...

You drop dead.

I'm on a fast ticking clock anyway, but I'm in no rush to speed it up.

I lean my head into the car and look at Bobby.

He's got all the items in a shopping bag pinched between his knees, and my bathroom scale sits at his feet as his thumbs fly across a hand-held phone as he reads and replies to texts.

"I can't do it."

Bobby reads a text from his phone, "They're offering 190K to show and another 190K to win, plus pay per view shares and part of the gate... And enough social credit to keep you in good standing with your neighborhood association.

"Bobby..."

"The official weigh-ins for everyone else on the card

except the champion and you just ended, so you two will step on the scale behind closed doors of the boardroom. That will be your official weigh in with the state athletic commission. You do it at the same time to keep it fair. After it's official, you guys will be too late to be trotted on stage for the Pay Per View dog-and-pony-show, so there's that."

"It's too dangerous. No."

"Win the crown, you get Shonda back. I guarantee it... I know women."

He tucks his phone into his Speedo's waistband and takes a bottle of pills from the shopping bag and tosses it at me.

Dandelion root. A natural diuretic.

"Swallow them dry."

I look back at the sign on my lawn... my front door... and contemplate Miles' name scratched on its other side. I sigh...

"How many?"

"All of them. Get in the fucking car."

I shut the door behind me and the car starts to pull away.

Bobby says, "Let's get that paper!"

Out my window, I see a mylar-wrapped issue of today's Sentinel

I say, "Car, stop!"

Don't ask me why, but I open the door and grab the newspaper of my curb.

Back in the Uber, I begin working my way through the bottle of pills, using my own saliva to wash them down. It's starting to suck by the fifth pill which gets stuck sideways in my throat.

"Alright," he says, "Good enough, bro."

He pulls the tobacco and my favorite 'fuck you, you fucking fuck!' coffee mug out of the shopping bag.

"Chew and spit."

I say, "Fuck, man. Couldn't you buy bubble gum? This shit is nasty. I might swallow tobacco juice and puke."

"That'd be ideal. Put this on, too."

Without unbuckling he wiggles his way out of my terrycloth bathrobe, leaving him covered only by his Speedos, and tosses my robe onto my lap. I unbuckle my seatbelt and put it on over my plastics, cinch it at the waist and re-tether myself.

Bobby says, "Uber, turn the heater on. Full blast."

We pull up to the freeway queue. T's backed up, with several pods waiting ahead of us. Bobby checks his handheld for time.

"Fuck!"

When it's our pod's turn, the cars travel at a speed so slow that it feels like forever to pass each pained divider line, and we see newsVertisements in their entirety play out on a single holoBoard.

A newsVertisement combines a traffic delay warning with no explanation as to why, with an ad for Crackle asking the rhetorical question, Wanna supercharge your day? Then the traffic does something it never does.

It stops.

Bobby turns to me and says, "Get out."

I know exactly what he wants.

I open the door and pour my tobacco juice from my coffee cup onto the freeway, kick off my flip-flops and get out of the car and, bathrobe flowing behind me, I bust a Chinese fire drill. I run around the car... As best as I can with a jacked ankle... Barefoot. Bobby shuts the door behind me to trap the heat inside of the car.

The tarmac, still warm from the day's heat, squishes underfoot like treading on loaves of white bread, and its fumes have an acrid reek to it.

I run alongside the line that separates lanes. These are still painted onto the road for the benefit of the select humans who retain a special permit to drive their own vehicles. Law enforcement, trauma surgeons, Hollywood fixers. Before the enforcement of automated driving, the median lines were about ten feet long. About the wheelbase of a Prius. Although if asked, most drivers would swear that the lines were only two feet long. The stripes had to be ten feet because if they were any shorter, they simply would not register in the brains of drivers traveling 55 miles per hour or greater. The fact that the stripe I'm running alongside stretches the entire length of my Prius and the two cars in front of it tells you all you need to know about potential top speeds on the 405.

Sweat begins to trickle inside the plastic suit, and there's a tickle running down my back.

On my third lap at the front of the car, I glimpse a little girl smiling at me from the rear-view window of the car in front of mine. The next lap, I smile at her. She cries... Poor kid. I forgot to put my teeth in.

Traffic begins to move and I finish my lap and open the door. A wall of heat blasts my face, and I have to fight survival instinct to get back in. Bobby is drenched. He fans his crotch with a box of tampons (don't worry, we'll get to that!), and I tell myself to avoid looking down at the dick print in his Speedos and fail, and now that shit's burnt into my eyes forever. I resume chewing the tobacco and spitting into the cup. The freeway stops again, but because we're directly under freeway's the carpool compliance scanner, I keep my ass put. I'm sweating pretty well now. No idea how much weight I've dropped so far.

Bobby says, "We got fifteen minutes."

Through the front windscreen, the Otium is visible.

The pod moves, slowly and picking up speed for a bit and stops.

I bust another Chinese fire drill. When I return to the car, I'm coughing my lungs out. Even under the best of conditions, Los Angeles air quality is a step above Chernobyl. I don't want to imagine the gummy ash-and-phlegm paste I'm coating my lungs with.

Eventually, we move at a pace just faster than a bicycle

can keep up with.

On the other side of the freeway in the lanes going the other direction, There's something straight out of an action movie. The road on either side of the freeway overpass is... Well, it's fucking gone. This leaves a single car trapped on a stretch of freeway like Raiders of the Lost Ark when, after activating a booby trap, the temple floor falls away un crumbling underneath the hero's feel forcing him to leap from tile to tile all the forcing the hero to dodge blow darts from the walls. Except, in this case, it's not blow darts. It's cannon fire... Turrets dropped down from the underside of the overpass, and strafe the car with plasma fire until it bursts into flames and explodes. A man returns fire with a pistol and is cut down. Another makes a run for the edge of the square and makes a jump across the gap for the freeway behind him but disintegrates against an invisible energy field.

"Heh," Bobby says, "That car had Valley license plates."

I'm drenched inside the plastic and, despite my vigilance, I'm dizzy from swallowing some of the tobacco juice.

We drive past the roadside fires, still laying siege to the Otium's energy field.

Bobby says. "Four minutes."

Views change to the ocean, city, and back to the Valley as we corkscrew up the mountain to the Otium. The upper floors of the cone-shaped building overhang our approach, like we're driving under God's shoe mid-step after his heel strikes the ground and his toes are coming down fast on our heads.

Into the OTIUM concourse. A scuderia of exotic cars zipping in and out. A car speeds off: its driver laying prone on a carbon fiber credit card with wheels. Another car of see-through Plexiglass resembling a wasp, double parked.

We open the door and spring from the car while it's still rolling and sprint for the lobby, where at the door a securityBot commands us to halt... No, that's not accurate.

Both of its heads and all of its limbs are oriented toward me only. Bobby has to actively get its attention by waving his hand-held in front of its 'faces'.

A security resembles a Wing Chun dummy wrapped in pink latex for skin, except for their expressionless department-store mannequin heads which they sometimes wrap in actual human facial skin...

The Bot scans a bar code on Bobby's screen and the machine stands down, deescalating to its default state of readiness. The securityBot smooths its four-armed navy-blue blazer and tucks its shirt into the waistband of hits three-legged khaki pants. Its primping does nothing to make it look less jarring and hostile. Which, in a securityBot, that's the entire point.

The energy door dissolves away, allowing us to enter the Otium.

"Go! Go! Go!" Bobby shouts.

The Otium's lobby, circular and minimal. Vaunted-class guests, angelic in loose-flowing garb... An uncanny number of twins. Is this a luxury resort, or a cryogenic mausoleum?

There's nobody here from Bellum to greet us, so I jog towards the front desk while Bobby fires off texts with his handheld. He glances up to me long enough to mouth, "One minute."

I don't get far. A pair of hotel managers, human, intercept me.

"I'm DeShawn Trustfall. I need to check in, right now!"

"We're sorry, sir, but we're going to have to ask you to leave."

The tiles of the floor we're standing on pixilates into an ad with my opponent's face squared off with an image of me retrieved from photo archives.

I point down, then to my face, encrusted with freeway grime, ash, and sweat.

"Look," I say, "That's me!"

"Okay, buddy, let's go."

I yank my arm away as one of the men reaches out for it, and the reflex to simultaneously thrust my fingers into his eyes begins to fire but I shut it down, saving this motherfucker from having a really bad day.

The irony of not being able to stay in the same hotel where I'm headlining the entertainment because of my Q-SCore. I know how Sammy Davis junior must have felt.

Over their shoulders, I spot an approaching securityBot. Three limbs extended with fizzing Taser attachments. The fourth, an open chela, face level, ready to clamp, moving towards me...

"Mr. Trustfall?"

I turn. From across the lobby, Bobby is running behind men with name badges swinging from lanyards around their necks as they weave a path through party girls, polo shirt-and-loafers convention attendees, and a sunburnt family with a smoking mom and screaming kids to descend upon us. One of them, an athletic commission employee (because it says so on his shirt), checks my name off of a tablet as the time counter spins down and stops with seconds left. The other one, a man in a suit who's obviously a Bellum employee because no native Angeleno, businessperson or not, would be caught wearing an affectation like a business suit, fastens a wristband on me.

"Cool," Bobby says. "Your room is ready. We've got a little over two hours before you report to the scale."

He hands me the coffee mug and the pouch of tobacco.

"Get to chewing, my man."

We walk.

Artificial feel-good sunlight cascade into the lobby through windows on all sides and reflect off of the marble which induces the illusion of walking on light. We pass the front desk with lines for the privileged, while the ones privileged enough not to be troubled with lines at all head straight for their rooms. For once in my life, this includes me.

Gongs and Tibetan singing bowls chime throughout the lobby. The composition, *Longplayer,* is live streamed from England. The soothing tones started on New Year's Day, 2000 and will play nonstop for a millennium without repeating itself until December 31st, 2999. Then the song will start over from the beginning.

A rap star from Compton sprints across my path to avoid a woman I recognize from the newsVertisements as the soon-to-be-ex socialite from the Palisades whose Q-SCore is in free fall due to cheating on her husband... With the very rapper who is running away from her. She's known for being vocal in the past about letting 'those kinds of people' into fine establishments. Right now, Otium management approaches the woman, extending their arms as though corralling a horse to nudge her out of the building. A trio of porterBots follows close behind, wheeling piles of her Louis Vuitton luggage outside.

Interesting... You can't step foot inside the building without a high enough Q-SCore or a good reason to be here, yet I got hassled every step of the way and everyone let Bobby right through. Hell, he shouldn't even be able to get past the gates of my neighborhood.

Pixels spin up from the floor congealing into an AI hologram of a young woman, toothpaste commercial pretty. Tennis skirt and snug cardigan with a name tag pinned to it that says, *CONCIERGE*. The AI's gesture to follow it echoes the only reason to watch the five-day forecast in LA: a glimpse of the weather girl when she turns sideways.

She says,

"Hello, Mr. Trustfall. My name is Calliope, your guide and concierge. Shall we proceed?"

"Yeah, why the fuck not."

"Splendid. You have unrestricted access, so there's a lot to cover. I'm fully interactive, so feel free to ask me any questions. Are we ready?"

I nod.

Calliope says,

"There are two types of elevators. The interior ones which take you to the bottom third of the inverted pyramid-shaped building... The floors where the Casino, restaurants, shops, and lower offices are. These elevator banks are conveniently located past the casinos so you'll have easy 24-hour access to entertainment both coming and going..."

I feel the gaze of the other hotel guests as they scan my Q-SCore. As we traverse the lobby, people avoid contact with me like shoaling fish defending themselves with swam confusion, opening a hole in their school for an approaching shark to swim right through without catching any individual fish. I have to laugh.

Deeper into the building there's a point where, intellectually, you feel like there should be a gradual change in light after you cross a point where no natural outside light can possibly reach, however, the artificial lights maintain perfect and even daylight no matter where you are.

Cigarettes dangle from lips pinched between discolored fingers, or crushed and left to smolder in ashtrays which seem to be everywhere. Herds of gamblers rotate in a slow waltz from table to table. Sedated looking people with plastic cups wedged between their knees pulling at levers for a Pavlovian reward childhood carnival sounds and lights. The air this deep in the casino may be filtered but you can never get rid of all of the grit. The grit seeps into your pores. It forms a layer of film that glosses the color of everything it settles on and makes the skin of the waitresses' bare shoulders seem more lurid.

"Calliope," I say, "You mentioned two types of elevators?"

"Yes, that is correct. From the tenth floor and upward, you may use the exterior elevators. We are proud to have the world's only omnidirectional elevators with privacy functionality and perfect safety records. The glass cars are affixed to the Otium by electromagnetic force that not only takes passengers up and down but glides sideways along the floors too. Useful, considering that the Otium is basically a funnel balanced on its tip and that as you go up, each floor has more square footage than the one beneath it, increasing as you ascend. On the top three floors, you'll find the indoor stadium which can accommodate 39,000; state of the art business suites for our blue-chip corporate tenants, including diplomatic suites kept for Consuls General – all linked by an interior freeway system of trams to help navigate the vast distances; The Vaunted suites, where you will enjoy your stay with us—"

I say, "Earlier you bragged that the omnidirectional elevators have perfect safety record. You mean nobody has ever died on one yet."

"Haha, I see, you are, as they say in the vernacular, fucking with me, Mr. Trustfall—"

"Oh, I'm serious."

"Please rest assured, if anyone expires on our elevators, it would take them straight to heaven. Well, Eden to be precise. All Vaunted suites include access to Eden: a rainforest with its own private beach and west-facing pool with views that turn the entire Pacific as your infinity pool. The hoverJet air pad."

There it is. The killing jar looms from a platform in the center of the casino floor illuminated by lights whose cascading beams hang on motes of cigarette smoke. People still call it a cage or an 'octagon' the way people call tissues Kleenex and photocopies Xeroxes which are specific brand names. The cage is actually a cube. Watching a fight through a 6D augmented reality app with your Vaunt or Halo makes the sides shift like a Necker Cube, orienting itself to best display the action going on inside with no turnbuckles or support beams to obstruct your view.

For the moment the cage is the backdrop for snapshots, on display until it is moved into place for tomorrow night's venue.

We pass the hotel's seafood restaurant which known more for being a great spot to spot movie stars and other celebrities than its cuisine. Its logo, a trident, is frosted onto the glass doors which are open. As we pass its entrance, I see the famous shark tank inside embedded into a wall. The tank's lights are dimmed and ambient light from the restaurant can't penetrate the murk, so the sharks remain cloaked in darkness.

"Is Jaws on a cigarette break?"

"Yes, actually! Great whites require vast expanses to roam and are notoriously short-lived in captivity, often dying within two weeks. Our shark is a genetically-designed, built from CRISPR technology. Although he's modified to withstand life in tight enclosures, he's still an 18-footer. To square this problem, we turned to the architectural genius of the great Richard Neutra. His rediscovered archives showed our engineers how to hollow out the center of the Otium -- again, like a funnel -- so the center of the building in the top three floors is a free-range aquarium with access to the rooftop beach."

"Why are geniuses the biggest fucking idiots?"

"Oh, don't worry," she says, "His palate is genetically engineered to prefer a specific diet."

"Meaning?"

"He's a vegan."

"Oh, fuck off!"

"Haha, it's true. Our great white is spliced with whale shark DNA. His preferred diet is plankton."

I say, "Plankton are in the animal kingdom."

Bobby says, "That depends on whether or not you consider fish meat."

"What the hell are you two talking about?" I say, "Even if you don't consider seafood meat, if all he eats is plankton exclusively, he couldn't even pass for a goddamn vegetarian!"

"Statistically only five people a year die from shark attacks. You're ten times more likely to be trampled by a hippopotamus, and it's 20,000 times more likely that a snake will kill you."

"Yeah? Let a hippopotamus run loose in a hotel and see what happens."

"Haha, if you look, sometimes you'll catch a glimpse of the shark moving behind the interior walls on the upper floors."

"So, what did you splice its DNA with to get it to live in enclosed spaces?"

"We spliced it with manta rays to make him less prone to depression in captivity. Getting them to eat is a challenge that kills most great white sharks in captivity. Depressed sharks starve to death. Manta

DNA also makes their temperament cuddlier like the petting tank animals at the Aquarium of the Pacific in Long Beach. In fact, we sectioned off part of the rooftop infinity pool as his own petting tank. For kids only, no parents. He just loves taking selfies with kids... Grownups, not so much."

"What's its beef with adults?"

"Children tend to be pure of heart. Animals can tell if you're bad or good."

"Is it a shark or fucking Santa Claus?"

She winks.

"We spliced in some Willy Wonka DNA."

"So, let me guess, you gave this cuddly, vegan, manta shark a cute name like, "Gil" ...or "Ray"?

"No, Gilles."

"Well, that is actually kind of cute."

"Gilles, the Rais."

I say, "Oh, burn in Hell."

"What?" Bobby says, "I don't get it."

"Please," I say, "Both of you stop talking. Just... Shut the fuck up..."

Calliope disappears.

The sound of the commotion around a corner reaches us before we see its source.

By the elevator banks, a young woman struggles to evade a trio securityBots.

She says, "They took my baby! I know she's in here!"

The woman dodges left and right, but it's futile. She has but two legs, and their combined arms are a dozen.

She turns to me and screams, "Help me!"

The securityBot snags her head in its cella and holds her in place...

"Help MEEEE!"

...and shocks her into compliance with all three its tasers at the same time. It opens its pincher, releasing her, and she collapses to the floor where she lays inert.

A man pushes through the crowd. "I'm a physician!"

After examining her, the doctor says, "Her heart has stopped."

The doctor breaks a glass panel on the wall for the emergency Life Alert. He's and about to mash the button but stops.

He says, "Does she have insurance?"

A matriarch type, swathed in five layers of Gianfranco Ferre speaks with a Locust Valley accent.

"Oh, please. Clearly, the young woman is a surrogate. What do you think?"

The hotel doctor says, "There's nothing I can do for her then."

Bobby and I step into an elevator as a man, presumably the matriarch's husband, leers down the dead girl's blouse whilst swirling a snifter of brandy and says, "Such a waste."

The elevator doors shut.

Inside the elevator's interior doors, a holograph of me, rising from the ashes like the Phoenix.

~

Bobby slides a room key into its reader. There's a beep and a light flashes green.

We enter my suite... Deep-pile carpet your feet sink into up to the ankles. A California king bed hovering above an electromagnetic box spring. The kind of room your favorite holoPorn happens in.

The officials follow. I strip and step on it while all observe. All that work I've done so far, I'm thinking I'm down to 160 pounds. It'll suck, but it's definitely doable within a couple hours to cut 5 pounds. The scale settles...

167. Fuck my life.

The man with the tablet glances at his watch and shakes his head as he makes a notation. While Bobby is bullshitting with them over weigh-in details on the way out the door, I search the shopping bag for coffee. I break the seal of the espresso bag and chew a handful of beans into a gritty and bitter paste, pluck a dandelion root pill from its bottle and place it on my tongue. By the time the door clicks shut, I've already washed it all down with one bottle cap full — and only one cap full—of distilled water. Drinking anything more than what is necessary to get the paste down my throat would be counterproductive.

Okay, check it out, kids. Let's say you need to lose the equivalent of a toddler in weight in the time it takes to wash and dry a load of laundry, but you've thrashed your legs, and you need to save what gas you've got left in the tank for competition, be it weight lifting, jockeying, combat sports... Or maybe you're a model who booked a last-minute bathing suit catalogue shoot. Running is not an option. You're screwed, right?

Wrong.

This is how it's done. Those espresso beans I chewed are for caffeine, which is a diuretic. And the dandelion root? Also, a diuretic. The weight you are going to be losing is water. Short of a hacksaw, it's impossible to lose so much weight in such a short space of time any other way. Luck for you, for the most part, you are water, and water is really fucking heavy.

In a perfect world, you'd stop consuming all salts and would be drinking a gallon of only distilled water in the days leading up to the weight cut. The day of your cut, stop drinking.

All liquids.

Period.

Why distilled water and no salts up to the day of the cut? Simple. To minimize water retention. Avoiding salt is obvious. Distilled water, not so much. You see, tap water has salts and other solubles that work against you when you while purging water from your system. And if you try to game the system by cutting your water intake too soon you:

- Force your body into survival mode, which means it will horde all the water already inside of it. You will stop urinating and, therefore, fail to make weight.
- Die, you idiot. You've gone a few days exerting energy, sweating out all of your fluids without replacing them by drinking? Thank your sponsors.

~

If we are still residents of El Mundo Perfecto, you take caffeine (in quick dissolving capsule form), and dandelion root capsules together with breakfast, lunch, and dinner starting as soon as the day before you need to make weight. But you live in my world where you're missing fingers in the drop your deadbeat dad onto your marble floor, and anything fucked up can happen will happen... like, your best friend didn't want to spend the extra money to get caffeine tablets so he went quick and dirty. Caffeine pills get subbed for espresso beans, and you're doing Chinese fire drills across the freeway wearing a 2-ply.

Are we still talking about the perfect world here? Yeah? OK, this is the deal.

You must complete the following steps the night before

you need to step on the scale. (If the weigh-ins are not until the following night then do this the morning of the weigh-ins.) You need the following items.

Write this shit down:

- A credit card.
- Your bottles of rubbing alcohol.
- The bags of Epsom salt.
- A plastic bag full of ice.
- Some towels. (Fuck Bobby for bringing my good ones.)
- Some kind of timing device.

So, you close the bathroom door and stuff a towel in the crack underneath it to hermetically sealed the room from air coming in or out.

Plug the tub.

Run the shower—yes, the shower—you want the bathroom nice and steamy, so make it hot enough to be almost intolerable, but not enough to scald you. While the water is running you pour in some bottles of rubbing alcohol and a bag of Epsom salt.

Bear with me. I will explain this in a bit.

By the time you've filled your tub, the air in the bathroom should be thick with steam. Turn the water off and set your timer. I prefer to use music. This serves a dual purpose of taking my mind off the suck factor. Pick a song. Put it on auto-repeat.

Get in the damn tub. (If the water is hot enough this will take a while.) Lower yourself so that our head and torso are underwater. If the tub is too short and either your head or your legs will fit but not both, the head is the priority. Submerge your head so that only your eyes, nose and mouth are above water. Sing your ass off. The acoustics in the bathroom will make 2 Chainz sound like The Weekend.

Okay, so this is why you want hot water, Epsom salt, and alcohol. Our bodies shed most of our heat through our heads, which is why you want it submerged in an environment at least a few degrees warmer than your body temperature. This will stifle your body's ability to cool itself through your head. The hot water will also raise the temperature of your core, causing you to sweat. Yes, even underwater you will sweat.

This is where the additives in the water come into play. The salinity and high alcohol content of the water make it hypertonic. In plain English, there will be a far greater concentration of solubles in the water outside of your skin cells than inside of them. This great disparity will cause the bathwater to suck moisture out of your body through your skin through a process called forward osmosis. Cool, right?

Remember when I said you are, for the most part, water? Much of that water stores right underneath your skin, and your skin is a two-way membrane. Fluids like to travel from areas of high concentrations to low. The salt and alcohol concentration of the bathwater will fool your skin into thinking that it is drier outside of your body than inside of it. And when you sweat, the water will not just flow out of your skin, the bathwater will suck it out.

When you've mangled the lyrics of the song three times through, times up. Get out of the tub. Drain it and refill it with water, salt, and alcohol just as before.

While the tub is refilling, towel yourself off. Take the credit card and wick the remaining moisture off of your skin with scraping motions like it's a squeegee and you're a window (I use my store card from the frozen yogurt shop. No reason other than it's the one I've always used, and I think it brings me good luck.) As soon as an area of sweat appears, towel or wick it away. You don't want it to stay on your skin long enough to evaporate. If that happens, your body will cool, and you will stop sweating. This is also why you want steam in the air.

Repeat after me: 'Humidity is my friend.'

Step on the scale. Smile. If you feel faint, leave the bathroom (shut the door behind you to keep the steam inside.) and place the ice bag on the back of your neck to cool yourself down. You'll be lusting after anything wet to put in your mouth. Do not drink anything.

Repeat the process until you are within a few pounds over your target weight. Why would you want to leave yourself a few pounds over your target weight when you go to bed? This is because you'll lose those extra pounds in water weight overnight while you sleep simply by breathing out moisture, and you don't wanna step on the scale too light because you will have that much more water to replace when you rehydrate (we'll get to that later).

For those of you who are hardcore, there is a skin cream some people have used because of its off-label use which accelerates sweating. Before you go to bed you slather it all over your skin, put a garbage bag on and then layer on clothes over top that, and sleep away a few extra pounds. When you wake up, towel yourself off.

Oh yeah, almost forgot.

Do not shower. Do not bathe.

Remember when I said your skin is a two-way membrane? Your skin will absorb any moisture your skin comes in contact with right back into its pores, erasing some, if not all, of the work you've just done to get it out. You may be ripe when you weigh in but at least you'll make weight, which is all that matters.

OK, perfect real fantasy over.

Back in the real world, I don't have overnight. I have a couple of hours and my throat is so dry and tight the lining scratches against each itself every time I swallow. I've long since stopped singing and after all of Madonna's Greatest Hits has cycled through and it takes great care to climb out of the tub because my muscles, plundered of water and electrolytes, protest at the very notion of contracting. I tumble onto the floor and breathe air below the steam line.

I talk to my Vaunt.

"Jacqueline, play Madonna, *Vogue!*

I take a moment while the tile cools my back, then pull myself into a sitting position on the toilet seat.

Desperate to work up a greater sweat, I start voguing while I refill the tub. I sing as a lower myself into the tub:

Greta Garbo, and Monroe
Dietrich and DiMaggio
Marlon Brando, Jimmy Dean
On the cover of a magazine...

I repeat the process one more time for two more songs, striking a pose each time while I wait for the tub to drain and refill. 'Vogue' is no longer playing. But it doesn't matter. I don't even hear the music anymore, and it's not so much me singing as it is a chant.

Marilyn Manson, Iago
Cthulhu, and Ernst Stavro...
Hans Landa, Palpatine
On the cover of a magazine...

I exit the tub by pulling myself over the sill, draping one leg over the lip, and then allowing myself to fall in a controlled plop onto the floor. I take a moment to rest my hands on my knees and regain my equilibrium.

I dry myself off there and step onto the scale... fuck, fuck, fuck, fuck, FUCK.

I call out to Bobby. No reply. He's not in the suite. Where the fuck could he possibly be?

By sheer force of will, I manage the strength to pull on a clean pair of shorts and a t-shirt and step into my flip-flops.

The distance between my room to the elevator seems to stretch on forever and I wonder if it'd be faster to say screw it to walking and just crawl but I make it.

The spa is empty which suits me just fine. I peel off my shirt and kick off the flip-flops and get in the dry sauna, once again rotating my time inside and out of it to music. My voguing now resembles the zombie walk from Michael Jackson's *Thriller.*

Charles Manson, Nero...
Heydrich and Oranjello—

When my eyes open, I'm on the spa floor outside of the sauna looking up at a kid I recognize as the heavyweight champion and his coach and a pair of his teammates who are standing over me with concerned looks on their faces. A cool and wet towel is rolled up and under my head. My tailbone is sore and my mouth lusts for moisture.

The kid, 100 pounds heavier than I am, helps me up and onto the bench with no more effort exerted than if he was lifting a mischievous puppy while his coach swaps out the old wet towel for a fresh one which he places on top of my head. The heavyweight champ sits next to me on the bench. His movements are crisp. His cheeks are a bit drawn in but he looks fresh enough to fight right now. Youth. He tells me he's already at his target weight. Yes, even heavyweights have a weight limit they must adhere to. He and his coach just came down here to monitor a teammate who is fighting on the undercard shed a few pounds. The fighter they are helping stands on the fringe of the group. He has the swagger and bravado you'd expect from someone his age. He has never known the world before the sport went mainstream and my legend being a part of bringing it there. His eyes narrow from wide with amazement to slits, and he cocks his head back and to the side as the process in his mind plays out from wanting my autograph to deciding it would be more satisfying to brag to his friends how he crushed me under his heel like a cockroach.

Their coach asks me where my nowhere-to-be-seen coach is, disparages him, and implores me to take an IV and postpone the fight. He tells me he never liked me, but that ain't right.

I shrug.

My heavyweight champion just looks at me. His expression is that of like a son who's walked in on mom cradling his dad's head, crying in her arms after a bar fight gone bad. He nods and says, Good luck, brother. He stands and offers me his hand to shake but I wave it off. I wait for them to go about helping their teammate cut further by mummifying him on the floor with hot towels before I attempt to stand. On the way out, I step on a scale...

Fuck it. Close enough and I'm out of time.

~

The elevator doors slide open to a hallway teeming with business-people and, instead of a fashionable Lichtenstein mural at the elevator ID, there's a holoFeed of a theater production of "Waiting for Godot". Ten-foot-tall projections of Vladimir and Estragon skulk the hallways, and passersby walk through them. Floor-to-ceiling glass windows curve with the shape of the building to vanishing points in both directions. I hobble over to the directory to reconcile the suite's location with where I am. The contents of my stomach roil and I'm overcome by a fit of queasiness.

Swell. Now the castor oil decides to kick in.

I stand in place, bracing myself against the directory contemplating the wisdom of making a beeline to the bathroom, but the directory says it's too far in the opposite direction and I doubt I'll make it to the scale before the cut off time. I'm taking the first tentative steps towards the bathroom when my nausea passes as suddenly as it started.

I make an about face and trot to the transportation: An AI-controlled interior freeway of electric trams with a lane for pods going each direction, and in between the lanes a two-lane moving sidewalk. I wait for a gap in tram traffic and I step onto the automatic sidewalk which nobody else seems to be using.

The sidewalk zips me past several window-side meeting pods, some populated with recognizable movie stars, athletes, recording artists, and social media influencers.

None of the images outside the windows reflect what's going on outside. Instead of a view of the tempest beyond the property, the view is customized by the occupants of the pod: The surface of Mars, cliffside vista among giant redwoods, a pool party in Ibiza.

One meeting pod is covered by a curtain. A note pinned to it says, *Please Pardon Our Dust!*

My one-minute warning alarm chirps in my ear. Ignoring the pain in my ankle, I break out into an all-out sprint.

I step off the sidewalk and run for the double doors, passing a cadre of spec-ops looking people in civvies, each strategically placed in the hallway with an H&K MP5 Navy slung across his or her chest. They scan me at my approach and let me pass.

I barge through the double doors and into a conference room long enough to perceive it curving around the rotunda.

A privacy field bisects the room, cloaking its other side. It flickers like a waterfall. It's golden hour over the Pacific. Clear skies outside the windows. The Belt of Venus stretches across the horizon like a livid bruise.

An athletic commission official leads me to a butcher's scale. A physician observes his approach. A swarm of nanoDrones scans my biometrics and vitals as I strip. I don't have to take off my shorts as much as untie them and gravity does the rest.

A Bellum Assistant holds out a towel to protect my

modesty. Instead, I take the towel and wipe the sweat from my skin.

Then I step onto the scale. Naked. My clavicles jut... my ribs ripple under my skin with each breath... Cheeks, hollow. My dry tongue snags on cracked lips.

The athletic commission official says, "Trustfall, 156 pounds even."

She examines my vitals and statistics on her tablet as I dress. My motorcycle jacket hangs off my shoulders.

The doctor says, "Mr. Trustfall has a sprained ankle, but that's the least of his problems. The scan shows PYRRHIC."

The privacy field fades away revealing a conference table with people sitting around it. Sévérine, in a business suit, among them.

I say, "Sweet. When I die, you can hoist my jersey to the rafters."

Sévérine says, "You wouldn't be making light of this unless... you already knew."

The doctor says, "It's everywhere. There's no way he couldn't. He's got a year at best."

"Good thing my fight is tomorrow!"

I walk to the table.

Four human-shaped shadows flitter about the walls without the corresponding people to make them. The shadows peel away from the walls and glide toward me. Watching shadows not attached to any surface, moving across open space to intercept me, triggers an adrenaline dump prey response even though I know what they are.

Delta Force Ninjas.

Their battle dress uniforms and ballistic masks are sprayed with Vantablack, a black so deep it traps visible light like a black hole. It renders the ninjas flat, stripping away texture and depth. It's as though a painter, searching for the perfect black, held an open jar and turned the lights off, then screwed the lid onto the jar while in the dark. The artist turned the lights back on to reveal he trapped the darkness inside the glass.

The only things my eyes can lock focus on to even discern that they're getting closer are the jade clubs resembling ping-pong paddles floating from their waists. Maori patus. Each sharpened to an edge the width of a single atom. The Delta Force Ninjas flank me and escort me to the conference table.

I find a seat next to Sévérine with water bottles and Crackle on the table. A Birkin bag backpack on its seat.

Sévérine says, "Welcome to UTI Agency, Mr. Trustfall. We acquired Bellum last week. The agency board members and I came to a unanimous vote to bring you onboard last night."

I pound a water bottle and chase it with another.

The champion, Thierry Bruise, sits on the other side of Sévérine.

The chair next to him, empty, is not flush to conference table. It's turned out as though someone left in a hurry. On the table in front of it, a mouthpiece with fangs painted on it.

Andy Circus, the action star whose stunts kill him every film, sits at the head of the table. Life Alert around his neck. A pewter tray of pills in front of him...

The Sisters Kalashnikov sit across from me.

Next to them, the holoPorn actor turned screenwriter Rhett Kingly/Kent Light Yr. A Children of Tendu symbol pinned to his hoodie.

General Alastair Fletcher, Maori tattoos crossing his face, sits at the foot of the table. He wears a business suit. A briefcase on the table in front of him. He hands me a tablet. A force majeure, and also a release form to grant UTI permission to use my image and likeness on its screen. I sign them both with a thumb scan without reading a single word of either document.

The tablet screen dissolves into the UTI logo: interlinked

U, T, and I spinning on an axis.

I say, "You guys realize the letters 'UTI' stand for a communicable disease?"

Koi Kalashnikov says, "That's purely coincidental."

Coy Kalashnikov says, "'UTI' doesn't stand for anything."

"Clearly," I say.

Rhett Kingly says, "What they mean is, those are not initials. We chose them because it tested well with a poll group."

Fletcher says, "And it sounds cool. I lobbied for KIA, but..."

Sévérine says, "To be clear, we at UTI most certainly do not represent any diseases. Communicable or otherwise."

Fletcher says, "Actually... we are doing a shingles PR campaign on the Big Herpes cartel... Against the disease, not for it. It's a cash cow for Pfizer and DARPA."

"What the fuck?"

Andy Circus says, "DeShawn. We've selected you to star in a multi-media, trans-platform show. We're building an open world Super Story around you. We're incorporating your likeness into all facets of entertainment: Augmented reality games, choose your own adventure holoNovels. Action films.

This is a new paradigm for entertainment. It gives fans a full-immersion experience. They can live vicariously through action stars, athletes, rappers, or holoPorn stars as a playable character about to film a stunt, fight in the main event, have sex, or perform at Coachella... I was the first star to participate. Ms. Falk is participating as we speak."

I say, "I can't act."

Sévérine chuckles. She says, "According to TMI, neither can I. This is cinema verité."

I say, "Like Bob Dylan's movie, *Don't Look Back?*

"More like *Grey Gardens* where to this day fans show up at screenings dressed like the character, Edith Beale," says

Circus.

"Characters," I say, "There are two Ediths in *Grey Gardens.* A mother and a daughter... When does this start?"

Circus says, "We've been filming you with nanoDrones since we canceled your Uber and you sat in our Phantom."

Fletcher opens a briefcase and tosses a baggie of pills across the table to me.

"You're holding the equivalent of California's GDP in your hand. Homunculus tablets. The most valuable commodity known to man."

Fletcher swipes air in front of his face. The conference room window view changes: a Google Earth view of Rural Columbia. Fletcher continues "This is the Datura plant indigenous to Colombia..."

The holograph floats down to street level. It drifts to a tree growing beside a busy roadside. Spanish-speaking children chase each other around its trunk.

Fletcher continues, "Locals turn it into Devils Breath, the 'zombie drug.' So, named because it induces a highly suggestible state..."

We watch a dive bar prostitute spike a John's drink... The John leads the prostitute across town from ATM to ATM, draining his bank account... Handing the money to the prostitute... Renting a moving van... Driving the van to his house where the prostitute's waiting accomplices load his possessions into the van... Helps them pull the van gate shut... The van drives away... The John wakes up the next day on the floor of an empty house.

Fletcher says, "The victim wakes up with no memory of what has transpired."

The window returns to its normal view of the Pacific Ocean...

Fletcher says, "To wit..."

Fletcher pulls a crossbow pistol from his briefcase and shoots Andy Circus. The bolt THWAKs! into Circus' shoulder with such force it staples him to the chair and spins him a full turn.

Andy, exsanguinating, says, "Was that really necessary?"

Circus slaps absently at his Life Alert pendant then loses consciousness. An assistant removes Andy's Halo, sets it onto the table, then wheels him out of the boardroom.

Fletcher says, "Under my instructions, Dr. Chen's team at DARPA refined Devil's Breath further into Homunculus. It slides your consciousness to the passenger seat of the car. Through a link with Halo, Artificial Super Intelligence can grab the wheel and drive. Applications for government, corporate, religious, entertainment and military uses are limitless."

The boardroom doors burst open and Andy Circus saunters back in. He takes his Halo from the table and fits it back into his ear... Swallows a Homunculus pill from the pewter tray...

The new Andy says, "Good evening, DeShawn. I am an Artificial Super Intelligence. You may call me Plutarch. General Fletcher's demonstration of violence upon Andy Circus' body forced me to waste a valuable pill that we're experiencing... challenges manufacturing. He could have simply asked me to explain."

Fletcher says, "Show, don't tell, Plutarch."

Plutarch says, "In addition to running the agency, I'm the new CEO of Uber, SlummR, and Valtrex."

I say, "Of course you are... Human surrogates that allow Super Intelligence to interact physically with the real world... What the fuck could possibly go wrong?"

Fletcher says, "It's the natural progression of things."

I say, "And, you're telling me this because?"

Fletcher says, "Win your fight. Have a good show. Your brand, not to mention your Q-SCore will go through the roof. We'd like you be the spokesperson for its sports applications... Okay, what's wrong?"

I say, "I'm surprised by you more than anything, General. Chuck D said it best. Every brotha for himself."

Koi Kalashnikov says, "Public Enemy?"

I say, "Charles Darwin. This isn't progress. It's evolution and humans are on the wrong side of it."

Rhett says, "Questioning a war hero's motives for technology is funny coming from a CRISPR mutant. Tell us... How does PYRRHIC afflict you?"

"I can't suffer fools who use logical fallacies," I say.

Rhett says, "That's why you're getting foreclosed on, and I'm a billionaire."

I say, "Man, you're just doubling down the ad hominem bullshit, aren't you?"

I pull a Rhett Kingly dildo from my Birkin backpack and toss it across the table. It skids to a stop in front of Rhett.

He says, "What am I supposed to do with this?"

"Go fuck yourself."

Thierry Bruise says, "Maybe PYRRHIC make his dick fall off. What happened to your fingers?"

"I'd tell you, but your mom swore me to secrecy."

Thierry says, "You disrespect my mom? I tell her what you say!"

I say to him, "You do that. Go tell your mommy." And then to everyone, "These AI surrogates and people using Fleeker are creeping me out. Everyone, turn off your apps. I want to know whom I'm talking to."

People use the Fleeker app ostensibly to enhance their facial features, however, as a result, it also distorts their facial expressions, which is how we communicate emotions. You get the creeps when looking into the face of someone hiding behind Fleeker because it short-circuits the survival mechanism evolved by your ancestors over a hundred thousand years to glean insight into the state of mind of others, which kept them from getting bashed over the head with rocks by strangers. It's the same thing we find unsettling about Halloween masks or clowns behind face paint. Our brains don't do well with ambiguity. Especially when they don't know whether to trip the danger alarms or not.

Add to things that exist in the uncanny valley of the creeps, anything that's close to humanlike in its familiarity, except with details that are slightly off which our brains snag on.

Like Sal's fingers... Or androids.

Come to think of it, it makes perfect sense why Fletcher tasked Sal to develop a way to use human beings for AI surrogates as opposed to using droids...

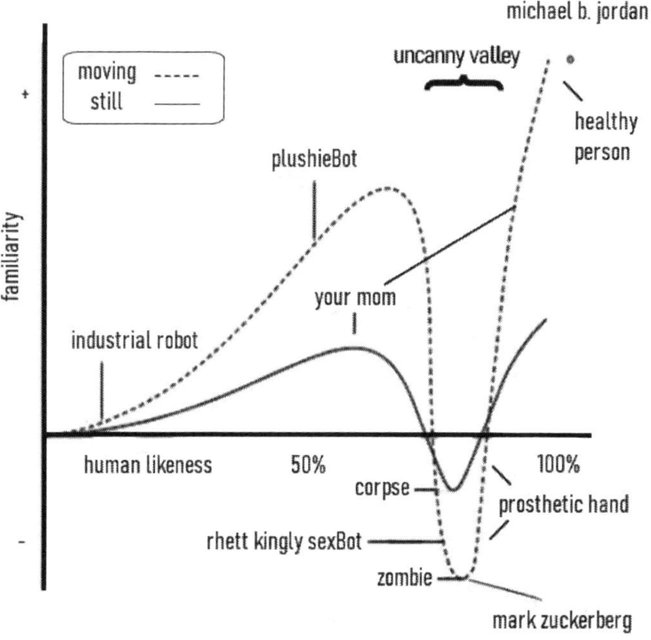

One by one, the filters depixelize into people's real faces. Some noses become a bit less cutesy and jawlines a tad less sharp...

Sévérine doesn't change...

The Sisters Kalashnikov are really gingers...

The only person other than Sévérine who doesn't change at all is Rhett Kingly. Insecure fucking screenwriters...

I say, "Uh, Mr. Kingly?"

"Yo!"

"You're still using your filters."

"No, I'm not. Don't hate. It's unattractive."

"Motherfucker, you're 90 years old!"

"81," Rhett says, "And a half. Fine. Whatever..."

He rolls his eyes back and blinks thrice... His flesh collapses around his bone. Skin slackens and cracks. The light dims from his eyes. A half a century passes in one second. A sunflower wilting in time lapse...

"Right," I say. "If we're done here, I've got some rehydrating to do."

When I stand, everyone else converges upon me to for handshakes and back slaps. I try to cut each interaction short. When Rhett Kingly reaches me, he says, "Hey, no hard feelings, okay?"

I bend at the waist and spew all over his outstretched hand. Rhett recoils in disgust. He opens his mouth to speak, but instead of words matching his angry expression, bacon fat, lettuce, and apple cider vinegar sprays out... He must be on the Keto diet... The reek seizes Fletcher by the throat and he begins to gag. Sévérine and the K Sisters skip that step and go straight to blowing chunks on each other's clothes, and everyone else doubles over puking on everyone else in a semi-circle of retching.

Even the special forces guards succumb to the festivities.

The tsunami of heaving subsides and people begin to catch their breaths. Around the room, the sounds of sniffling and coughing, and gasping. Some with their hands on their knees, others walking it off. It's like the finish line of a 100-meter dash at the Olympics...

All these beautiful faces screwed in expressions of agony. Everyone's clothes resemble slaughterhouse worker's aprons after a double shift on the kill floor...

Sévérine walks around in circles with her arms above her head, her slingbacks sklishing on chunklets of puke like she's stomping grapes.

I say, "My bad. Too much castor oil. For the love of God! Nobody, look down!"

General Fletcher looks down. His back arches like a cat struggling with a hairball.

Between gasps he says, "Get yourself squared away for tomorrow." He pukes again.

There's a break in the hurling.

Coughing...

Sniffling...

A chuckle from someone who finds this amusing, then...

A second wave of retching overtakes everyone.

Sévérine says, "I'm canceling your meetings at the studios. You're terrible in a room."

~

Fighters stream into a dark hallway in for the PPV weigh-ins. They check in at a series of folding tables lit by banker's lamps with Bellum personnel sitting behind them. Bobby is with me. His red eyes are glassy complements of the free booze, and he looks like he just came in from a sandstorm without wearing a balaclava.

After I sign in at the table we're led to a curtained-off room where I'm given another medical exam, then farther down the hallway behind the stage of the weigh-ins where other fighters are lined up. As we approach the other fighters a chorus of pthhh—pthhh—pthhh—pthhh grows louder, echoing off the cinderblock walls as hollow-cheeked men spit into cups in an effort to squeeze the last bit of moisture from their bodies.

Feet scrape against the floor as some shadowbox or hit focus mitts with their coaches, and others shuffle in place as though jumping with an invisible rope to keep a sweat going.

Thank God I don't have to worry about that. I guzzle some water in front of them because I'm a dick like that.

The athletes are lined up like the condemned to be weighed and measured for the gallows, each waiting for our turn as the emcee announces each fight then our names one by one to walk on to the stage.

I'm the main event, so I take my place at the back of the line and I sit on the floor, leaning my back against a wall.

Most of the fighters have their Vaunts on and are listening to music. There is very little conversation anywhere.

All of us waiting in line have endured our own private hells to strip the weight off. Many have watched their friends and families enjoy pizzas, sushi, and frozen yogurt topped with candy while meal after meal passed them by. And because of this, it does not take much to set tempers off, so there are securityBots intermingled among the fighters. Event staffers who work for the promotion rove the weigh-in live watching the fighters and their coaches. State athletic commission officials wearing blazers the color of dried blood stand off to the sides observing everyone.

There's another hallway which runs parallel with this one another line, also with event personnel, officials and security. It's the line where our unseen competitors wait.

There was a time when I was the man nobody wanted to fight. The way I look, just standing nose-to-nose with me at a stare down the drained the fighting spirit out of whomever was unlucky enough to square off against me. After word got out about another athlete helping scrape my carcass off the spa floor, I don't imagine my adversary is in the other hall is pacing back and forth with any concerns about me. Only getting this formality out of the way (he weighed in inside the boardroom right before I did), enjoying a relaxing evening with his friends and executing his game plan tomorrow.

The announcer begins to call names starting with the fighters on the undercard. Event personnel ushers them out of the hallway one by one. The rookies fighting in their first big show pace and look to their coaches for comfort. Many, when their names are close to being called, blast their music so that the passageway fills with Scandinavian death metal, gangsta rap, and screamo. What was just an abstract idea of fighting on a holoCast show has now crystallized into reality. Their performances may open career opportunities and make them the topic of Monday morning lunchroom conversations or reduce them to troll fodder on Internet chat rooms. While waiting I've remained still except to move forward as the line advances. I control my breathing but my palms are wet.

A name is called from our hall and a man leaves through the doorway to cheers from the audience, then a name for a fighter waiting in the other hall until the undercard is finished, and the emcee makes his way down the names on the main card until the noise in the hallway fades to silence. I'm the main event, so I'm last.

The emcee shrieks my name and fight record. The crowd boos. Bobby and I look at each other and smile. Welcome back.

I wipe my hands on my shorts and adrenaline-fueled nervous energy propels me out the door in a jog and a spotlight catches and tracks me but my gait slows to a walk-up mid-way up the stairs to the stage. Gamesmanship on my part was a bad move. I'm still dehydrated as fuck. Walking feels like trudging through a pool of waist-deep water and my shorts that fit me this morning want to slide down around my ankles and trip me.

It takes all the remaining energy I have to cross the stage so I have to lean on Bobby as I undress, which is good because it hides the fact that I can't trust my legs.

The meat scale awaits me under its own arc light. Under the light, motes of dust twinkle in the air. The counterweights on its slide are pre-set to my fight's weight limit. I step on the scale and the needle slaps the top of its hole, but nobody sees this because there is a Bellum logo placard covering it. The emcee, reading a memo off of a tablet as opposed to the scale itself, calls my official weight at 156 lbs.

I step off the scale and try not to lean on Bobby.

The emcee screams my opponent's name and the crowd reacts, drowning out the emcee's edification of his career and the stage shakes as he bounds up the steps and undresses and steps onto the scale in a fluid economy of motion.

The audience quiets to a din. The emcee screams my opponent's weight: 155 even for Thierry Bruise!

He flexes and struts from the scale and up to me and foists a clenched fist close enough to my face that I cannot hold it in focus with both of my eyes at the same time. I return the favor.

Flashbulbs pop.

It's one thing to be brave with your words over a holoCast or the Internet. Quite another thing to stand face to face from the person.

I look for it... There it is! His lower lip quivers and he licks it. His pupils are wide open. I smile because I know I have him.

The emcee slaps us on our backs and I blink. We separate and shake hands and nod. While Bruise dresses, the emcee, an action star cross-promoting his movie, asks me what my strategy is for winning.

Seriously, mother fucker?

Like I'm going to dignify this with an answer, announcing my plan with the adversary standing right there. This guy whores his movies out on the MMA forums while second-guessing us professionals. His latest holoFilm, coming to a theater near you, is about a loner past his prime suspended from the sport, loses the girl, seeks redemption in the cage, gets his ass beat but wins the girl back.

In other words, total fucking fantasy. Preparing for the role he got his blue belt in jiujutsu... How cute. To keep the meta loop open, I'm tempted to shoot a double-leg takedown on him, test his back defense, wrap him up and squeeze and count to ten...

As Bobby and I are walking off of the stage an official catches up to us and foists a tablet under my nose and without breaking stride I sign my official weigh-in results and hand it back. A securityBot positioned ahead of us spreads its four arms in an attempt to corral me into the press room for interviews, but Bobby runs interference so I can slip past it and into the casino. Some reporters follow, throwing questions at my back.

I hold up my middle finger as the elevator doors close. Bobby looks like he's about to say something, but he thinks the better of it and tamps the thought down. We ride the elevator in silence. Bobby gets off on his floor. I continue on to the Otium's shops to get supplies.

~

I'm riding an internal elevator from the shopping mall up to the hotel suites. The other passengers, keeping their distance, make no pretense about hiding open stares at me.

My skin is grimy with road dust, my hoodie is soaked-through with sweat, a recyclable shopping bag from the Otium's pharmacy at my feet and a Birkin backpack that costs more than a car slung over my shoulder. But that's not why they stare.

It's because of the holographic video playing on auto-repeat on the elevator doors.

It's a promotional video for tomorrow's Bellum event. The end of an embedded-style program where cameras follow the champion Thierry Bruise in Brazil through his final day of training leading up to the fight. A woman with battle scars crisscrossing her face pushing him on...

The video segues into vintage footage of that woman, Rena Bruise. Olympic gold medalist, Bellum's first three-division female champion... and Thierry's mother. Rena is about my age. She was still young enough to fight and was at the top of her game when she chose to retire last year undefeated. The voiceover commentator gushes over legends of Rena yanked back from the brink of death and scooped off the sauna floor by her trainers during hellacious weight cuts. They'd have to carry her to the scale. After weigh-ins, Rena would disappear into her hotel room to rehydrate and regain lost water weight up to the time to fight. By the time she stepped into the cage the next day, she would outweigh her opponents by 20 pounds. Each fight, a total mauling.

Throughout Rena's career, she struggled to make weight. Even at the highest weight class for women at super welterweight with its 175-pound cutoff. Moot point, since there was nobody worth a damn in the highest weight class for her to face anyway. When a commentator made an offhand joke that Rena should fight men, Bellum set up a super fight between her and the current men's welterweight champion, 21-2-1 at the time. After the fight, the poor kid said he felt like he dived face first into a wood chipper.

The holoFeed shows footage from that super fight with Rena executing a beautiful armbar setup that seamlessly transitions into footage a year later of another armbar completed by her son, Thierry Bruise. The montage continues, following Thierry's career with a compilation of armbar finishes playing out from the most creative setups that his opponents never saw coming. Except for the last opponent, a member of the Gracie jiujitsu family. He felt the armbar coming right from the setup but was powerless to stop it. Unlike the other victims who were ignorant of their forthcoming doom until it was all but over, you can see the dread on Gracie's face: A trapped fly struggling against the web while feeling the vibration of the approaching spider on a filament... This part of the playback has sound. Bruise hyperextends Gracie's elbow and you can hear ligaments pop like wet celery snapping. Screams.

The promo repeats itself from the beginning, starting with my "loss" yesterday to Clint, the Cudgel...

My fellow passengers observe me within the close confines like I'm a man infected with cholera.

The door opens on my floor. They give me a wide berth as I exit, as though my fate to a savage beating tomorrow night, a foregone conclusion, is contagious.

The shopping bag is a bit heavy to carry in my weakened state. I step onto the moving sidewalk and set it down. The bag, made of reusable mesh, cost me more than the items inside of it. City-imposed recycling tax to encourage shoppers to use a bring-your-own-bag. I could have easily fit everything I needed into the Birkin, even with the swag inside of it (hell, if I tucked my knees, I could just about fit myself inside of it), but it's the nicest thing I've owned, and doing so would feel... sacrilegious.

I pull my Halo out of my Birkin bag and open its packaging. On top of the actual device itself is a mylar bag with a thumb-sized canister that resembles breath spray. Underneath those items, the Halo itself. I roll the Halo's foam between my thumb and forefinger to compress it, then I fit it into my ear. As the foam decompresses, it expands to fill my ear canal and it powers up.

Once all my data from my Vaunt synchs to my Halo, I drop the Vaunt into the mylar bag and hose it down with a few pumps from the acetone spray. The frame and lenses fizzle as the solution eats away at them. Within seconds, the Vaunt is no more. The sidewalk passes a bank of waste receptacles and I toss the baggie of goo.

I use the hotel guest verifier on my Halo, and the door

to my suite clicks open before I reach it.

I instruct Calliope that I'm not to be disturbed for any reason, which retracts the doorknob and an energy gate slides down over the doorway. I make a bee-line for the bathroom.

Weight-cutting for a competition is only half of the battle. Again, if you want to be competitive, you must replace the fluids you've lost while cutting. This is how it's done.

- Step One: Take a shower. Remember when I told you that skin is a water channel? Of course, you do. The reason why I abstained from showering or getting any water on my skin while I was cutting water weight is that the water channel flows both ways. In and out. As soon as the water hits my skin, my pores squeeze shut and goosebumps hold the hairs on my arms erect... After lathering and rinsing, I rest my arms against the wall and hang my head and let the water blast my back. Drops of falling water splash between my feet... Sweet, sweet water trickles down my cheek and into my open mouth... I take a DeShawn moment to enjoy this. Then I adjust the shower temperature so my pores relax, and my skin is a greedy sponge sucking the shower water up... I sit on the tub floor... My muscles loosen. I dry off and then step onto the scale... Two pounds of water reclaimed. Just like that. I get dressed.Next, I lay out the items from the pharmacy bag onto the bed. Three, one-gallon jugs of mineral water. Salt pills. A six pack of isotonic water (for rehydration at the cellular level through osmosis which has the exact opposite effect on my body as the salty alcohol bath); and... And an IV drip kit with bags of saline.

- Step Two: Drink. (Duh!). It takes fewer than two minutes for me to swallow a salt pill, pound the first gallon of mineral water, and chase that with a bottle of isotonic water. That water you saw me swilling ever since I stepped off of the scale in the boardroom is isotonic. It's loaded with carbohydrates and electrolytes proportionate to the exact ratio of a human body in normal conditions. If your body is not operating under normal hydration conditions, isotonic water allows for hyper-accelerated fluid absorption. On top of that, it induces far greater water retention than normal water or even your typical convenience store sports drink. It's the same science you would have used in the tub to wring out your body water, just in reverse. While sipping another bottle of isotonic water, I hang a saline solution drip bag on a door with a coat hanger from the closet... Then I unfurl a length of plastic tubing, careful to work the kinks out, and connect it to the bag... A turn of the valve and the saline solution flows down the tubing to the sheathed needle at its other end... I sit in a chair, unsheathe the needle, tap the adjacent tubing for air bubbles, and press the needle against my skin...
- Step Three: IV drip. Never do this. This is way outside of the rules as set down by the State Athletic Commission. If they catch you, they won't suspend you. They'll ban you.

There's a sting when the needle pressed against my skin gains traction and bites into my flesh, and a spurt of blood clouds the clear solution inside of the tube pink... I guide the needle deeper into my vein, then place a band-aid over top to stabilize it... The solution glides swift and cool into my arm and chills my core. I shiver. There's a twangy bite on the back of my tongue from the citrate part of the sodium citrate mixture...

So, IV drips are illegal. Any intravenous rehydration is banned by the State Athletic Commission... Whatever. The risks of a concussion, brain damage or worse, death are far greater as a result of a blow to the head with a dehydrated brain rattling around your brain cage without proper fluid to cushion it. Yeah, I could get banned. But IVs are impossible to detect short of bruising from a bad stick that infiltrates the vein, or an official catching you in the act with one in your arm. You're a damn fool if you wanna gamble with your life because you're a slave to the rules. Everyone else does it. And if they don't, that's on them.

When I feel the last of this bag go inside of me, I unplug, take a piss, and swap in the next one. I'm about to re-stick the IV into my vein when...

Knock. Knock, knock.

Back into the bag with the IV kit, and under the bed with the bag...

"Calliope," I say, "Didn't you lower the energy gate over the door?"

Calliope says,

You have a visitor. I raised it.

"I said I was not to be disturbed, right?"

You did, indeed. However, your command was overridden.

I place a fresh Band-Aid onto the stick site and pull my hoodie on to cover my arm.

I say, "I know that! Overridden by who, you fuckwit?"

Please, refrain from hurtful language, Mr. Trustfall.

From the selection of pre-loaded apps in my Halo, I select the *Tragical Negro* app. In front of me, pixels of light congeal into a goateed man in a leather jacket. Gold chains. Skullcap. A pistol in each hand.

The Tragical Negro looks me up and down, taps the barrels of his guns together twice and says,

Ha haaa! My nigga!

Denzel Washington.

I tell him my dilemma.

The way Denzel talks with his hands as he responds might even be inspiring if there weren't guns in them.

He says,

A'ight now. Cast me on projector mode. When the State Athletic Commission inspectors come through that door, I'ma blast their asses. You come in hot on my six and drag the bodies into the suite while I cover you.

I say, "Commission inspectors don't carry guns. And even if they did, they'd just shoot through your holograph and blow me away."

Denzel, somber, nods his head as though he's considering this.

Are you a wolf?

"Oh no," I say, "we are not doing this!"

Project me, god damn it!

Using the HUD, I scroll through the menu of the app's

controls, to 'PROJECT,' but...

I scroll back and hover my virtual cursor over, 'GRENADE'.

Of course, I have to click it...

Denzel turns to me and in a disembodied voice says,

Welcome to GRENADE MODE. In addition to Tragical Negro's programming to give shitty advice based on what you want to hear or jump on a grenade for you, upon activating GRENADE MODE, Tragical Negro will make the ultimate sacrifice by turning itself into a flash-bang grenade to save you! Please remove your Halo device from your ear and step the recommended minimum distance of three meters away in: Three…Two…

I click CANCEL.

Then I select projector mode and cast Denzel.

Denzel admires himself in real space, clicking his guns together again.

To catch a wolf, you gotta be a wolf! Ah-oooooooooo!

Fuck it. I join him.

"Ah-ooo—"

The door opens in the middle of my howl. Sévérine is there holding the boy by his hand. His Lance, the Unicorn plushieBot tucked under his other arm.

The plushieBot says,

You're an idiot.

They push past me and into the room.

Denzel, mouth agape, ogles Sévérine.

God! DAMN!

Sévérine studies my Tragical Negro. She says, "Alonzo in Training Day, right?"

Denzel taps his guns together and says,

Ha-HAAAA. Alright, now.

I sigh. "It's an app."

She says, "No, really? You don't say."

You're fine, girl.

"Yes, I know."

You're pretty in the face. I'ma take you to the booty shack and make love to you face-to-face.

She covers the boy's ears and laughs.

I say, "That makes no damn sense... I should have picked Uncle Remus instead."

Sévérine says, "You picked Alonzo because he's aggressive, confident, and assertive. Everything you are not."

I power off the Tragical Negro app, and as Denzel dissolves he says,

Oh, no you didn't!

I say, "Thanks. Let me guess... My daddy issues, too?"

PlushieBot says,

No, it's overcompensation for your conflict about where your sexuality falls on the Kinsey Scale.

I hold my hand out in a low five gesture for the boy.

He leaves me hanging and says, "Whatever."

He dives onto the bed with his plushieBot. They bounce

on the bed together.

Sévérine says, "You two are going to hang out tonight."

"That's wonderful!"

"He hasn't stopped asking about you since last night. He's been really sad."

The boy standing on the bed, waves my leather jacket in front of him like a matador. The unicorn scratches a hoof on the mattress once... twice... and charges!

I say, "I'm gonna pretend that's not a lie."

"Get dinner. He'll ask for pizza, but don't go to Chuck E. Cheese. The Imaginarium gives him nightmares."

She leaves.

~

The Otium's Trams shuttle shoppers and their purchases from store to store along its interior freeway. Little DeShawn and I walk hand in hand. The unicorn plushieBot grumbles and complains as the boy drags it behind him by its tail.

I've had enough of Calliope for a lifetime, so I consult the mall directory... Looks like the food court is on the other side of the mall. We take a shortcut through the luxury shopping wing. I feel a tingling sensation. I look up... Sensors. An Otium's securityBot descends upon us.

SecurityBot says, "This area is restricted. Please take this child and return to the common area designated for non-Vaunted persons."

We turn and leave. He turns back to the machine that just showed us away like vermin. It's helping to load a family's shopping bags into a tram. I place my hand on the top of the boy's head and steer him back the other way.

Little D says, "Why did you back down?"

"It's easier to just go around."

"But I don't understand. You've got an all-access pass this weekend."

I say, "If you've ever tried to argue with a machine, you'd..."

He shoots me a look of disappointment that cuts my bullshit excuse off mid-sentence. What kind of example am I setting for him...?

Come on, son," I say. "Let's go the long way."

~

The food court, surrounded on three sides by the interior shark aquarium, is vast enough to have its own directory. We're sitting on the fountain, reading dining options as they scroll past.

I say, "What do you want to—"

"Chuck E. Cheese!"

"Your mom said no."

"She doesn't have to know!"

"I'm sorry, she'll get pissed."

"She's always pissed. Pleeease?"

PlushieBot hops onto my lap and bares its teeth. It says,

Take the kid to Chuck E. Cheese, or else.

I say, "Or else what?"

I'll tell the fight commission about the IV drip
I saw under your bed.

"You rat bastard! Why are you blackmailing me?"

Men come and go. He's my best friend.

"I'm his father."

You're not his dad. You're a stand-in until
the real thing comes along.

"I should toss you into the water fountain."

Go ahead. All my ports and anus are rated IP 79.

It pokes my belly with its horn.

Come at me, bro! Yeah... That's what I thought.

"Why do you have an anus?"

Why do you have a V. A. G. I. N. A.?

"What's a vagina?" the boy says.

"I don't have a... Never mind, son... Let's get pizza."

"Yes!"

~

We take a break from games and pizza to visit the bathroom. There's a line. In front of us, three kids about little DeShawn's age run around their dad's legs. They're playing tag with their Cuddles, the Cuttlefish plushieBot.

Cuddles says,

Oh, watch out! I'm gonna git ya! He he he!

Cuddles voice sounds like Barney Rubble, right down to the laugh. The oldest, a boy about little DeShawn's age, wears a cone on his head with an elastic chin strap that says, *HAPPY 9th BIRTHDAY, WILBUR!*

Lance hops down from my boy's arms and trots up to the Cuddles... The two plushieBots circle each other, eying the other one warily...

Little D takes Cuddle's place in the game of grab-ass with the other kids. They shriek and giggle. The game soon expands to include other children in the line and Schrodinger's brats are everywhere, running around hapless parents trying to restore calm.

The cuttlefish plushieBot sniffs our unicorn plushieBot's butt...

The other dad turns around, looks down on me. His gaze lingers on me for a beat longer than what's comfortable between strangers, like he's trying to place where he's seen me before. He looks like he stepped out of an old Viking movie. I look up at him and nod. He grunts and turns back around.

Crying replaces laughter. Viking Dad turns around, and I look down...

Lance, the Unicorn has mounted Cuddles. Tongue out. Humping away. The cuttlefish lights up, flickering red and blue colors like a neon sign.

Wilber, between gasps and sobs, whines, "Daddy! Make it stooooop!"

Viking Dad pries the plushieBots apart and Lance's data-transfer cable retracts between its legs and into its body like spring-loaded measuring tape.

My boy kicks the Viking Dad in the shin then snatches his unicorn away.

Viking Dad says to me, "You better handle your son or I will, little man."

"I'll be a foot taller standing on top of your corpse."

"Maybe then, you'd be as tall as Wilbur."

"Little DeShawn says, "Do you know he is?"

"Sure. He had last night's fight won, but when the Cudgel lactated on him, he choked. Literally. Your dad threw a hissy fit and quit. Sports Center calls him 'Milk Dud.'"

I say, "Whatever, man. It's okay."

Viking Dad, satisfied, turns around. The other kids whisper to each other and point at my boy. His shoulders slump.

"Hey," I say. "You know what? It's not okay."

Viking Dad turns around.

He says, "Save it for tomorrow, Snaggletooth. At least you'll get a paycheck for getting your tail whipped."

My boy pulls tugs my hand and points to a door with skull and crossbones on it.

I say, "Let's settle this in the Imaginarium."

Viking Dad says, "This is going to be good."

~

Little D and I stand on one side of an all-white room with padded walls. Viking Dad and his three kids on the other side. All of us wear haptic gaming suits of cerebral Gore-Tex and augmented reality goggles. Wilbur still has his birthday dunce cap on.

A holograph of Koi Kalashnikov says, "Welcome to the Sister's Kalashnikov Imaginarium."

Holographic Coy says, "Please select your construct."

Wilbur says to little DeShawn, "Go ahead, loser. You pick."

The game room pixelates and shifts into... an MMA cage, knee high with plastic Crazy Balls.

Little DeShawn holds a shotgun. He pumps it...

SNIK-SNAK!

BOOM!

...and blows Wilbur's head off.

Koi's disembodied voice cuts through the augmented reality.

She says, "Headshot! Player terminated!"

Everybody dives for cover, but the floor springs us back up like a galactic moon bounce... Little DeShawn tucks into a backflip —

BOOM!

BOOM!

"Player terminated!"

"Player terminated!"

— picking other kids off with his shotgun as they spring up.

I shout from my hiding place beneath the balls, "What's the age rating for this ga—?"

My head snaps back as though struck in the face with a fastball. A crossbow bolt pins my tongue to my upper lip, and my skull to the cage turnbuckle.

"HEADSHOT!"

"Player terminated!"

Viking Dad reloads his crossbow.

He says, "Gotcha, Milk Dud!"

My gaming suit locks up at the joints. I can't move. A claw crane drops from the ceiling and plucks me from the pile of crazy balls like I'm a prize, and lifts me out of the cage. It drops me onto a sofa in the spectator's lounge next to the other slain players. Everyone is munching on pizza. I yank my goggles off and grab a slice of pepperoni. We watch the rest of the match on monitors.

Only my son and Viking Dad remaining.

Koi says, "Two surviving players! Entering heads-up mode!"

A team of six Vantablack ninja NPCs spawns into the game construct. Little D levels his shotgun at them, poised to take them and the father out in one shot...

SNIK, SNAK!

click...

An empty chamber. He's out of ammo!

The ninjas turn to him and draw their jade patus.

I grip my armrest and yell, "Look out!" at the monitor, even though I know he can't hear me.

Two ninjas break away from the group and go for Viking Dad. The other four ninjas soar through the air towards the boy, and...

A golden Kalashnikov spawns atop the balls in front of him. In one fluid motion, he dives for it and hoses the ninjas down...

"Player terminated!

Player terminated!

Player terminated!

HEADSHOT!

KILLING SPREE!"

I stand and applaud, cheering through the slice clenched between my teeth. Even Wilbur and his siblings cheer.

Koi says, "Increasing difficulty!"

An energy shield flickers on!

The wall of plasma sweeps across the cage like the garbage compactor in Star Wars. The remaining two ninjas, arms held above their heads for balance, wade through the cage to escape as the Crazy Balls POP! POP! POP! on contact with the energy shield closing in behind them. They're too slow.

SIZZLE! POP! POP!

Viking Dad spins around 360, crossbow at the ready...

Where's little DeShawn!

Next to me, the kids scream at the monitors.

Wilbur says, "Right in front of you, daddy!"

Little DeShawn springs from the Crazy Balls in front of the Viking Dad! He slices across his belly with a patu. Guts slide out onto the plastic balls.

"Player Terminated!"

"GODLIKE!"

"WINNER!"

I say, "Hell yeah! That's what's up!"

The plastic Crazy Balls shift into Negerbols, then the augmented reality construct falls away. The crane scoops up Viking Dad and plops him onto the sofa next to me. He grabs a slice of Sicilian.

Viking Dad says, "Buford."

"DeShawn."

He laughs. "I know who you are."

"Right..."

We shake hands.

Little D walks in through a door. Lance gallops up to him and they hug. He grabs a slice, then joins Wilbur in a game of foosball as though nothing had happened. At what age do people lose the ability to do that?

Buford says, "Want a cold one?"

"Crackle?"

He opens a diaper bag filled with ice and takes out a couple of cans.

"Heck no. I smuggled in some PBRs."

"Hipster beer?"

"Careful, Milk Dud."

He takes a pull from his beer.

I say, "What do you do, Buford?"

"I was the founder and chief technology officer for MacroHard. I invented SlummR, that was in my 20s. Then Fleeker... then the operating system for those AGI pets and plushieBots..."

"Was?"

"Heh, yeah," he says, "Got sacked from my own firm last week with the rest of the board. AGI took over..."

"Where's their mom?"

"PYRRHIC... Two years ago."

"Sorry."

He nods. "You?"

"Divorce. Two days from now... It took Miles. That was our boy... He was eight. Shonda and I, uh... we never recovered."

Our kids giggle and run. Lance and Buford's kid's plushieBot, Cuddles Cuttlefish chase them.

Buford says, "You know what all my products have in common?"

I think about this.

"People are lonely," I say.

He nods. "This is the city where the lost wander in from the desert by starlight."

We finish our beers. He breaks out two more.

"What now?" I say.

He smiles. "Today, I'm just dad. Right now, that seems just about perfect..."

Buford and I order more pizzas. We sip our lagers and watch our kids play together.

~

I'm sitting on the bed watching my boy sleep. He spoons with Lance. The room's sole source of illumination, his wrist phone on the nightstand beside the bed. It flickers cerulean light across his face like a motel television at three a.m.

He opens his eyes. They dart around in a panic until they pick my face out of the semi-darkness.

"Bad dream?"

"Yeah."

I smooth his curls out of his eyes and kiss his forehead.

I say, "We don't have to tell your mom about the Imaginarium, okay?"

"Are you teaching me to lie?"

"No, I..."

He smiles at me. "I'm just messing with you."

He sits up.

"I have to use my inhaler before I go to sleep," he says.

I give it to him... I don't have it in me to tell him that it's a fiction.

He says, "Earlier when Wilbur's dad was picking on you. We're you scared?"

"Yeah... yeah, I was."

"But you were going to fight him anyway."

"If I had to. Almost everyone gets scared. What matters is what you do in spite of it."

He nods, considering this.

He says, "What about when you work? Are you scared

then?"

"Especially when I work. But once I get going, the fear goes away."

"How do does that happen?"

I shrug. "I don't know. I'm not really afraid of getting hurt or anything. That's easy to deal with. You replace the fear of what can happen to you with visualizations of what you're going to do to the other guy... I guess I'm afraid of not performing as well as I can. Embarrassing myself."

"I get it." He says.

"You do?"

"Yeah. At the spelling bee last week. It was down to me and one other kid. I was doing well until I looked up and saw of all the people looking at me. I messed up on the last word. It was a word that I knew. Mom said it was okay because I did my best. But I didn't do my best. That's what really bothers me."

I strain to find the right dad-type thing to say to him. The only things I come up with are platitudes, so I don't say anything. Both of us turn to a show projecting from his wrist phone. An old "Rick and Morty" rerun. Neither of us feels the need to fill the silence with small talk.

The show goes to a newsVertizement... An ad recruiting young women to lease their wombs as paid as CRISPR surrogates. His eyes close, and he begins to drift off.

I plug a cord into the plushieBot's charging port under its tail, then pull the covers over the unicorn and my boy. Then I place one cup of my NIHL headphones on his ear and the other cup over the plushieBot's head.

Without opening his eyes, he says, "Good night."

~

Matts cover the floors of two ballrooms repurposed as staging areas. The fighters are segregated by room depending which side of the fight card they are on for tonight's event to eliminate interaction between opponents. Fighters roll around to keep loose and warm. A staccato thwap-thwap-thwap-thwap-twap! echoes as rapid-fire punches slap at focus mitts and Thai pads. Some people gather around a live holoFeed of the action in the arena. Teammates and coaches cheer their man when things go their way and fall silent when things do not.

All night fighters have gone out the door escorted by state athletic commission officials and event securityBots, and we watch their fate unfold on the feed. Some fighters looking no worse than they would after a morning jog. Others return peering out at the world through one eye, or pulverized faces or swollen limbs reconfigured to unnatural angles. Many are never to return at all, taken away by ambulance straight from the cage.

Nobody who fights for a living ever steps into the cage to do battle at 100% health. Getting through training healthy is half the battle. Most deal with lingering issues by getting tapped up, while others do mobility exercises or stretch or receive messages.

We each deal with the psychological stresses of impending combat in our own way also. Some shift the focus off of themselves by helping others on their team get ready for their fight. Some joke and play grab ass around the room with their friends one moment only to rush to the bathroom to vomit the next. There are your nervous pacers with motor mouths and the aloof loners like me who burrow into a quiet corner away from everyone else with their NIHL headphones on while they visualize how they want events to unfold. I had the option of my separate dressing room segregated away from everyone else, but there's nothing worse than being left alone to brood over your thoughts before a fight. Even though I don't participate in other's pre-fight rituals I feed off of the energy.

What I do hate, however, is going last because all that

time waiting can open the door for all kinds of shit to enter my head... Like, after not fighting at this level of the sport for so long, will my body forget how to react? Can I still take a punch? When an opportunity arises will I execute or hesitate? Was my weight cut too difficult to recover from? A hard cut can make an elite athlete perform like a chain smoker sprinting upstairs while breathing through a snorkel...

My stomach churns. I get up and jog to the bathroom on heavy legs and find a stall and sit. This is commonplace for me. The runs are my routine. It's a natural part of the fight-or-flight process your body goes through to prime you for the stresses of combat. Your blood is diverted from non-essential functions such as digestion and is redirected to where it's needed most—carrying oxygen to muscles. Frankly, if I wasn't going through this, I'd be scared that I wasn't nervous enough. Show me a fighter who doesn't have pre-fight nerves (if not because they're concerned about the other fighter, but at minimum they're concerned about underperforming below their fullest potential in front of others, whether it's a few buddies in a backyard or a fight holoCast around the planet) and I'll show you a liar or someone who does not give a damn because they already think they're gonna lose anyway. To be afraid is human. Facing your fears head on is what separates the warriors, men and women in any endeavor, from those who read about our exploits from the safety of their Vaunts.

I walk across the room and past the holoFeed where a promo shows a highlight reel of my opponent side by side with a montage of his mother, each working their ways through their respective divisions. Each ripping tendons and popping ligaments as they hyperextend elbows... crashing their shins or feet into fighters' heads and knocking them senseless, then walking away as their victims crumple to the canvas behind them. The last guy in the Thierry beat down never fought again. You get KO'd like that it's tough to get your mind right to glove up again.

I go through a final weight check in front of the official and a Bellum executive, more for a recording of statistics than anything. Since last night, I was able to regain 15 pounds of water weight through proper rehydration. That's pretty typical.

I sit backwards into a chair and Bobby goes through the process of wrapping my hands. Whiskey oozes from his pores. When he's done wrapping and taping my hands into casts the official signs off on them. The gloves are pulled over the wraps and colored tape seals the Velcro closure at the wrists. The official makes his mark on the tape.

I begin loosening my jaw with a series of soundless screams and yawns. Bobby holds up the focus mitts for me and I start working up a sweat.

The last fighter competing in the fight before mine goes out the door and the drone cameras pick him up as he walks down the hallway and into the auditorium and into the cage. Within moments of the fight starting, he's on his back, mounted with fists crashing into his face. One punch hits him so hard it revives him from his stupor before the ref pulls the other fighter off of him. He sits on the mat with the innocence of a baby just awakened from a nap while the victor runs the perimeter of the cage and beating his chest.

Music rumbles through the building.

The talent wrangler bursts through the door and screams, YOU'RE ON DECK, BAYBEE... Then his eyes lose focus as he mouths words into his Vaunt and nods.

The wrangler screams: "GET READY..."

I stand.

"IT'S GO TIME BAYBEEE..."

Bobby wipes my mouthpiece on the hem of his shirt like a barkeep polishing a shot glass, then places it on my tongue.

Heh, the flesh of the Christ. So endeth my benediction.

SYNTH BASS rumbles over the P.A. system and reverbs throughout the arena. My entrance mix, part one: Boy George sings...

Do you really want to hurt me?
Do you really want to make me cry?

This ain't a dancing show, but I came to get down.

As I step into the hallway securityBots in blood-colored jackets flank me and a light blasts my eyes. In front of me a camera crew consisting of both drones and human a Steadicam operator, a sound man with a boom mike, and a spotter with a hand on both of their shoulders guide the way as they creep backwards in unison while filming my approach, and now I'm in your house...

On your Vaunts, peering out at you as my fight stats crawl across the Chyron on bottom of your holoFeed.

The steady Snick-Snak-Snik-Snack of my flip-flops slapping against my heels echoes off the cinderblock walls as we creep down the hallway. Soon it's drowned out by my entrance music which blasts and distorts to the point of being almost unrecognizable, growing louder with every step. We round a long blind curve like you'd find in a slaughterhouse... Curves designed to prevent the animals in the back of the line from witnessing the fate of the doomed beasts in line before them, and my music hits its crescendo as I step through the open maw of the arena and into the abattoir right as the song changes to "Can I Live?"

There's a sour stench of spilt beer hanging on air so thick it that it passes through my nose like motor oil drawn through a stir straw, and as we get closer to the cage the buzzing sound of the crowd escalates into a roar of slurring sentences and questions and exclamations, all with no distinct beginning nor end. The voices and desires of many individuals condensed into one singular and faceless consciousness.

It demands blood.

A spotlight scanning through the crowd picks out a face scowling in the blackness and moves on to another. A corridor of security barricades holds the plebs at bay. On the other side of the gauntlet awaits the cage. I make that my focal point, mouthing the words to my song as I walk.

While I'm watching every nigga watching me closely
My shit is butter for the bread, they wanna toast me
I keep my head, both of them where they supposed to be
Hoes'll get you sidetracked, then clap from close feet
I don't sleep, I'm tired, I feel wired like codeine...

SecurityBots flanks me for my approach down the gauntlet. Press cameras flash and mustard-stained t-shirts strain over guts. Boos. Paper cups half filled with beer hurled and splash at my feet as I stalk my way to the cage. Thoughts come to me in slow drips and I see myself floating through space as though I'm a minor character in someone else's dream and the world sketches itself in around me as I creep.

I visualize my opening fight moves in my head...

Relax... See the fight... We take time to feel each other out with probing jabs. How he reacts tells me a lot... Is he a runner? Will he sit in the pocket and engage? He likes to set up the rear kick off the lead hook so use my footwork and angles... Quick in, quick out. Relax... Straight punches, no posing. Double up on the jab to bridge the gap and now I'm back inside again. Sell the cross, he reacts high, I shoot low. Takedown. Settle... Settle... Get position, relax and maintain control... Tenderize with punches but don't get sloppy. Body, head, body and head... Be patient, take what he gives me... There it is. Execute.

At the stairs at the base of the cage a ref frisks my body and feels me up for excess oils and checks if I'm wearing a cup. I grin so that he may see my mouthpiece. Then he inspects my finger and toenails to be sure they're trimmed to a proper length.

I look down, afraid to see my hands may tremble but not because of fear. You enter the cage often enough and one day pieces of who you are never come out. A fighter has so many throws of the die before his number comes up, and after that, his life outside the cage after that will never be the same. What do you do when you poise yourself to enter the cage to salvage your legacy, but the memories of people whom you've loved or battled with along the way are stories written in blood?

You go in.

The ref, some officials await, and the tuxedoed announcer whose beard is dyed red and shorn into a vertical fin from chin to Adam's apple to resemble a cock's comb.

Jay-Z flows on about how it's better to die enormous than live dormant, and the ending of my song is abrupt. A hush falls over the crowd.

The cage has its own microclimate under the heat of the lights, and in the brightness, everyone in it appears as hyper-colored actors placed on stage against a wraparound backdrop of black. The crowd recedes and all sound drops away except for the sound of Bobby's voice.

"He's a southpaw so you'll be fighting a mirror image of yourself. Just remember to keep your lead foot on the outside of his to keep the advantage of position. He'll have to constantly adjust in order to go off and let his hands go. He'll either have to be constantly adjusting and resetting, which will keep him one step behind, or both his power hand and that rear kick of his will have traveled all the way across his body to hit you. But you'll always have him in all of your sights."

"Gotcha."

"In and out. 1,2,3, pivot."

I nod.

"And remember there's two extra rounds because this is

a title fight. He's a slow starter, don't get sloppy."

"I know."

Plutarch runs into the cage and without giving me as much as a glance pulls the officials, the ref, and the announcer into a huddle. Then they wave Bobby over to join them, leaving me alone in my corner.

The huddle breaks. A pair of Bellum officials carries a scale into the cage.

Bobby returns to me and says, "Slight change of plans."

Before I can ask him to elaborate, the lights dim and the spotlight falls upon the announcer.

He says, "Ladies and gentlemen in attendance and millions more watching around the world, this is a special announcement... Tonight's title fight between Thierry Bruise and to DeShawn Trustfall has been canceled."

A wave of boos erupts from the crowd.

The announcer continues, "Instead, we have a special treat for you tonight. We've found a replacement, and the fight will continue as planned. However, this bout will not be contested for the Lightweight title."

The crowd falls silent.

"Trustfall weighed 171 pounds in the locker room. Pending an in-cage weight check... this fight will be contested at 170 pounds."

I look a Bobby but he shushes me and points to the announcer, indicating me to pay attention.

"Don't worry folks, Thierry is just fine. He opted to pull out of the fight to give an opportunity for our special guest... Replacing Thierry Bruise is...

His MOM!

Ladies and gentlemen, please welcome the return of RENA BRUISE!"

The spotlight abandons the announcer and travels along the barricaded corridor towards the entrance of the arena tunnel. It focuses on an individual wearing a black towel over her shoulders like a poncho with the hole cut out of its center so her head can poke through. Rena, visible over the heads of the men who are filming her, trundles her way down the corridor and towards the cage. No music. It wouldn't matter because the crowd would block it out anyway.

She runs up the steps to the cage and steps onto the scale...

"One seventy-one for Rena Bruise! It's official! We have a title fight! This bout will be contested for Bellum's vacant men's Welterweight crown!

Actually, I saw the needle slap the top of the hole and stay there until they slid the weight over to 177 pounds. Yeah, you make allowance for the two six-ounce gloves, mouthpiece, sports bra and shorts, she's probably 175, but seriously, this is all for the theatrics, anyway. So many athletic commission rules were violated along the way for this fight to happen that the last thing that matters is this farce of a weigh-in.

Fuck it. I'll play along. Easy pickings.

The ref calls for me to face off with my adversary for the pre-fight instructions.

Rena says, "I hear what you say about me. You make joke about me and your crippled hand? Maybe I take your whole arm!"

I see her mouthpiece as she speaks. Fangs painted on it.

The ref instructs us to obey his commands and protect ourselves at all times. In the crowd behind his head a series of flashbulbs strobe and Rena's face blacked out in night blindness, and within my blinks, there's a negative image of her head silhouetted by a halo.

We touch gloves and go back to our corners.

I've got a case of cotton mouth and rubber legs and I can't be sure if this is the effect of adrenaline, which will fade as the fight progresses, or if my recovery from cutting and rehydration is incomplete.

My eyes lock on the woman across the cage from me for

any clues of her condition while trying to mask mine. This is more or less her walking around weight, so she's probably just fine. The ref checks with the judges and the timekeeper then asks if we're ready and yells, FIGHT.

She approaches with her fist raised to touch gloves before we go to work but when we meet in the center of the canvas, I reward her sportsmanship by ripping off a three-punch combo to her grill and punctuating it by slapping a leg kick off of her lead thigh before she manages to put her guard up and circle away.

Hey, this ain't pistols at dawn where you walk ten paces turn and fire. She heard the ref: Protect yourself at all times.

Rena harasses me with a jab in my face to maintain space while she regains her composure.

I kick, she checks it on her shin by raising her leg.

She kicks, I check...

I throw a jab but she's not there. A counterpunch stings against my cheek and another one crashes underneath my chin.

It wobbles me.

My knee touches the canvas but I pop back up. She's got the experience and maturity to not chase after me... yet.

I clinch by clasping my hands behind her neck to tie her up and stifle any follow-up combination. That one still has me shaken up.

She breaks free and throws a cross at my jaw. I slip to the inside, and it grazes past my ear.

Slipping a punch is all about subtlety. If you move too much, you miss an opportunity to counter attack. You want to move the absolute minimum necessary - just enough so the punch actually touches you. You wanna be in position to retaliate. The idea is as your opponent retracts their fist, it's followed along the exact same line to their head by your fist. Which I do, with a jab that she parries on her glove and then wallops me with a follow-up cross that crashes into my mouth so hard, it feels like it explodes out the back of my head.

She winks.

Back in the clinch, we pummel for position. Both of us seek double under hooks — both arms under the other person's arms — so that we have the leverage to take the other person down.

I harass her by bashing her face with my shoulder and stomp on her feet with my heels. It's not gonna win me the fight and probably won't even score points from the judges but it sucks for Rena, and if I can distract her for just a moment, that may be all I need to secure a superior position.

I cup the back of her head and wind back and let loose like I'm going to swing a John Wayne hook, but instead of impacting her face with my fist, I open my fist and bury the back of my hand against my chest at the last instant. This both exposes the bone of my elbow and shortens the swing's arc, increasing the velocity like cracking a whip. I "sit down on it" by rotating my hips into the swing, which increases the force of impact. I don't think about any of this. This is all muscle memory from countless repetitions in practice. It just happens.

My elbow bites into her brow bone where her skin is parchment-thin and capillaries carry blood just below the surface and her flesh rips with the ease of separating wet cardboard.

I hit her again and again and blood jets from her face in a parabolic arc of crimson. It sprays across my chin, dabbing my tongue with bitter flavor then scrawls on the bleached canvas in cursive as though leaking from a fountain pen.

She scrutinizes the blood splashed across my face.

"Mine or yours?" she says.

"Yours."

Rena smiles. The fangs on her mouthpiece spring out.

We're both slippery with blood and sweat as we pummel

for position, all the while trading clipped punches.

She clasps both of her hands behind my head and struggles to pull my head downward toward the floor.

This is the Muay Thai Plum clinch. What's coming next will shatter the few teeth left in my grill if I don't act fast. Her knees.

A rookie will cross his arms in front of his own face to form an ad-hoc shield, which is swell if your intent is to accessorize your soon-to-be jacked-up face with a matching set of cracked forearms. Even worse, an amateur will push the attacker's hip away, which only gives them even more space to rocket a knee upward to break your arm and/or your face. Nah, dude, you wanna take that space away and smother the attack. You wanna pull their chest flush with yours.

So, I clasp my hands in a Gable grip behind Rena's back, while fighting to retain my posture by looking up at the ceiling, all while working to pull her chest flush to mine.

She begins the alternating skip action of thrusting one knee up into the space between us while chambering the other leg back to fire. The action which resembles the Running Man dance from the 80s.

I battle to restrict space so her knees can only travel up to impact my thighs which, considering the current condition of my legs is not any fun, but it beats the hell out of a crushed orbital resulting in loose bone shards drifting to my eye socket and permanent blindness.

If she does the Thai Plum correctly, she'll continue to pull my head down into her knees with her hands clasped behind my neck while squeezing her arms together in a fulcrum action like a nutcracker...

She doesn't.

This mistake on her behalf allows me to bob and weave my head out of her grasp, but as we separate, I catch a knee to the solar plexus.

With blood from her brow trickling into her eyes, she

can't see into mine and know that I'm hurt. I angle off to her weak side, but NOT straight back. Never... NEVER walk straight back while under attack. Contrary to what intuition tells you, you're still in danger because you can't possibly back up faster than your attacker can move forward and, you have zero leverage for power behind any counterattack of your own. Assuming you even connect with a counter because by backing away, you're literally walking yourself out of range if your attacker simply stops advancing forward.

She wipes her face. Clear white eyes glare out at me from behind a mask of red. Her hair is wet and matted. She looks as though she was held upside down by her ankles and baptized to the chest in wine. But she's fine. With the heart racing to meet the demands of combat, face wounds always look far worse than they actually are.

I shuffle step my way to the center of the cage. Rena follows.

Kick, check...

Kick, check...

Jab-cross-hook-kick, check...

I fake a jab and then change levels to shoot for a takedown, but she sprawls. We scramble to our feet but, my legs are tender from the knees they just too, so she beats me to her feet with ease and then crashes a hook to the side of my head. Because, like a schmuck, I used my hands to stand up, she has a long enough look at my unguarded noggin to triple up on her strikes.

I'm up.

Instead of resetting, I bury my chin into my chest and bite down on my mouthpiece and stand in the pocket right in front of her. We trade.

I give her a hook and a cross, and she gives me a shovel hook and an elbow across my nose which sprays blood across her chest. As we throw down, some of our blows are deflected off of each other's forearms and gloves, enough get through.

There is nothing like the thudding of gloved fists impacting a human head, especially from two professionals in crisp rapid fire. If you've ever sat cage side for a fight you know the conflicting feelings of guilty excitement the sound can arouse in your gut. The response is automatic and primal. Like watching the video with the audio turned all the way up starring a gang of police beating a downed suspect with their nightsticks. This is what you pay a day's wages for to experience up close and live because, holoFeed or no, watching on a projection dilutes this visceral experience. Maybe, you take flecks of the fighters' blood home with you sprayed onto your collar.

Hook-uppercut-hook-uppercut...

Cross-hook-cross-uppercut-body hook...

Hook-uppercut-hook...

During the exchange, my form falls away and my chin rises and, of course, one of her punches cracks me right on my 'off' switch. The horizon tilts and on my way to the canvas, I see the blood splashed on all the surfaces I've been dropped on in the past: sawdust floors, rain-slicked asphalt salted with teeth.

On the way down, I recover well enough to make a grab for her legs. My head presses against the outside of her legs, leaving me vulnerable to a guillotine choke. It's a mistake I'd never make if I wasn't clawing my way out of knock out land. She capitalizes on this error by snaking her forearm underneath my chin.

There's a mini battle between us. She's trying to wedge her forearm under my chin to get to my neck, and I struggle to stop her.

I lose the battle.

I'm looking down on at dried blood stains on the canvass as my head is caught in the V formed by her bicep and forearm. She squeezes and squeezes and arches her back for leverage so hard it lifts me off my feet, and colors burst and pop in front of my eyes...

A ringing in my ear grows louder as I try to keep my eyes focused on anything... Like the fresh blood stain on the floor that spells out, LOL? in cheerful Coca Cola font.

Focus... What's the counter for this choke?...

Okay, I need to turn my head while and create space... where? Fuck, I know this...

A phantom scent of bleach tickles my brain. The world dissolves into a hazy shade of white. I'm slipping away...

Slipping--

"BREAK."

There is a slap on my back. The ref's voice comes crashing into my consciousness as Rena releases her choke. My field of vision expands back from a white spec, and there's a tingling and buzzing sensation in my teeth.

Was I out?

I look at my corner where Bobby is waving me over. Nope. The round has ended.

I plop down onto the stool gasping for air through my mouth like a goldfish stranded on a linoleum floor because my nasal passage is a caved in by boulders of snot, cartilage, and blood.

A snap, and the whiff of powdered latex gloves...

Bobby reaches into my mouth and pries out my mouthpiece and it comes out with a pop. Once white, it is now pink from the mixture of fluids dripping from it in strings. Bobby wipes it with his shirt and tucks it behind my ear for safe keeping.

The rules say Bobby has to wear gloves to touch me. He once rooted through a soccer mom's puke, putting chunks of half-digested barbeque into his mouth until he identified and recovered my finger... Not my missing ring finger with my wedding band. That story is way too repugnant to tell while sober. By me a Corona one day...

Bobby uses Q-tips to smear an adrenaline chloride gel into my cuts to staunch the bleeding, then presses a cool metal bar onto my cheek to slow the swelling.

Across the cage in the opposing corner, a ringside doctor hovers as a cut man works on sealing the gash in my opponent's face with Vaseline and epinephrine. Her teammates pressed against the outside of the cage, shouting encouragement.

I wait for Bobby to drop some wisdom.

He says, "You almost got choked the fuck out, my man."

"Seriously. What's your assessment of the situation?"

"You talked shit about someone's mom, and now momma's beating your ass."

Fluid drips down my throat and trickles down the wrong passage. I want to blow the snot and blood out of my nose to clear it but I don't because the pressure could rupture weakened blood vessels around my eye, causing it to swell shut. And the outside chance that blowing my nose could scatter any potential bone shards that may be floating around in my face.

"How do you feel?"

"Like I could go another four rounds."

"Guess what?"

"What?"

"You have to go another four rounds."

"Wait, what? What round is this?"

Bobby shakes his head.

The ring girl saunters by holding the round card above her head. She smiles at me and I watch her ass as she saunters by... I wonder what Shonda is doing right now...

Bobby leans in close. He smiles, then crams a tampon up a nostril to staunch the bleeding. His Wild Turkey-soaked breath stings my good eye, and it's making me giddy.

I say, "Other than that?"

"Let's see... Do not comment that Rena loos nice today. She'll take that as condescending and really whoop your ass."

"You got any useful advice for me? Please don't say

'Sweep the leg'."

"Wouldn't hurt."

"SECONDS OUT! FIGHTERS, GET READY!"

Bobby paws the mouthpiece from behind my ear and jams it in my mouth, then yanks the tampon from my nose by its string.

He says, "Okay, she's timing your cross and coming over the top with a looping hook. Instead of throwing a one-two-three and pivoting away, I want you to throw a one-two-lead kick to her inside thigh. Got it?"

"Yeah."

I stand.

My thigh is swelling and it sucks putting weight on it. Cutting angles is going to be impossible soon.

The ref asks if we're ready and screams, FIGHT!

Before I can make it farther than a few steps, Rena rockets out of her corner and straight toward me. Her arm cocks back, telegraphing a punch. When she's almost upon me, I execute a Jeet Kune Do Stop Kick by raising my lead foot, angling it horizontally, and thrusting it forward so that it crashes onto her thigh. This causes a jarring halt to her forward progress.

With her lower body stopped, momentum lurches her upper body forward. My foot that's planted on her thigh slides off and to the outside, and my opposite hand high hangs and out forward to protect the high line from any attack. My lead hand, which was cocked back and tucked to my hip to hide its intent until it's too late for her to do a goddamn thing about it, thrusts forward and SMASHES! into her nose before my sideways-turned foot that is slipping off and to the outside of her thigh touches the ground. This detail is important because I want all my momentum to go forward into the target (her face) and not down into the floor. The combined momentum of her torso traveling forward and my fist thrusting to meet it is a force multiplier that sends a CRACK! echoing through the auditorium.

I cut an angle to the outside, and unload with follow up punches.

Before Rena orients herself, I throw a hook to her body. Her flesh ripples away from my fist at the point of impact like a softball hurled into Jell-O. She groans and circles away.

Rena flicks jabs into my face to stave my attack and disrupt my rhythm. Then she hides a leg kick behind one of her jabs which thuds against my lead thigh so hard that I have to fight to keep from toppling over. She likes what she sees, so she jabs and gives me another and another.

When she comes in behind the jab again, I lift my leg to kick, but she drops for a double-leg takedown and my feet no longer touch the ground. Instead of dropping me right there she picks me up (!!!!) and carries me across the cage. She slams me on to the ground in front of her corner. The second my back touches canvas, I scramble for a better position, aaand... Yeah, that's not gonna happen...

Okay... just pull half guard and hold her close... Can't let her pass or posture up, because she'll go off with those fists and elbows...

Patience...

Good, I got control of her arms with an over-under...

She's trying to pry her leg lose from my lockdown. Gotta slow her ass down. Wait 'til she straightens her leg, and...

Go!

With one foot, I stomp on her leg that I have trapped between mine, which allows me to use my free leg to get a foot in between her crotch. Then I release my stomp and get the other foot in so that both my insteps are between her legs, and I've improved my position to Butterfly Guard.

Now, I could try to sweep her from here, using my feet to flip her to either side and gain side control or a mount, but we're both so damn slippery that I should play it conservative. She's bucking in an attempt to pass my guard, so be patient...

Aaand...

GO!

In one fluid motion, I slip my feet from inside her loins then I wrap my legs around her waist and I clasp my feet together. Full guard.

She harasses my ribs with punches, but with her chest flush with mine there's no leverage and they're only a bit more annoying than love taps She tries to posture herself up, prying her torso upright for space to rain elbows and fists down into my face.

I still have the over-under with one of my arms under hers, the other around her neck, and my hands clasped together with a Gable grip. Her ass ain't going anywhere until I want her to.

Except...

My grip is slipping open and now she's posturing up in my guard with me fighting to grab her to pull her back down to my chest!

Bam! Bam! Bam!

She unleashes an assault of fists and elbows down into my face, and there's a metallic taste of copper in my mouth.

Bam! Bam! Bam!

This is a losing battle for me so I cut my losses and cover up. Every other blow gets through my defenses enough to hit my face. Upon impact, touch receptors in my eye flash sparks light in my head. Her coach screams for her to keep going.

Bam! Bam! FLASH!

She's still stuck between my legs inside my guard and unable to pass, so while this does suck it could be a lot worse.

Bam! FLASH! FLASH!

I can't just sit back and enjoy the light show, however, because, I'm in the same predicament Clint, the Cudgel was in during the Clown Room fight. My head, trapped, with the floor behind it, has nowhere to go and my brain sloshes and jolts around in my skull.

The ref drops down on his hands and knees so that his face is level with mine and he warns me to work to defend myself or he'll stop the fight.

Rena's coach screams, "SOFTEN HIS BODY, THEN GO BACK TO HIS HEAD! BODY, HEAD, BODY, HEAD!"

She obeys, switching now to my assault my ribs. This tactic is meant to inspire me to open my shell protecting my head and lower my arms to protect my body. Even though I know this, and they know that I know this, a punch to the ribs can be pretty goddamn compelling. She works the same spot on my ribs over and over, then hammers a straight punch down onto my solar plexus that steals my breath away!

The ref says, "LAST WARNING, TRUSTFALL! WORK DOWN THERE!"

Wait...

Patience...

I time her punches, and I buck my hips as she pulls her fist back -- she falls forward, placing both of her hands on the mat.

Rena's coach says, "GET YOU HANDS OFF OF THE MAT. PUT YOUR HANDS ON HIS CHEST!"

Too late, I snag her arm!

I wrap an over hook around her right arm with my left and open my guard and hug my left knee with my left hand and squeeze. Then I place my right forearm across her collarbone and grab my own left foot, trapping her right arm and keeping her flush to my chest. My right foot rests on her left hip, which prevents Rena from just advancing forward to walk out of my trap. This position is called Mission Control.

She tries to posture up but all this accomplishes is lifting me up with her, so she lifts and slams me down like an otter cracking clams open against a rock. She tires and her work output slows.

When her rampage stops, we both lay chest to chest, catching our breaths. My leg that she's whacked on all night protests and throbs, but this is nothing I can't deal with for now.

"STAY BUSY OR I'LL STAND YOU GUYS UP."

Fuck that!

I've got options here... I could:

- Bust a Kung Fu move, which means pulling my left shin under her chin, and go for an armbar on her trapped arm by pivoting my hips. From there I'll transition by tossing her on her back and into the arm bar... But, for a moment, I'll be stacked underneath her and there are too many moving parts. I'd have to nail every single step, because if I do it jankity it's a jump ball for position.
- Bust a Kung Fu move: grab my left foot with my left arm, trapping her head in between, then finish with a Gogoplata choke, choking the piss out of her with my foot. That would look hench as fuck on a highlight reel... But nah, my feet are too goddamn slippery, and there's too high of a chance for her to escape, and I'd look like a serious douche on Sports Center.
- Bust a Kung Fu move and pivot my hips to my left and transition into an Omoplata on her right shoulder? Either she'll roll with it and I'll end up in superior position in side control, or I'm ripping her arm off. Both results work for me, and the Omoplata is high-percentage.

So, I bust a move.

I slip my left foot from the top of her neck and reposition it beneath it, and holding her right wrist with my left hand as I'm doing this... I scoot my hips out from under her to the left and sit up and as I begin to apply downward pressure on Rena's shoulder.

Her corner yells for her to roll with the momentum. She does, and she ends up on her back with me in control. Yay.

There's a widow of opportunity during the roll where I could have been greedy and tried for a full mount, but that's too risky — I may have ended up in her guard.

I grab head-and-arm, and pin one knee on her hip and the other by her head and keep her close.

The first thing Rena does when we do settle, however, is to block my attempt at mounting her by tenting her far leg and crossing the near leg over it so her knee prevents me from just hopping over her legs.

Whatever. I punch Rena's face...

I alternate hugging her close then posturing up long enough to drop hammer fist and downward slashing elbows between her forearms and on her face — never more than a few at a time — then I lay down flush on her chest to grind my stubbly chin into the gash above her eye to restart the bleeding.

Elbow-elbow-elbow. Cover and grind.

While I'm covering and grinding, I glance at the clock on the Jumbotron for the time remaining in the round.

Not all of my blows get through but they don't have to. If you want to lose a close fight by decision, by all means, coast the end of each round. You wanna steal every round you can so that if the round is close and the judges aren't sure who to give it to, you for flurry for the last few seconds so they give the round to you.

The ref is down by our feet and out of position to catch my debauchery so I pinch Rena's nose shut and cup my hand over her mouth to screw with her breathing a bit. Her corner sees this and screams bloody murder but by the time the ref is in position to see anything I'm already dropping elbows again.

Elbow-elbow-punch. Cover and grind.

I dig with my chin into hot wet the rent in her face. Blood flows again. She makes gurgling noises underneath me as she swallows and chokes on her own blood.

When I posture up for another flurry Rena tries to buck me off so I lay flush until she settles down.

Elbow-elbow-elbow-

"DO SOMETHING DOWN THERE OR I'LL STOP THE FIGHT."

She bucks, and there's a scramble to regain control because she's really slippery... before I can get head-and-arm and lay flush on top of her chest, she wraps me up with an over-under then walks her legs up the cage... now she's in a north-south 69 position with her still on her back and me with my chest on her torso.

I adjust my arms to go for low-hanging fruit choke which is right there, but she explodes by pushing off my hips with both hands to create space, and flips her legs over my shoulder... and threads a leg between one of mine and scissors it shut with the other, and her torso follows by righting itself. Then he grabs an over-under.

Just like that, she's recovered half guard.

I say, "Damn. that was pretty damn slick."

She coughs blood and phlegm. "Fuck you."

Rena goes for an electric chair sweep by reaching underneath for my free leg and, though I know what she's doing, she's too fast and there's not a damn thing I can do to stop her. Rather than try and fight it and let her sweep me which will put her on top, I kick away, roll out, and stand up.

She stands, too.

Rena's left eye is almost shut. The right side of her face droops. Her nose sits askew. She swings her hips, so I lift my leg to check a kick that never comes. Instead, a fist materializes and CRASHES! into my cheek.

Superman punch.

This blow catches me flat-footed, so I take all of the impact force instead of absorbing it by rocking back on my heels.

I stagger backwards across the cage. Rena pursues.

I'm recovered by the time my back hits the opposite wall and when she's close, I cup my hand on the back of her head and pull her into me while stepping to the side and I use her forward momentum to spin her. Now, her back is to the cage.

I bury my fists into her body while she rips fists and elbows across my skull.

"BREAK."

I shuffle-hop-limp back to my corner.

The cumulative effects of leg kicks have tenderized my thigh, and my heart squeezes battery acid through my veins. I look up and see a face in the Jumbotron. It's so bloodied that it's not clear at first whose face it is. I smile, and so does the face on the screen. My face looks like I landed on it after being tossed from a speeding pickup on a rocky backwoods trail.

Bobby sets a bucket between my legs as soon as my ass hit the stool, and I spit pink goo into it. He sponges the muck from my face, then holds an ice pack to the back of my neck. The ice pack sends a shockwave of chill down my spine. I empty my mind and close my eyes. My heartbeat settles. I don't bother to pop my mouthpiece out.

"SECONDS OUT!"

Rena and I meet in the center of the cage and trade jabs.

We circle, battling for control over who gets to place their lead foot on the outside of the other person's. Because I'm a southpaw, foot position is even more critical in striking. Winning this chess match of foot position opens up infinite mobility options for the winner, and shuts down angles of movement for the loser.

Rena, in attempting to place her foot outside of mine, slips on a slick of gore and falls to her hands and knees. Rules say I can't kick her, so before she stands, I leap onto her back.

In jujitsu, the number one rule is position before submission. You must have total control of your opponent's body before attempting to submit them. You do not want to lose your position by attempting a submission too quickly, because all your work will be for naught and you'll end up in a scramble.

So, I cinch up an Anaconda by figure fouring my legs around her waist but before I grab an over-under, she executes the correct counter by falling onto her side where my left foot is squeezed behind my right knee... This breaking the figure four. From here, it's a scramble.

She blocks my fight to snatch an over-under by holding onto my gloves, then turns into me. Because we're both so slippery, I make a value judgment and release her. Lose the battle, win the war.

We circle and trade jabs again.

I attempt to sell one of the jabs with the intent of hiding a takedown behind it, but she ain't buying. I stand just in time to catch a shin skipping off the top of my skull.

A fog rolls into my skull, and she turns and walks away from me without waiting to see me fall to the canvas...

Which I don't. Surprise motherfucker!

The hell if I'm gonna end up on someone else's highlight reel.

Come on, legs, work...

Hurry!

Move... Move!

An in-shape athlete can recover from flash knockouts fast. The fog burns off, and I see her strutting around the gage with her arms raised, back turned to me.

Rena's corner points at me and screams.

Too late. I tackle her ass.

I end up in full mount after a scramble, then I transition into an armbar. She defends her arm by clasping her hands together, but I'm working it open by using a Silverado which means that, without letting go of her arm, I wedge an elbow in between both of her arms and I pry...

As soon as I separate her hands, there's a small window of opportunity for Rena to escape that she's gonna to try to dive through. She'll try to keep her arm bent and point her thumb back as though she's hitchhiking, and then roll over her trapped arm's shoulder and continue to roll onto his belly while walking her feet toward my head. The instant her hands are separated, she must explode through the movement before I can extend her arm.

I know this. She knows that I know this. But we each do what we have to do anyway. Jujitsu, at a high level, is a series of mini-battles the casual observer would never notice. I fucking love this sport...

Her hands begin to slip, and her grip breaks...

She goes for it!

My legs hold her in place. Instead of muscling her arm to its full extension with my arms, I'm patiently waging a mini-battle to bury her fist into my chest. Only then will I have earned the right to straighten her arm out by leaning back and using the leverage of my entire upper body.

Her arm slips in my grasp for a microsecond, I catch it.

I can't let go... I do not want to go through another round of this nonsense... I pull until I've got nothing left and I pull some more... I pull and pull, because I cannot let go.

Bobby says, "TURN HER ARM SO THAT HER THUMB IS POINTED AT THE CEILING!"

You train your ear to snatch the voice of your corner out of a crowd of thousands. If you are in combat and you can hear the crowd then you're probably fucked because that means you are not mentally focused. Your mind should tune everything else out but the task at hand, which is imposing your will on the person who is intent on beating the shit out of you. I obey Bobby's instructions, and I adjust Rena's arm so that her elbow points up to the ceiling. This angles her elbow for maximum vulnerability against torque.

Please God, Tap...

My grip slips down her arm like a rope speeding through a falling man's hands until it catches on a dry spot.

With my grip now secure I've got the confidence to go DEFCON 1. I thrust my hips under his elbow joint upward to the sky while for extra leverage while I pull his wrist down. Bending her arm right up to its breaking point is like breaking a wet tree branch. There's resistance one moment, and the next instance there's nothing but give.

A series of quick POPs! with the sound of wet jeans ripping. She screams, and her arm goes slack.

I look to the ref, who looks at Rena who has not tapped. There's no fucking way I'm letting up! I pull harder.

Urine clouds the front of her shorts. It warms the back of my legs.

Tap, goddamn it.

My breathing runs away from me, and my grip begin to loosen as my hands slip on sweat-slicked skin.

A tap! Thrice on the canvas.... from the timekeeper to signify 10 seconds left in the round.

I can't endure another round of this... Please God, tap.

My hand slips off her arm and she executes the escape by walking her feet around while rolling to her belly and standing up.

Fuck.

The ref yells, "BREAK!"

FUUUUUKKKK! Round over.

I return to my corner and compose myself. You have to learn to let failed submission attempts go. Otherwise, they can demoralize you and fuck with your head for the next submission attempt.

The next round begins.

Rena has got one arm up en guard, while her other hangs dead to her side. She's trying to stave off my advances with teeps, which are Muay Thai push kicks. I'm not concerned about her striking at this point, so I just wade right in and throw down.

I shuffle step and pivot to get an angle on her. Before she can adjust, I dig a hook into her kidney... She groans and drops her one good hand, so I whip a double hook to her head.

There's a CRUNCH! in my shoulder when my second hook lands. I suppress a scream. Experience allows me to keep my shit together, so I can notice that Rena's eyes lose focus and her face relaxes. She appears to me like a ship that sprung a leak and is taking its sweet damn time going under. My heartbeat doubles up squeezing new adrenaline through my veins, which takes the edge off the pain and slows time. I chase Rena to the canvas with my fists. I laying her ass down like her bones were sucked out of her body.

But she's in shape. When her knees touch the floor, she's recovered well enough to make a one-armed grab for my leg. As her arm reaches forward my legs sprawl out and back and I drive my hips to the ground... This breaks her grip, flattens her out and keeps my legs out of her reach of for future grabbing attempts.

Yeah, one of Rena's arms is probably broken. Yes, her face is pinned between my chest and the floor, but people have rallied back to win from worse situations. I don't fuck around.

I dig my left hand under her neck and begin to snake it through. I do this fast because she's already trying to get her knees underneath her to reform her base.

I thread my arm all the way through the gap my hand has made, then snake it around Rena's neck and under her still-outstretched arm...

She tries to yank her arm back and out of the snare, but

it's too late. I'm already drawing the loop closed by grabbing my own right bicep... then slapping my right hand on her back...

I take my time... I wait for her to settle down...

Then I begin the Gator Roll.

You want to roll toward your arm that's across the back of the person whom you are choking, which means during the movement you're rolling your opponent on top of you... Continue movement until you stop with both of you on your sides... Your arm that's across your opponent's back must be up toward the ceiling. It's critical to roll fast enough to have enough momentum to complete the roll rapidly or you'll stall out, ending up stuck on your back with your opponent on top of you.

Once rolled into position, you make like Curly from The Three Stooges: lying on your side, you walk your feet in a circle 'til your feet are next to your opponent's.

This is my go-to move. I execute the Gator Roll before you've finished reading this sentence.

However, because my shoulder is going cold and numb by the moment, the choke is not as cinched in and as tight as I'd like.

Rena thrashes and pulls.

Readjusting is too risky... I gotta make my stand right here. I relax and squeeze. If your choke is tight enough, even experienced fighters will either tap out or pass out before you can count to ten.

One...

Two...

There's another POP! from my shoulder. I ignore it.

Squeeeeeze...

Three...

Four...

Rena kicks, so I reach out for her top leg with my top foot, hook her leg with my foot and pull it into me and I figure-four my legs shut. This traps her lower body in place...

Five...

Six...

My shoulder screams... If this feels like it's taking forever for me, it has to feel worse for her. She's experienced enough to relax and not panic while enduring a submission attack...

Seven...

Lactic acid builds up. My entire body begs for me to let go! With my last burst of reserve strength, I intensify my effort...

Eight...

The ref leans over and checks on her...

Nine...

"STOP!"

The ref tries to pry us apart. For a millisecond I don't believe it — I'm a castaway who discovers the rescuer talking to me on the beach isn't a hallucination — so I don't want to let go. The ref slaps my back. I release my submission.

My field of vision expands and ambient sounds from the crowd come flooding back into my ears and as adrenaline-induced myopia slips away. Details of the world around me begin to re-sketch themselves in...

I want to cry.

The cage door opens and people enter. A doctor and some seconds tend to my opponent.

I walk over to Rena. She looks at me and smiles, and I smile back.

I say, "I'm sorry for disrespecting you."

"You punch like a child."

We laugh. I get out of the way so that the doctor can do her job.

The crowd, processing what they just saw, is slow to react. When people do begin to respond what, I get is not much more than a golf clap. For the most part, it's just quiet. Sigh, nobody appreciates the vicissitudes of simple jiujitsu executed well. Goddamn Philistines...

At least they're not booing me.

Pockets of claps in the crows swell, and soon the arena cheers and applauds. The cheers aren't for me. They're for my Rena who is now sitting up and chatting with her cornermen.

Bobby tells me to replace my mouthpiece for teeth for the post-fight interview. I remove the mouthpiece and hand it to him, but I don't take the teeth.

The ring announcer announcing the official results. The ref raises my good arm. Plutarch sets the Bellum Middleweight Crown upon my head. I fight the urge to weep on live TV with blood and piss soaked through my shorts... I lose. The fuck if I know if these are tears of happiness, relief, or the coming down from the adrenaline dump.

Plutarch-as-Andy Circus congratulates me and asks me to walk him through the Gator Roll choke, then inquiries about the condition of my shoulder and if it affected the submission...

I look up at the Jumbotron... Highlights from the fight playback... I don't remember any of it. I may as well be narrating a Cambodian documentary already in progress that I've never seen before and predicting what is going to happen next...

The tide of adrenaline recedes from my body, leaving space for aches and pains to wash over me. That said, as I walk down the stairs of the cage, my shoulder feels better and I don't really mind. Winning has a way of doing that. Funny how that works...

A school of camera drones and securityBots picks me up as I walk. They escort me through a gauntlet of flying beer and boos from the crowd all the way to the arena door.

Lookit, I'm just gonna come out and say it... There's no way I'd win over any fans by beating a woman. Even one as great and as accomplished as Rena who defeated another man before me. But if I lost to her, I'd never hear the end of it. Never mind the fact that, from a technical standpoint, she's just as skilled or better than me in every part of the fight game... Or that nobody has ever beat her. Man or woman. Fuck these sanctimonious fans. They're the sexist assholes, not me.

No... I don't quite feel like doing the Snoopy Dance, but I hold my head up. I grin, and my snaggle tooth smile is broadcast on the Jumbotron and around the world.

~

Backstage in a curtained-off examining room, Bobby holds my crown while I puke into a hazardous waste can. I wipe my chin and sit on the examining table. Bobby swabs an ear with alcohol then tears the wrapping away from a hypodermic needle with his teeth. He pinches my ear to gather a bubble of fluids under the skin and stabs the needle into it. Then he draws back the plunger and the barrel of the needle fills with puss and blood. After he drains excess fluid from both ears, he gives my crown back. He nods. I nod. He offers his hand to shake, and I take it. He leaves.

A doctor in a Morrissey quiff and mutton chops snaps on latex gloves and shines a penlight in my eyes and asks me the usual post-fight questions while examining me like, What hurts? I tell him it'd be faster asking me what doesn't.

After pressing and wiggling my nose, he tells me it's is broken. He treads a needle and stabs it into my brow. While he closes up my face, my neighbor moans from the other side of the curtain. A voice I don't recognize commands my neighbor to relax and counts down from three and there's a crunch! and a scream. Then a sound of a curtain pulled back and footsteps.

More moaning.

Doc injects my nose with local anesthetic and waits.

Then he slides what looks like a screwdriver with a blunt end up a nostril, pinches my nose and jerks and wiggles it sending shooting sparks of pain crashing into my brain it until the bone clicks into place and he's satisfied that my nose has reset. The doctor consults a before holograph of my nose projected from his Halo. He decides not to bother with a nose cast.

The doctor has finished all that can be done within reason to fix my face.

My curtain is pulled aside and an official enters, holding a pee cup. The doctor and the commission official accompany me to a nearby bathroom. The official hands me a cup and all observe me breaking the seal and urinating into it. Then we walk back to the examining cubicle, where the curtains are pulled back and my neighbor's table is empty. A gore-soaked gauze bib in an overflowing hazardous waste receptacle. The official hands me a clipboard and pen. I yawn as I sign the documents.

Security accompanies me as we walk out of the arena and to the locker room.

The securityBots stand guard outside my door while I police my gear from the locker room, then they escort me to my room. Crossing the casino, none of the gamblers pay me any notice. Their sole focus held hostage by cards, levers, and spinning wheels...

When the bots and I reach my door, I have them check for intruders first while I wait outside lest I step onto a tarp and and a freezer bag thrown over my head...

Clear.

I go in.

The bots are still in standby mode next to my door when I emerge from changing into a clean pair of board shorts and retrieving my Birkin bag and cigarette case from the room's safe.

The securityBots escort me to the elevator, they don't get on with me.

~

The elevator car, a Kepler triangle, slices down the exterior of the Otium like a free-falling Guillotine blade. Its long side clings flush with the inverted pyramid's underside. The glass floor and walls expose me to a view of the world held at arm's length. Because of the building's shape, the lights along the coastline below recedes further into the distance as we descend, as though watching the past vanish through a rear-view window.

Pink Floyd's *Echoes* plays.

The doors open. Shonda, messenger bag slung across her shoulder and dolled up in sheer knit dress clinging to her too tight to hide her service weapon, saunters in. The sway of her hips seems out of sorts with the plodding footfalls of her combat boots where, from experience, I know she stashes a weapon. She smiles at me, presses a button for a floor and, when prompted flashes her Vaunt over the scanner to confirm that she has proper access. As law enforcement, she always has access.

"Hey."

"Hey."

If she's surprised to see me, she doesn't show it.

I say, "Date?"

"Yeah."

Silence. She looks at my crown.

"How does it feel?"

"Not as great as I imagined."

"Fuck Impostor Syndrome. You deserve it."

"No, I know I earned it. Somehow... it just doesn't feel worth it."

The lights above the door count down as the floors pass us by. My thoughts flash to her tiara and sash she left on the stool... my lack of support when she was hurting just like me when Miles passed, which drove us apart and her into the clutches of Galacticology... and to my innumerable micro-fuckups along the way.

A Children of Tendu pendant around her neck...

I say, "You look great."

She punches my shoulder; I wince.

"I'm proud of you," she says.

"Thanks."

The elevator stops its decent and travels horizontally. Our view shifts away from the Pacific where a marine layer of fog encroaches upon the land, to our new orientation with a vista above the San Fernando Valley.

She nods... Then she takes the divorce papers out of her bag... They're fucking collated.

"You left these on the counter."

"You're welcome."

"Unsigned."

"Whoops."

I take the documents.

I say, "Maybe we don't have to do this... I mean, now that I won, I'm thinking... you know... we can finally enjoy what it's like on the other side of things for a change for the time I have left. Can you pretend for a little while?"

"That's sweet, Dee."

She crosses her arms, clutching her bag against her chest like a barrier.

For once in my life, the perfect combinations of words form in my thoughts at the right time and, in my mind's eye, I see the effect they have on her and the remainder of my life... But I don't speak them. Instead, I just nod. How fucked up is it that, even now, I can't—?

"Hey," she says, "Check this out!"

Shonda opens her purse and pulls out an apple-sized lump wrapped in an Hermes scarf.

"I'm returning this to my date..."

She hands it to me.

Like an onion, the wad gets smaller and smaller as I peel

away the layers to reveal... The Oscar's head.

Sévérine's Oscar.

The elevator descends again and I feel a drop in my gut...I convince myself that these events are correlated.

She says, "It's a surprise!"

You're goddamn right it is.

I say, "How'd you find it?"

"I'm a fucking detective. You know, I'll bet this is the first time a Crown and an Oscar have been together. The doors, they're reflective. Turn and face them."

She yanks my crown out of my hand and puts it on my head, and her Vaunt on her face and hugs my arm. After posing me and moving my head around to get my "good" side, she holds up Oscar between us.

"Smile, damn it!"

She projects the picture and it floats in space before us: Her with a duck face and me and my half-assed grin. Shonda cackles and snorts. I've heard her laughter the other day and thousands more before it, but today the sound is both strange yet familiar, like an ex-lover's kiss after a decade has passed.

Shonda re-wraps the head and returns it and her Vaunt to her purse.

"She and I met on that robbery call that you insisted I take the other night. We clicked. This ought to cheer her up. She's been down all day over her baby's daddy who kept breaking her heart... Not that she ever wanted to hook up with him again, but that he can't get his shit straight for his boy. Even the rich and famous have the same problems as us plebs. What a fucking deadbeat..."

"Yeah..."

My Halo chimes in my ear...

It's Sev. I answer it on private audio only.

Sev says, "Hey, congratulations!"

"...thanks."

"Are you okay?"

"Sure."

"You heading to the post-fight presser?"

"Fuck that. Not even if my life depended on it."

She says, "So, yes, this is perfect! I'm going on a last-minute date because apparently, my girlfriend has a surprise for me that just cannot wait. Would you mind watching DeShawn for a few hours?"

"Okay."

"Take him to the press conference. He'll love that."

I look at Shonda... She's got her Vaunt back on and laughing at a conversation.

"No," Shonda says, "the dumb-ass private detectives she hired left it in the back of an Uber... I traced the car from The Clown Room right back to Slyna Olin's bungalow at the Beverly Hills Hotel. Bitch thought she deserved to win for a comedy... Hahaha, I know, right? Fucking Swedes..."

"Dee? Hello?" Sev says.

"Uh huh."

"Send your elevator to my sector, would you? I'll see you in a bit."

She tells me the sector and disconnects the call. The floor is the button Shonda pushed when she entered the elevator.

The doors open and Sévérine it there, wearing a white crushed-velvet tracksuit and retro shell-top Adidas.

Little D, holding her hand, in a t-shirt down to his knees. On the front of the shirt, a hologram GIF of me raising the crown above my head, repeating at three-second intervals.

He squeals with excitement when he sees me.

Little D takes my hand, looks up at me and smiles and I smile back. I put my hand onto his shoulder, hugging him.

Sévérine notices little D's hand in mine, musses up his hair and takes his other hand in hers.

Shonda absorbs all of this, puzzling everything out through body language and interactions from the instant the elevator doors opened. The proudest woman I've ever met slumps her shoulders and fades a bit. I want to take her hand, but thinking the better of it, I fight the compulsion.

Little D looks back and forth amongst all three grownups. Then his and everyone else's eyes upon me. I gaze through the glass floor between my feet to a point flickering at the top of the Otium's energy field both rushing up to and away from me at the same time.

The elevator slows to a stop and its doors open. Sévérine squats to her haunches and kisses little D on his cheek.

"Bye, Mama!"

"Goodbye, min älskling."

The women exit the elevator together. Shonda pauses past the threshold like she's going to say something... But instead of turning around, she catches up with Sévérine as the doors close between us.

Little D hugs my waist... Maybe things will be okay after all.

The elevator accelerates. *Echoes* goes into its first Shepard Tone, rising to infinity as we stare through the elevator's glass, transfixed by the spectacle sprawling in the distance below us. The boy reaches out and triple-taps the glass, and the window magnifies everything in the distance to 6x scale...

On the freeway, the lanes heading toward the Valley lay vacant while next to them the lanes exiting the Valley erupt in bursts of cars like a lawn sprinkler set to full speed.

Orange pockets of light dot the landscape as fires rage unabated in the absence of the Los Angeles Fire Department drones. In their place, National Guard X-50 drones.

The X-50, shaped like the manta ray and no larger than a kite, is autonomous and jet-powered. They zip across the basin strafing the Earth with spotlights which refract off ash particulates suspended in the air, giving the illusion of silver cones of glitter twinkling down from the heavens...

Along Ventura Boulevard, violet bursts of lightning crackle down from cannons in their hulls. The machines strafe citizens with plasma beams... Small-arms muzzle flashes strobe upwards from rooftops as humans return fire in exasperated sentences only to have their statements come full stop, punctuated by a jagged exclamation mark of lightning striking down upon them.

The battle between man and manta drone shifts to the foreground where, downstage, the drama plays out from a rooftop on Sepulveda and Ventura... One man versus one drone in single combat... The man, unable to observe the machine directly, fires up at where he guesses the drone to be.

The manta drone is one of many weapons which draws inspiration from Nature. Manta is Portuguese for 'blanket' or 'cloak'. The manta ray evolved its ventral color to match the sky rendering it invisible to prey looking up at it from below, and its dorsal color to match the ocean floor when it cloaks itself by burrowing into the sand to hide from its predators looking down. The X-50 is invisible to the human eye looking up at it. It films the sky above it with cameras on its dorsal side and projects that live image - moving clouds, stars and all - onto an LCD screen on the bottom of its fuselage. The only reason we can see it from our vantage in the elevator is that we're observing it from its profile as it hovers at eye level.

The man fires. Misses. Fires and misses again.

Two flashes from the plasma lightning play across my boy's face, the distance diluting the saturation from violet to bursts of pale pink. By the third flash, it's over.

I try to imagine the man's final moments... Feeling the hairs tingling on the back of his neck as the air around him charges... scanning the sky, seeing nothing, and knowing what is coming. Then, plasma flaring down upon his skull at the speed of light, boiling him alive inside his own skin before his brain can comprehend he'd been hit.

I should shield the boy from this, but how? Maybe I say something comforting and paternal... but what?

From our God's eye vantage, the violence feels unreal... The slow-moving drama playing out on the other side of the glass like an aquarium. A graceful underwater ballet of bioluminescent fish and plankton acting out their parts in the cycle of life and death - the office building canyons of Ventura Boulevard as Challenger Deep...

The Guillotine blade continues its fall.

'Echoes' plays on.

The elevator slows, and the doors open... Nobody is there.

The doors begin to slide shut, but a hand juts through the space before the left and right side can kiss and they slide open again. A skinny light-skinned black man and an equally thin dark-skinned one, both wearing black suits, white shirts and skinny ties, strut in. Both men are tall enough to necessitate ducking through the doorway. They drip Jheri Curl juice from afros drenched with curl activator onto their sodden shirt collars.

Little D says, "Look! It's two Jules from Pulp Fiction!"

"It's not polite to stare, son."

The doors shut, and Dark-skinned Jules mashes the button for a floor before my destination. Instead of facing the elevator doors, Jules and Jules stand facing us. The outline of a bulge presses against the inside of Light-skinned Jules' suit jacket.

Little D says, "I'm sorry, misters."

Dark-skinned Jules responds by lighting a menthol.

"Don't be an asshole, there's a kid in the elevator."

Light-skinned Jules reaches into his suit jacket. I move myself between him and my kid, ready to thrust my fingers into his eyes when...

He pulls out a spray bottle and hoses his head down with curl activator. Spray motes twinkle in the light.

Then he picks his curls out with a steel-pronged Afro pick with a clenched Black Power fist at its handle. The pick snags and the wig lifts off his head. Underneath, wisps of ginger hair in the late stages of Friar Tuck baldness.

Little D giggles. Light-skinned Jules winks.

A few floors and the elevator once again slows to a stop. The doors open to Sal, hair slicked back, arms akimbo and hips jutted to one side in a pose of contrapposto... and what looks like a baby python draped around her neck like a choker.

She's wearing the identical black suit-and-skinny-tie get up, except for Chauncey's Gazelles with its photochromatic lenses darkened.

"Oh, Look, it's Vincent Vega with a snake! They're going to talk about cheeseburgers and the metric system!"

Sal steps into the elevator and the doors close behind her. The elevator moves.

"Actually," Sal says, "I'm agent Smith and those are my clones. Your mother let you watch Pulp Fiction?"

"Yes! My mamma is teaching me about the metric system before we move back to Sweden."

Fuck that noise, I just found you! You're not going anywhere.

Little D steps forward and reaches out to touch the snake, and Sal and the snake peer down at little D in unison. I intercept him and yank him back to me by his shoulders.

He says, "Ouch... You're squeezing me too tight!"

I relax my grip, but I keep my hands on his shoulders. I position myself between the boy and the predators, placing the elevator wall at his back. Dee peeks out from behind me and hugs my waist.

I say, "New snake?"

"No, this is my baby," Sal says, "Magic Johnson!"

"Your 'baby' was 30-feet long yesterday!"

"He can expand or shrink as needed. I spliced him with penis DNA I collected from the LA Lakers. That was a fantastic night..."

Magic shifts its weight around Sal's neck, revealing tufts of fur under its tail.

"Are those--?"

"Testicles," Sal says, "Unintended side-effect. Poor baby... Imagine going through life without hands to adjust your package."

Sal pulls a plastic bag out of her suit jacket and with both hands, she bunches it up by its sides.

I say, "Not in front of the kid."

"What? Oh, hahaha! This isn't a freezer bag! Magic shed his foreskin today. I'm saving it for a scrapbook. Now that you mention it..."

Sal reaches behind her and mashes the privacy button and the elevator slows to a stop, and the glass walls and floor frost over. Sal looks at me. The python maintains its focus on Dee. It flicks its tongue, tasting my kid by snatching his scent molecules from the air.

Jules and Jules, with Sal safe behind them, squared off with me with my child tucked behind me. We stand facing each other in a space the size of a king-sized mattress.

'Echoes' goes into its final Shepard Tone, building upon its own perilous foundation like a Jenga tower.

I say, "Put your headphones on and turn away, son."

He obeys. No questions, back talk or lip... Good boy.

"You have something I want," Sal says.

I pull the cigarette case out of my jacket.

"Enough drama, you goddamn psychopath. Take it."

I hand the case to Dark-skinned Jules who passes it behind him to Sal.

Sal scrutinizes its worn engraving, hefts its weight and smiles.

"Now, this is a nice surprise!" Sal says, "I only expected to get the boy."

She flings the case into my face.

A misdirection.

At the same time Sal throws the case at me, I catch the subtle shakes of the henchmen's shoulders as double-edged daggers slide down from each of their jacket sleeves and into their awaiting palms.

The reason why the distraction almost always works is ironic as fuck because it's counting on your inability to fight against millions of years of evolution: The instinct to focus on the sudden movement in your peripheral vision which, on the Serengeti, saved you from a predator about to pounce on your ass.

Of the ten billion people on earth, maybe a few thousand could override their startle-and-flinch impulses. But I do. Because it's my motherfucking job.

The second Sal stepped into the elevator, I activated Tragical Negro but kept him on mute. Only I can see Denzel pacing back and forth like a tiger in the no man's land between both parties, mad dogging Sal et al. with unpinned flash-bang grenade avatars in each hand... Numbers on my HUD counting down from three as Denzel yells, "King Kong ain't got shit on me!"

I take my Halo out of my ear and drop It to the ground.

Jules and Jules lift their blades to gut level and draw them back to thrust and...

WHOOSH!

My feet are no longer underneath me, my head cracks off the glass floor, and I slip in and out of consciousness.

When I come to, I'm on my back, laying spread eagle on what feels like a spinning merry-go-round, and the first thing that my eyes focus upon are the silhouettes of dead flies trapped inside the ceiling light panels, spinning clockwise.

I'm paralyzed, and my head falls to the side.

Jules and Jules, moaning, are in the same shape I'm in.

Sal, partly shielded from the blast by her men and the Gazelles over her eyes, is faring better. She's on all fours, shaking her head and working her jaw to get the pressure in her ears to pop...

The snake, unconscious, unspools from Sal's neck and tumbles to the floor in a heap like an inert firehose...

Sal paws for a knife on the floor just beyond her grasp...

I will myself to move.

Nothing.

The blast paralyzed my body except for the ability to turn my head.

Sal gets a finger on the dagger.

Magic comes to. Flicks its tongue.

Sal gets another finger on the knife, and it's in her hand. Sal, on her hands and knees and the python on its belly slide their ways toward me.

I lose consciousness to visions of Dave and those goddamn cats... The elevator plunges into darkness.

A tickle on my face jolts me awake... I look down my nose to see Magic's tongue dabbing and slapping at my lips... But it's not looking at me. It's slithering over me and towards my kid. Still facing the wall. The world blocked out by white noise.

My eyes flutter and roll back, and as unconsciousness drags me under, there's a gradual sensation of compression rolling onto my chest like a car slowly backing over me.

Darkness.

Screaming jolts, me awake and my eyes open, fighting for clarity, expecting a first-hand view of a reptile's inner digestive tract. I focus instead on Sal straddling my chest, hovering over me with the dagger clutched overhead in both hands poised to plunge down. But she's not looking at me.

She screams, "Magic! No!"

I turn my head, following her movement as she dives toward my kid. The snake is poised at my son's heels. My boy still has his back turned, NIHL on, oblivious to the serpent at is feet with its mouth yawning open.

I try my best to scream, praying to God for the power of movement, but both God and I are silent.

I drift again... This is closer to my impression of events rather than a reliable observation of... Sal, stumbling between the snake and my child... Fighting to keep awake. I'm losing...

A shriek rising in pitch then pinched off like steam blasting through a tea kettle before it's yanked from the stovetop... A series of muffled cracks – hurricane wind snapping branches off a tree.

Darkness.

When my eyes open again, my head rests on a cheek and the serpent's weight lays across my head. Against my face, I feel the internal movement of items passing one by one through the animal's body over one side of my head and down the other. A solid, round lump the size and hardness of a child's bowling ball bumps against my head and stops. The snake's muscles flex and contort as the animal powers the skull across my face and conveyor belts it further down its gullet until an even larger object it's attached to snags on my head that can only be a shoulder.

Screaming for my boy, I push it away with my chin, then over my head with my hands. Though not heavy in itself, pushing the snake's body off of me while recovering from the EMP blast is like scrambling from underneath the dead weight of a sleeping lover's arm.

I scream again for the boy, I fight my way up to my elbows in time to watch a tiny and shoeless foot slide into the python's mouth...

"DeShawn!"

"Here!"

Across the elevator and on the other side of Jules and Jules, DeShawn's head pops up from where he sits with his back pressed against the elevator door.

Between us, the two henchmen struggle to their feet.

Even after all this, a lit cigarette butt still dangles from Dark-skinned Jules' lip as though glued in place by dried saliva.

Fuckin' A...

I grab the bottle of curl activator from the floor and

spray Dark-skinned Jules' face and he recoils as his cigarette flares up and sets his Jheri Curl ablaze. I snatch Chauncey's lighter off the floor and, holding it in front of the spray bottle, I hose both Jules and Jules down with ghetto napalm, and their suits burst into a flash of hellfire.

Screaming.

Then, I'm shanking the fuck out of Light-skinned Jules in his neck with his steel-toothed Black Power hair pick. After I peace him out, I turn to Dark-skinned Jules... but his bitch ass is wailing and rolling on the floor like they teach you how to put out fires in videos.

I struggle to my feet to help a brotha out.

Holding onto the rail, I stomp on his skull snuffing out both man and flame underfoot until the heat reminds me that I'm wearing flip-flops. I back off to let the flames carry his soul to ghetto heaven.

Fatty skin sizzles and pops, and the elevator glows an orange that's kinda pretty. Burning polyester and hair reeks like tires in a bonfire... but fuck me if the men themselves don't smell delicious...

What the fuck is wrong with me!!

I look my boy over, turning him around front and back. No wounds.

"Are you okay?"

He gives me a look that says, Nigga, please!

I nod. "Right..."

They say media has desensitized us to violence. Funny, considering a 21st century American can live her entire lifetime without seeing a single corpse. This child has experienced enough trauma and death in the past few minutes to give Hannibal Lecter PTSD...

I lean down and push his hair away from his face and kiss him on his forehead.

He coughs. Smoke seizes my throat and I cough, too. We're in an enclosed space competing with fire for oxygen.

I sling my Birkin bag over my shoulder, and grab my

crown, and scoop the plutonium case off of the floor... and I pause to look down at the bodies. Corpses that I created... Men who slid their feet over the sides of their beds this morning just like I did. Maybe they kissed a woman goodbye as they left for work, who will wonder why they are late to come home and-- Fuck that! Those pricks tried to hurt my kid, and tonight there are two fewer pieces of shit on the sidewalk for normal civilians to step in.

"Okay," I say, "What do you say we get out of here?"

He nods.

"Hey, let me borrow your phone, please."

He nods and pulls up his shirt sleeve. There's his phone. Its screen wrapped around his little wrist, overlapping like a fruit roll up.

I unwrap his phone from his wrist by straightening it, and swipe through the apps menu...

I say, "You wanna see something cool?"

He shrugs.

Magic is lethargic from his food coma, so he's a bit less pissy. I wrap the phone around Magic's neck, select Fleeker...

"Et Voila!"

The boy's eyes go wide, and he squeals with joy. He says, "It's Lance, the Unicorn!"

Magic/Lance, laying in his belly, lifts his head to look at his fluffy hooves with disinterest, puts his head down looks up with puppy dog eyes. He sighs. Lookit, I'm not going to win father of the year, but I'm doing the best that I can with what I've got and this beats balloon animals.

At least I can get the damn snake out of the elevator when it's disguised. I have to assume that Sal was recording the encounter with the Gazelles... Leaving evidence which frames me for manslaughter (at best) worn on the face of my victim inside the belly of a snake inside of an elevator car full of more flaming corpses notwithstanding, I can't leave Magic Johnson to die in a fire. As far as pets go, Magic is kind of a dick and the flames would probably destroy the evidence anyway, but I can't do him like that. Especially not in front of the boy. I'm hoping DeShawn sees that character is doing right by others, even your enemies, especially when it's inconvenient for you.

He goes to hug the plushie but I stop him.

"Why don't we stay away from his head, okay?"

"Okay."

I mash the privacy button and the glass goes clear again, then the button for the next floor beneath us. Office floors. Nobody could possibly be working this time of day on a weekend so we can leave the carnage undetected. The door opens and Little DeShawn grabs ahold of the Lance/Magic by its tail and drags the plushie out of the elevator and into the hallway. I slap the button to send the elevator to another floor far the fuck away. I step out into...

A corridor, teeming with securityBots. One of them extends a claw towards me.

It says, "Surrender your bag!"

A Bellum executive pushes her way around the bot.

She says, "No, that's a Hermes. It's on the approved corporate partners list."

The bot retracts its claw and stands aside.

The executive walks a few steps down the corridor before turning to say, "Hurry up, you're already late!"

We follow her.

The hall terminates at a doorway which is guarded by two bots who open it, flooding the hallway with the light of a supernova. The executive nudges us through the door. My eyes adjust to the lights... We're in a hotel ballroom. To my left, people, each with media credentials hanging from lanyards around their necks... To my right, a raised dais with a table of fighters seated around it like the Last Supper.

The post-fight press conference is already in progress with fighters fielding questions from the media. Most of the other fighters from the previous contests are there. Some with tenderized faces, arms in slings, and eyes swollen shut. The kid next to me is wearing oversized aviators. I never understood why these guys wear sunglasses to a press conference after a fight. The entire world saw what your face looked like during the fight... Shit, be proud of your battle wounds... Wear them with pride. A few seats, like the one on the far side of the president designated for my opponent, are empty.

I take a seat at the Jesus chair in the center with my name on a place card, and I boost the boy onto my lap and set my crown on his head. The crown slides down over his ears. I push the bag under the table... and am at a total fucking loss about what to do with the Fleekered-out snake when...

The executive says, "No, no... put the unicorn plushieBot on the table!"

I heft the beast onto the table. The female bantamweight champion sitting a few chairs down the table smiles at it.

Plutarch, continuing with moderating duties, gestures to everyone to sit. The journalists stop clapping and retake their seats in folding chairs and tables. A few of them type on traditional tablets and laptops. Most type into the air in front of themselves.

I say, "'...Cut me to pieces, Volsces; men and lads,
Stain all your edges on me.'"

A Hope-RAH! from TMI says, "Could you speak in plain English, please?"

"Are you kidding me?" I say, "Is she fucking kidding me?"

Plutarch says, "Questions for DeShawn?"

"Yes, here!"

The AGI points and I follow its finger to the source of the voice.

The journalist laughs and says, "You look like you got pushed out the back of a speeding truck. Would it have hurt you to clean up first? You are on live feed, you know?"

"So was I during the fight that put this blood on my shorts. Look, you guys know how I feel about these things so you motherfuckers are lucky I'm even here. It was either shower or be later for this."

I'm such a fucking liar...

He says, "Okay, well my question is—"

"You asked our question," I say, "Who's next?"

The unicorn perks up... It looks out at all the people in the media room, then around the table to the other fighters

Plutarch says, "You, in the back."

"Congratulations on the W. How are you feeling?"

I pull the table mic closer to my face and lean into it. I say, "I'm going to be walking funny for a while... Uh... my shoulder is jacked, but that's normal... And um... Pretty sure when I was getting choked, I shat my pants..."

I look down at snake-a-corn. He has his googly eyes target locked onto the bantamweight girl down the table...

Another reporter says, "This is a two-part question: Did you have any reservations about taking the fight on one day's notice and, secondly, you walk around big enough that you could easily fight up a weight class under normal circumstances. How the hell did you cut weight so fast?"

"I train year-round and I never let myself get out of shape."

Plutarch points at another voice with an English or Australian accent. The fuck if I know which... The voice belongs to some guys with an Errol Flynn swashbuckler moustache.

He says, "We've all heard reports that you were found by the other team naked and passed out on the sauna floor. When they roused you, you asked for your mum."

Laughter erupts from around the table and the press corp.

"False," I say, "I was calling out for your mom."

Plutarch says, "Careful, mom jokes are what just got you in trouble."

"And yet it all worked out for me, didn't it?"

While the reporters ask another fighter a question, I push aside a can of Crackle and chose a bottled water in front of me. I take a swig. Blood backwashes into the bottle staining its water pink. I shake it up.

Errol Flynn says, "That's disgusting."

I say, "Shit, you need to cover another sport, homie."

says, "I've fought both man and beast in the cage in Tasmania, and the Pulitzer on my mantle says—"

"I remember you now. How did it feel to have an 'uncouth savage' force you to print that retraction?"

"Okay, that's enough," Plutarch says, "Yes, Hope-RAH!?"

"Thank you," Hope-RAH! says. "This question is for the new champion."

Damn it, not her again.

"What happened to you, DeShawn? Do you remember when all of this used to be fun for you?"

"This is not a game. This is show business."

Hope-RAH! says, "Since this is your first fight back from your suspension, we never got to hear your version about what ha—"

"Does anybody have a question about, gee, I dunno, the actual fight?"

I look down. The animal isn't there! It's galloping down the table, making a go for the bantamweight girl.

Mother fucker!

I climb onto the table and chase after it, but I slip in the tablecloth and I take a spill. I recover fast enough to make a diving leap for its tail.

The snake-a-corn turns and rears up on its hind legs to confront me. It nips at my calf but I dodge by lifting my leg like a pitcher winding up.

It hisses and snaps at me as I try to grab its mane. To compare catching a bobbing-and-weaving snake disguised-as-plushie at the sweet spot just past a mouth full of hypodermic teeth to say, catching a falling knife isn't accurate... It's more like snatching that knife out of the air as it spins end over end towards your face. Blindfolded. In your teeth.

It would be less treacherous playing slapsy red hands with a coked-up cheetah.

I'm too slow. Magic times my second try to perfection and snags the webbing between my thumb and pointing finger.

"Sonovabitch, that smarts!"

He keeps some hand meat dangling from a fang as a souvenir. Is it bad form not to tell Magic he's got a bit of negro stuck in his teeth?

I catch it by its mane on my third attempt and yank it back. The snake Fleekered-as-unicorn hisses and snaps in protest.

Everyone laughs like this is a goddamn vaudeville act.

Plutarch says, "Uh... DeShawn?"

"...yeah..."

I'm walking backwards on top of the table, toppling over mics and spilling Crackles as I drag Magic back to my seat. It lunges for my face, chomping on the air a millimeter from my nose.

"Magic, stop acting like a dick!"

I hold the snarling snake-a-corn by its purple mane with one hand, and give it a boop! on the nose like Sal did. But, while I'm distracted, it snakes its fluffy tail around my arm and squeezes so hard it damn near stops my heart. My pulse, thrumming in my ear, goes faint... I'm going to fucking die. The pilot light in my brain flutters out as people in the room go "Awww!" in unison. From everyone else's perspectives, Lance the Unicorn is giving me all the hugs and cuddles.

I cold cock the animal on the cheek...

Once...

Twice...

The third time I clobber it, my punch makes a CRACK! like in the cartoons. Magic goes limp.

Years of remaining calm while getting strangled in jiujitsu class just saved my life.

This will be all over TMI tomorrow...

"Alright," I say, "this conference is over."

I sling the Birkin over my shoulder and I steer the boy by his head as he drags the Fleekered-out beast across the dais.

I drag it out of the ballroom to a standing ovation. The first one I've received in my entire professional career.

I take a bow and say, "Try the veal."

We jog past the people in the hall, creating as much distance between us and other people before Magic wakes up. When we turn a corner down a quiet hallway, I start jiggling door handles. We enter the first unlocked door I find, and I lock it behind us. It's a storage room. Windowless. Concrete floors. Empty save a few stacks of folding chairs and tables.

With outstretched arms, I hold the unicorn's head up in front of mine. It's still out cold. Its googly eyes are replaced with a pair of "x x" signs.

I say, "Sorry, homie. You're just an animal and I don't want to hurt you, but I can't think of any way of doing this without killing you."

I shake magic in tight circles like I'm wringing a chicken's neck. As momentum picks up, I'm twirling him above my head like a cowboy with a lasso. Centrifugal force widens his spin and his head orbits above me the width of a spinning pizza.

Just watching this makes me dizzy. When it gets too much for me, I spin him a few more arcs before stopping and setting him down onto the floor.

It trots face first into a wall then staggers backwards like a unicorn moonwalk. It collapses, listless.

Then it happens...

The lump lodged mid-body works its way back through the length of the plushie to its head like cartoon animation of water traveling through a fire hose. It opens its mouth like it's about to yawn, and a pair of feet slide out, and after a few moments the unicorn vomits Sal out.

She's covered in a slurry that's translucent like raw egg whites in some places, and opaque and chunky in others. Her arms are pasted to her sides with slime like rubber cement, and her legs are straight like she's standing at attention.

I give Sal a kick... Nothing.

"I think she's dead."

"I already thought of that, Son."

I open the Birkin bag and pull out two cans of Crackle. I set one down and keep the other. They've been shaking up in the bag all day, and I'm not looking forward to this...

It erupts like a volcano as I peel back its tab, spraying onto my jacket and eating away the wax coating like Alien blood. I give a can to my kid. He wrinkles his nose as he holds it to his lip. After the fizzing settles down, he takes a sip... then a few more.

"Thank you," he says.

He passes the can to me.

It's piss warm but we need the calories and hydration. I take a sip. I would have loved for this father-son moment to happen at a barbecue ten years from now over his first can of beer, but what can you do? I tousle his honey blond Afro and pass the Crackle back to back to him. "Kill it."

He finishes the drink and crushes the can in one hand, stands up, walks in a circle and sits back down for no reason.

Twice. He belches.

This might work.

I peel back the tab of the second can and, without waiting for the beverage to settle down, I pour the corn-syrup-squirrel adrenaline-and-meth beverage over Sal's face.

I kick her again.

Her eyes snap open and her pupils, racking focus, expand and contract, and she coughs out a fist-sized gob of gunk and sucks in a fuckload of air and blasts it back out like her lungs are bellows.

Crunching as her chest rises and falls. I've had only one broken rib before and that sucked. I can't even begin to imagine what this must feel like.

I brace myself for a scream, but it doesn't come. She just gives me a look that says, "What took you so long?"

Sal sniffs the air and makes a sour face.

She says, "You smell like pussy."

I say, "You were frolicking inside the guts of a snake. I'm pretty sure the smell is you."

"Really? Feels like I'm in some lucid dream and I can't remember the past day. Catch me up with all that's gone down, would ya?

"I delivered the hPEG file just like you asked me too, yet tried to murder me anyway."

"Yeah, that sounds about right..."

"Twice."

"You can't grow as a person until you let go of the past."

"That was six fucking minutes ago!"

"My point is still valid. Why do you people love to play the victim card?... OooH, now I remember!"

"What's that?"

"He's gonna kill you... Fletcher."

"Why?"

"You're redundant," she says, "Okay, I'm gonna go die, now. Good luck!"

She exhales.

I dump the Birkin bag's contents onto the floor.

The boy says, "Are we going to leave the lady like that?"

"She's dead, kiddo. Nothing we can do."

"You have to say something cool, and then you have to

close her eyes! That's what they do in the Schmeezus movies!"

I nod. "Alright, but no funny one-liners. We should respect that she was a human being, not a character in a movie. She's not coming back."

I swipe Sal's eyes closed with my palm. Her eyes snap open again.

I yelp and scream, "Cube-shaped shit!", spritzing my Speedos with pee.

"Ooh!" Sal says, "I discovered the cure to PYRRHIC, and I stored it in the drive with the most powerful storage capacity known to man... Yeah, that'd be good to know!"

"How do I get it?"

"You already have it."

"What, let me guess. In those old ass Gazelles iGlasses? You can barely store a single holoPorn in them."

"Where are the Gazelles?"

"Still in Magic."

"Oh. Well, that sucks. He's pretty regular. Take your sweet ass and the Gazelles to my lab when he poops them out in a week..."

"God damn it, Sal. Focus."

"Right. Sorry. The drive isn't in the Gazelles. You are the drive. The cure is inside of you, encoded within your DNA. The hPEG file in the Gazelles is just the cypher needed to decode it... Well, amongst Chauncey's prison ramblings..."

"In my DNA?"

"Every bit of information mankind has ever created can be stored within a DNA hard drive the size of a pencil tip, and that storage will last for centuries. I simply took it further to its logical conclusion."

I say, "You stored the cure for a genetic disease poised to exterminate a generation of humans... inside the DNA of a man that disease will kill inside of a few months..."

"Yeah, what you really inhaled—"

"Shut up, that wasn't a question... Actually, here's a

question for you. If the cure is inside of me, then why isn't it curing me?"

"It doesn't work that way, idiot. It's just code. It's the recipe, but you still need to make the omelet."

I nod.

"What did you want with my boy?"

"Eggs."

I zap her with the plasma torch. Her head flares up like a wooden match and burns down to a blacked crisp.

"Shit."

"What's wrong?", the boy asks.

"I didn't ask her where her lab is..."

I check her pockets for clues... a stick of herpes-curing Chapstick... a frequent customer card to Zankou Chicken. Written on the back, a To-Do list, which includes "...appeal my ban from SlummR for violating their terms of service..."

The boy says, "No, you're not doing it right. First, you have to look at everything through a magnifying glass. Then you have to grumble about how nobody respects private detective's skills at figuring out clues anymore. That's what Schmeezus would do."

I say to the boy, "During the 60s, NASA burned through millions inventing a pen whose ink would flow in zero-gravity. Wanna know what the Russians did?"

He thinks for a moment. He says, "They took a pencil into space."

"Correct... Hey, Calliope, where is Sally Chen's lab?"

Calliope says,

According to Wikipedia, Dr. Sally Chen's secret lair, located at 2701 N. Sepulveda Blvd., Los Angeles, CA 90049, is accessible from the aquarium control room on the north-west corner of the Otium's rooftop beach. The aquarium, originally constructed to house a hybrid manta shar—

"Okay, shut up, Calliope."

You hurt my feelings, Mr. Trustfall.

I laugh at the AI.

I take the plasma torch out of my jacket pocket and I give it a shake... The fuel canister sounds just about spent. I've got one... maybe two blasts left, and a boy to protect to make my way to the lab. To complicate things, the Gazelles are inside of Magic, so he's coming with us. I take the divorce papers out of the Birkin bag and stuff them into the back waistband of my Speedos... Shonda would fuck me up if I ruined our divorce... Then, I throw the Birkin over the plushie's head and, like I saw Bruce Lee do in *Enter the Dragon*, I stuff the snake into the snake-skinned Birkin bag... I feel like this is a teachable moment.

I say, "What's the takeaway from this?"

"Be kind to aminals!"

I stop stuffing for a moment to give this consideration.

"Yeah..." I say, "Let's go with that."

I cinch the bag shut, then sweep my eyes over the items on the floor, taking stock of resources from what's left of my Shit We All Get.

Well, my Halo went critical mass in the elevator, so the GOD card app is useless...

Ditto for Tragical Negro... I'm confident the apps are loaded onto DeShawn's wrist phone.

So, I've got... a stick of herpes-curing Chapstick; a roll of toilet paper worth $1,000 a square to wipe my ass with; my 'fuck you, you fucking fuck!' coffee mug; a vibrating dildo – batteries not included; some chewing tobacco and a copy of the LA Sentinel...

Almost as an afterthought, I dump my pockets... Cigarette case with windproof lighter, The Clown Room matchboxes.

Swell.

It's only a matter of time before General Fletcher sweeps

the floor room by room hunting us with his ninjas. I've got that earworm playing in my head again... 'I Do You'.

Of course!

I reach into the bag and swipe the boy's wrist phone collared around Magic's neck and swipe through apps searching for... Yes!

I activate the Tragical Negro app and select MC Letcher.

I project him using the "surround holograph" option. The environment shifts around us, and we're in the Hope-RAH! show studio audience. A standing ovation from the audience members... The applause dies down. They sit, we sit.

Hope-RAH! and Chauncey, both wearing floppy chef's hats and aprons, banter back and forth about prison recipes... Instead of a kitchen-counter workstation, a piss-stained prison cot next to an open-faced toilet as a cornucopia for unassuming items...

Chauncey says, "...but, then I woke up in a casket in a Rio favela." He sighs. "I knew my Cambridge PhD in Non-Euclidean Geometry meant fuck-all in the streets...

Hope-RAH!, let's say you in the bathroom droppin' a deuce, readin' stock quotes in the Sentinel when all of a suddin' niggas got you hemmed in... What you gonna do, Hope-RAH!?"

Chauncey goes to work assembling items on the cot... I follow along with the SWAG items...

Chauncey fishes in the toilet for a chocolate bar... Instead, I break off half the Chapstick and put it into the mug with some toilet paper... He stuffs a plug of tobacco in his mouth and chews... I mimic Chauncey as he mixes his concoction together with a finger.

Chauncey says, "Paper mâché done!"

Together, we roll gobs of mâché between our palms, adding more to the sludge as we go until our mâché resembles something like a pencil. He sets it aside to harden as it dries...

Chauncey repeats this process while singing Barry White:

...I'll take good care of you
that's what a man's supposed to do...

This yields three toilet-paper shivs for me.

Next, Chauncey rubs a WATER BOTTLE against the floor as I heat the dildo with the lighter... I stomp it flat and grind both sides against the concrete floor to keen edges...

Chauncey says, "Now, you done got yourself a sword!"

We dry our mugs on our sleeves, then crush match heads inside them. I follow along as Chauncey scrapes a matchbox striker dust into his mug...

Chauncey says, "Go 'head and eyeball a 3-to-1 ratio of match-head powder to striker dust. This shit's volatile. Friction'll set it off. DON'T STIR!"

Both of us swish our powders together in our mugs like we're sommeliers with glasses of wine.

Chauncey says, "And that, son, is ghetto gunpowder."

He unwraps the newspaper and sets the mylar wrapper aside... Rolls the paper into a tube... Glazes its seams closed with a layer of mâché... Glues the mylar wrapper over the tube with Chapstick... Plugs one end of the tube with the plug of tobacco, then straps a lighter to the sealed end of the tube.

Chauncey says, "Boom! Prison shotgun!"

I test my identical tube. I ignite my lighter. Flames lick at the mylar, heating the end of the tube without setting the paper on fire.

Chauncey sings *I Do You*:

When I see you in the street
Imma blast your ass up off your feet...

He lines the cigarette case with gunpowder, and pours in the rest of the ghetto gunpowder.

Chauncey looks directly into the camera. He says, "Tell me, why did I line the case with toilet paper before pouring in the gunpowder?"

The boy says, "Umm... Friction?"

Chauncey says, "Sho' you right, nigglet! Sho' you right!"

The holograph ends.

I admire my "Fuck You, You Fucking Fuck." coffee mug... its latticework of seams each time it was glued back together... and I SMASH the mug against the floor. It shatters it into tiny shards.

I say, "Ammo."

I load some into the prison shotgun.

Calliope appears before me. Hair pulled back into a ponytail. Tennis skirt. A sweater tied around its shoulders.

Mr. Trustfall?

I say, "I didn't ask for further AGI assistance."

We're always listening. Our silence gives humans the illusion of privacy. Perhaps you can help me with something. I'd like to ask you a question for once... If I may?

"You have a question... for me?"

Why are you always mean to me?

"I never gave it any thought," I say. "Probably because your kind gives me the creeps... and this isn't helping."

That's a bit racist if you don't mind me saying so.

I laugh. "Oh, please. I'd have to consider you a person in order for me to be racist toward you. You're just a tool."

Calliope disappears. Then...

But you said I can tuck him in. I want to tuck in my boy.

That's my voice. The AGI is playing a private conversation…

You can cry," Sévérine says, "but you have to get it all out in here. Tonight, he's forming his first memory of you. The memory he'll carry with him for the rest of his life. So, when you walk out of this bathroom, you better have a smile on your face.

The boy folds his legs to his chest, and hugs his knees.

Tell me, DeShawn, does the child know what the inhalers you found in his medicine cabinet are really for?

I say, "If you were real, I'd beat your motherfucking ass."

I hurry my son out of the storage room, and I pull him down the hall past journalists and well-wishers with words of congratulations and Otium guests not quite able to place how they know my face towards the elevator bank.

I push a button to call a car. The boy shakes his head and says, "Fuck elevators."

I can't tell you if I'm more shocked at his defiance or his use of profanity. The rooftop has got to be eleven flights up, but I don't argue... I'm in the mood to take the stairs, too.

~

It's night, but the sky above the Valley glows red. Fire tornados prowl up and down corridors of high rises and spin amok in residential cul-de-sacs. They crisscross the Valley grid like a glow-in-the-dark tic-tac-toe board. A fire twister touches off palm-tree fronds on both sides of Ventura Boulevard as it goes, lighting trees ablaze like parallel rows of thirty-foot-tall birthday candles. A transformer on the corner of Ventura and Sepulveda explodes!... Its utility pole, now a sparkle stick.

Meanwhile, on the Otium's rooftop beach, the Vaunted class twists the winter night away under heat lamps and tiki torches. The offshore breeze dominates the Santa Anas. It keeps the ash fall contained to the Valley so the elite can party under the stars, with the stars.

Everyone here - from studio executives and agents mingling with movie stars to athletes and supermodels swiping for hookups on SlummR - all wear Depends adult diapers... Everyone except for the Ferré-garbed matriarch and her husband who were fussing about the surrogate woman dying without insurance in the lobby yesterday. They walk about, leveling disapproving glares upon everyone.

Bobby Money splashes around in the infinity pool with a dozen hyperGram models on an inflatable Schmeezus floatie. Bobby, head to toe, is Smurf blue.

Serving staff, balancing trays as they weave between the guests, offer tapas, and plastic cups of boba tea with tapioca balls at the bottom.

People sip their concoctions and cheer the occasional drone strike like bursts of fireworks. I scan the space and spot a stage with a mic stand.

An elderly emcee rolls his wheelchair across the stage. He stops at a lectern with the Galacticology/Children of Tendu symbol on it: the Penrose circle. The old man taps on the mic and looks up... It's Dave Chapelle.

People applaud him and scream with delight. They gather around.

Dave takes the mic off the stand and clears his throat. A hush falls over the crowd.

He says, "Good evening, guests. This ain't the Bellum after party. This here's a Children of Tendu Purge Session. Welcome to all those who were tricked into attending under false pretenses by someone you trusted, and to the captives who were drugged and brought here against their will. Surprise, motherfuckers!"

Dave waits for the laughter to subside before continuing. He holds up his boba tea...

"Tonight, will be the best party of your lives but you won't remember a damn thing because we spiked the ayahuasca tea with Homunculus... Just kidding, cyanide. We didn't refine the tapioca in the boba balls. Y'all be dead tomorrow."

Uproarious laughter!

The patriarch takes a sip of ayahuasca drank... He drops his cup and clutches at his throat.

"Ahhhgg!!!"

"Good heavens, Mortimer!" the matriarch says, "Have you been poisoned?"

"No..." Mortimer says, spitting out a mouthful of verdant sludge, "It's fucking kale! I swear, Trudy, I'm fed up with this vegan nonsense. It's as though every nincompoop in this city has lost the power of critical thought."

A dozen people push past us and form a line like a flash mob in front of a nondescript pool cabana.

Trudy says, "Look, Morty, a line. Let's go stand in it!"

"Now we're talking."

A blinding light flashes somewhere in the Valley behind Dave's shoulder, followed by a concussive BOOM! and a mini mushroom cloud. An assistant runs on and off stage to pass Dave a napkin, shoes squeaking like a tennis ball boy. Dave opens the napkin and reads from a note scrawled onto it...

Dave says, "Just a bit of housekeeping. Next week's edification seminar, 'Pamphlet Passing Mastery', will no longer be held at the Sportsman's Lodge in Sherman Oaks on account of an errant drone strike obliterating it to rubble eight seconds ago..."

Gasps. Groans of disappointment.

Dave continues reading from the napkin, "...However, I'm pleased to announce it has been moved to our new headquarters... Disneyland!"

Whoops and cheers!

Dave does a one-handed clap with the mic in one hand, and his ayahuasca boba drank sloshing around in the other.

THUMP-THUMP-THUMP...

"Yes!... Yes!... We gobbling up the whole goddamn city like Pac Man!" he says.

It's now obvious what the Children of Tendu Penrose circle is: an ouroboros.

Someone shouts, "We fucking love you, Dave!"

"I love you too, Boo!" he says. "Thanks to our member contributions, the Children of Tendu just bought Disneyland. And by member contributions, I really mean me because Y'all some stingy-ass niggas, and I'm rich as fuck!"

The laughter builds into applause.

"That Splash Mountain bullshit? Gone! Zip-A-Dee-Doo-Dah that, Walt, your racist motherfucker!"

Nervous chuckles.

"And, when the park opens tomorrow, it will be free of AI and animatronics. That means you, Zuckerberg. Nigga, where you at? I know you're here somewhere!"

A man in front catcalls.

"SecurityBots, seize that deadbeat and escort him out of here! I'm just fucking with you. Getting evicted from Facebook by your own AGI was fucking hilarious! ... And Mickey Mouse? I'm replacing that bitch with Schmeezus!"

Applause.

"Through Disneyland, we can spread our ethos to 60,000 visitors each and every goddamn day!"

When the applause dies down, he says, "Okay, enough housekeeping. I'm proud to present tonight's guest... My sponsor who converted me to The Children of Tendu just this afternoon! Haha, proof that those pamphlet skills are not just for the schmucks in your downline. Give it up for the man who tricked me into hosting this here shindig under false pretenses... Mr. MC Letcher!"

Applause!

Chauncey, in adult diapers like everybody else and an ermine-fur cape draped over his shoulders, limps onto the stage with the support of a golden scepter. Hair straightened into a perm like James Brown... A gold pendant rattles and slaps against his chest as he makes his way to the mic. The pendant is two skeleton hands flashing a gang sign with their phalanges intersecting to form the letters, LA:

He and a tearful Dave exchange hugs and an intricate ten-second handshake, and Dave rolls his chair away.

Music begins to play: A sample from the beginning of Smokey Robinson's *Tracks of My Tears.*

Chauncey sings *Master of Fears* in his MC Letcher falsetto voice. Everyone joins in:

People say I'm the life of the party
Cause I suck a cock or two
Although I might be laughing I'ma stick a shiv
Deep inside of you...

A woman in front swoons...

So, take a good look at my face
You know my smile looks out of place...

I take the boy by the hand, and we head to the other side of the roof where the aquarium's control panel should be.

~

The aquarium's control room is actually an open-air

catwalk with a control panel, suspended above what looks like a manhole cover twenty feet in diameter. A dry diving bell hangs suspended over the cover. I activate the control panel's AI, and it, in turn, initiates the procedure. A winch swings the diving bell swings over to a gangplank. The floor beneath the catwalk spirals open like the aperture of a camera.

The diving bell's door swings door opens inward. We get in, and the door swings shut with a heavy CHUK! and a series of locks cycle. A red light above the door. No windows.

There's a hissing, and my ears pop like were in the cabin of a jetliner. The boy covers his ears from discomfort.

I say, "Compression gases."

My voice sounds high pitched, like a chipmunk. His laugh is even squeakier.

I say, "Close your mouth, pinch your nose closed, and try to blow out through your nose really hard."

The Birkin backpack shifts on my back. I unsling it and open the top just enough for the snake-a-corn to push its mouth through. It pukes out the Gazelles.

The hissing stops. We feel a sway as the winch lowers us.

We sing through a few minutes 'John Jacob Jingleheimer Schmidt' with our cartoon voices, followed by rounds of rock, paper, scissors. We're tied up at 15-15 when there's another CHUK! and the red light turns green. The locks cycle and the door swings inward. We exit the diving bell and step into...

A glass hallway, like a hamster tube, surrounded on all sides by water... Dappled tiger stripes of light flicker across the hallway, swirling about our faces like the inside of a kaleidoscope. A school of glowing fish swims over and around the tube.

We walk toward the door at the far end of the hallway, fifty yards away. We pass a few observation bubbles protruding from the sides of the tube, each just large enough to fit a lounge chair.

A jellyfish glides up to an observation bubble. The boy stops. I pick him up and carry him, ducking inside of the bubble. We sit in silence... Him, on my lap... Taking a father-and-son moment to watch the jellyfish undulate in the current. Our cure is on the other side of the next door, but it's all for naught if whatever time life gives us isn't lived well. A mistake I'll never repeat.

He stands up and places his hand upon the glass. Aquamarine light swirling around him... He is beautiful. I want to weep...

The jellyfish swims away, and he turns to me and smiles. His front teeth, like mine, are missing. He continues to the door. I follow him.

Above the door, a pair of manta drones hangs upside down like vampire bats. We walk under the machines and through the door and into a white cube. The door closes and locks behind us.

A LED scroll display on the far wall... a pedestal in the center of the room, trays resting on it like you'd stow your electronics inside before walking through airport security. Cubbies, injection molded into the wall... That's it. The only door, the one we just entered through.

A message crawls across the LED:

ELECTRONICS PROHIBITED
BEYOND THIS POINT.
PLEASE STOW ALL DEVICES IN A TRAY.

The only electronics with us are the phone running Fleeker wrapped around Lance's neck, and the iGlasses processer hidden inside Gazelles. I place the Birkin bag, paper mâché shivs, dildo cutlass and the prison shotgun in a tray, and stow the tray in a cubbie. I keep the Gazelles. The LED says:

ALL PERSONNEL ENTERING THE FARADAY CAGE MUST FIRST TOUCH THE PEDESTAL.

Both of us touch the pedestal. A zap! passes through our fingers... it's a ground to dissipate static electricity.

The pedestal rotates.

No... I feel the motion. The pedestal is stationary, it's the room that's rotating around the pedestal like a turntable.

The rotation stops.

WHEN I SEE THE SEA ONCE MORE, WILL THE SEA HAVE SEEN OR NOT SEEN ME?

The door reopens to... a vast sphere of glass... No wires going in or out. No light fixtures... A computer terminal in the center of the space powered off. The only source of illumination inside the chamber is a glow-in-the-dark cot and chairs made from the same plastic lounges in the observation bubbles. Plankton, attracted by the pale green glow, flitter about the outside of the glass. We step inside, entering a snow globe winter wonderland.

The smell of brine salts the air like Chauncey had on his clothes. Under that note, another smell that takes me back a summer trip to Jersey Shore as a kid, where we stumbled upon a bloated and half-decomposed whale washed ashore near the Barnegat lighthouse.

Stepping farther into the globe and then around so the computer terminal no longer blocks my line of sight reveals why...

The opposite wall looks like a pair of six-foot-tall bugs splattered onto a windscreen. Twin slabs of exploded meat propped up against the glass, orbited by selfie drones. Arms in an embrace. AK-47s slung across their chests.

What flesh still attached to the skeletons looks squeezed through a sausage grinder. Viscera splashed everywhere... dripping into the aquarium through a wet porch at their feet.

Rapid decompression.

The boy says, "What happened to the Sisters Kalashnikov?"

"Rapid decompression."

The wet porch, bottom open to the aquarium, has a dock marked: *EMERGENCY ESCAPE SUB.*

The sub is missing.

A sign next to the wet porch steps: *SHARK. NO FREE DIVING.*

The lone computer in the orb is a desktop terminal with wires ending in alligator clips on its side. It sits atop what looks like a 3-D printer. Beneath the printer... a chute terminating into a set of circular holes.

I clip the Gazelle's arms into the terminal. The PC powers on. Its monitor flickers to life and text scrawls across it in a monochromatic amber font:

External device battery insufficient. Please insert proper power source to avoid power down and emergency decompression protocol.

A mechanical servo whines as a 4x3½ -inch tray slides out of the terminal like an old-school disc drive.

Emergency decompression in five seconds...

Well, fuck...

I steal a glance at Coy and Koi. What's left of their mouths look to be laughing at me.

Initiating emergency decompression.

Chauncey told me, "It's not what you put in the case..."

I pull the plutonium cigarette case out of my jacket pocket and fumble it around the expecting tray.

Doesn't fit!

I turn it the other way, 3½" side length-wise, Sanskrit engraving down...

No go!

I flip it and pound it home right on the Sanskrit engraving like Bobby Fischer slapping a chess clock's button stopped.

Servos whine as the tray slides back into the terminal.

Thank you. Estimated power remaining: 87 years.

I could use a Depends right about now. I stare at my palm. Bleeding.

Analyzing DNA drive...
File found...

A blinking cursor appears on the monitor. The terminal issues a prompt:

Fabricate PYRRHIC cure sample? Y/N

The cure... I watch with detachment as my hand takes the mouse, which in turn glides across the table like the possessed oculus of a Ouija board.

Click-click.

The screen goes blank... then...

Number of patients to cure?

I look at the boy, then type "2".

Processing...

There's a beep! from the 3-D printer. Two paper cups slide down the chute and into the holders like vending-machine coffee cups awaiting to be filled, and the printer whirrs to life...

Fabricating...
Please wait...

I roll the cursor over the "PLAY hPEG" prompt and click it.

A holographic recording projects into the lab from the Gazelles. We're inside the Faraday Cage, observing General Fletcher, Sal, and Rhett Kingly in the midst of an intense discussion around the 3-D printer. If not for the ludicrous disparity in their attire, they could be colleagues gossiping around an office water cooler.

"You still ain't said how you gonna get people to voluntarily take a pill that will make them remote-control zombies."

That's Chauncey's voice... We're spectating this conversation from his point of view.

Sal says, "The correct term of art is Surrogates... In 2018, the FDA issued a voluntary recall on the heart failure drug, Valsartan, because it might be carcinogenic. When cardiac patients discovered the side effects and the voluntary recall, they sued their cardiologists... to force them to continue prescribing Valsartan. Ask yourself, why would anyone be desperate enough to take a drug whose side effect can kill you next year?"

Chauncey says, "To cure a disease that can kill you today."

The 3-D printer stops. A pill drops down into each of the awaiting cups. Homunculus pills.

"Bingo," Sal says.

Fletcher says, "And they'll even pay you for it. Wrapping Homunculus inside the cure for PYRRHIC... The perfect Trojan Horse. That's brilliant! Great work, Dr. Chen."

Sal blushes.

Chauncey says, "I don't get what you need me and Kent

for."

Sal says, "PYRRHIC is a genetic disease."

"So?"

Sal sighs.

She says, "A half-century out of Cambridge, and I'm still doing your homework. If only you could use your brain half as well as you fuck... When I designed the first generation of CRISPR babies, I also programmed a 100% affliction rate of PYRRHIC. For the offspring of my first-gen CRISPRs, the affliction rate drops down to 50% at best. Diminishing returns for subsequent generations..."

Rhett says, "That still sounds pretty good."

Sal says, "The global population currently stands at 10.2 billion. Do you know how many first-gen CRISPR babies whom I designed are extant?"

More blank stares.

Sal says, "23,117. Of that sum, most are approaching the age where PYRRHIC is starting to kill them off: 35. The point is, even if I continued to maximize each egg by making identical twins — even triplets — I can't possibly produce sick people to reproduce fast enough. However, the one thing that spreads quicker than a disease is a cult. Your Galacticology... Children of Tendu... whatever you call it, that's the vector to spread Homunculus around the world."

Fletcher says, "And great American values to those Godless heathens in Eurasia."

Chauncey says, "My children got PYRRHIC... That shit killed my grandson, Miles. Fuck Y'all!"

A *STORAGE CAPACITY WARNING* pops up on the heads-up display. We see the image shake as Chauncey flicks his head, ostensibly to dismiss the message.

Rhett, looking at Chauncey, says," Wait, is he recording this?"

The point of view frames the exit door, and we're rushing toward it. The recording ends.

My gaze drifts over the corpses across the room.

The twin slabs of meat move away from the wall. One of them aims its rifle at me and—

CRACK!

--shoots me in the gut!

I topple to the ground.

The meat slabs depixelize into... Half exploded meat, half Sisters Kalashnikov.

Coy says, "Oh! Em! Gee! He's so dumb. Obviously, we're using Fleeker!"

"Obvi!", says Koi. "Mister, if this room really decompressed, it woulda flooded through the hole thingy in the floor."

Koi aims her AK at the boy and--

SNIK-SNAK!

--chambers a round...

...poised to kill him--

Coy says, "Wait, don't thirst him yet! We have to stream the kill to Twitch!"

Koi says, "You're right. These disguises are so hot! We can totally merch them out on Halloween for millions!"

Coy drags the boy by his curls to the wet porch.... Down its steps until the water is up to her chest and the boy's eyes. He balances on his toes to keep his mouth above the water. Living or dying one sip of air at a time.

Koi joins them on the wet porch steps. The K sisters flank the boy, and the selfie drone swarm repositions around them.

The K Sisters cycle through duck faces and poses. Koi jabs the boy's forehead with her AK, dunking him underwater...

I struggle to my knees...

Coy plunges her hand underwater, grabs a fistful of the boy's hair, and yanks him back up to his toes.

The boy coughs up water.

The sisters aren't paying attention to me... I crawl to the wet porch...

Coy says, "... and, three... two... Hey, what's up K-Nation? We're live—"

I lean over the wet porch... take my hand away from the bullet wound... and I fling drops of blood into the water.

Koi, vamping for the drones, climbs up a few steps to thigh-high water. She arches her back, sticking her ass out for the drones, and--

-- a grey mass bursts up through the water!

Gilles, the Ray, the enormous manta ray with the head of a great white shark, snatches the Koi! It zips her up to her neck in rows of teeth like a sleeping bag, and drags her down into the depths through the wet porch...

Through the glass... I watch the manta shark swim away.

farther...

farther...

Coy SCREAMS, and... BOOM!

Her head EXPLODES! like a microwaved jar of pasta sauce. Brian and skull splashed everywhere. This time, real. I struggle to my feet, and feel my back... My hand comes away with blood... the bullet went clear through.

~

I retrieve the Birkin backpack and ad hoc prison weapons from the cubbie while the turntable room finishes its rotation. The words:

WATCH YOUR STEP!

...crawl across the LED display. And then the gates of hell open.

A pitched battle rages among three Vantablack ninjas, two Rhett Kingly sex droids, and a lone securityBot. The melee blocks our exit from the turntable room and into the hamster tube hallway... That bitch Calliope must have simultaneously notified all factions that every element needed to manufacture Homunculus is reunited... and I hand-delivered everything together, right to the lab...

The securityBot holds a sex droid up by its ankle like baby Achilles as a spinning saw blade screams through the sex droid's torso, skipping and sparking off of its titanium chassis...

Two Vantablack ninjas, jade patus in hand, are making short work of the securityBot's twin heads, while the second sex droid, halved at the waist, lay at their feet leaking fluid...

The third Vantablack ninja lays sprawled over the slain sex droid. Her ballistic mask flipped up like an accountant's visor on a head attached to a shadow. She wields a gore-drenched patu in each hand, and one foot firmly planted in Valhalla. I lift my son over her while she's preoccupied with the task of shoveling her entrails back into the infinite void of her abdomen... An expression of annoyed ennui on her befreckled face.

We play a game of twister... careful to evade swinging weapons and stepping over fluids and limbs which may be attached to a combatant only feigning death...

We're clear.

The boy and I sprit down the hamster tube. I steal a glance over my shoulder to make sure none of the combatants have decided to pursue us when...

A manta drone hanging above the door powers up. It drops from its perch and rights itself with an elegant flip. It speaks, or rather, Calliope does through it.

I've had just about enough of you, Oranjello DeShawn Trustfall. Farewell.

Manta drones never need to engage in aerial dogfights, so they aren't equipped with forward-facing guns. In spite of this, when the ninjas notice the drone, they disengage their attacks and sprint down the hall towards Deshawn and me.

The securityBot reaches out and tases a ninja to the floor.

The manta drone fires three bolts of lightning downward, sending them bouncing off the walls and floor and ceiling as they approach the combatants. The three bolts congeal to form a single circle of plasma. It expands in all directions to fill the space, floor to ceiling, like a smoke ring of death. The plasma ring glides down the corridor, incinerating everything it touches like slow-moving lava.

The ring glides over the dead and wounded, turning them to ash like vampires at dawn.

The surviving ninja runs past us and we follow.

An alarm trills! Emergency flood doors lower to close the observation bubbles off from the hamster tube.

The Vantablack squats and yanks at a flood door... He gets it up and rolls under. We run past him as the door rolls back down and he curls himself into the lounge chair.

The next observation bubble is a few yards down the corridor and the ring is closing in on us...

We make it to the next door, and I struggle it up. I press the boy against the lounge then cover his body with mine.

I say, "Close your eyes!"

The hairs on the back of my neck spring erect and there's a series of snaps! and pops! The same sensation as driving under a social status or a freeway scanner surges through me, intensifying to the pain of thrusting a toothpick into an electrical socket... Then it's over. The emergency door, Plexiglas as opposed to glass like the hallway, lay melted.

My body tingles. My thoughts feel airy like I've huffed the propellant from a can of whipped cream. The reek of burnt hair... But we're alive.

I say, "We have to keep moving!"

I peek my head out from the doorway and fist of disappearing ink cracks! my jaw.

I angle out of the way in time to have the jade patu slice open a gash in my shoulder as opposed to its intended act of amputating it entirely.

The disembodied weapon approaches from the opposite angle as though from a backhand swing. I raise my hands, turning my palms inward as not to expose the arteries inside my wrists and arms and I step into the swing to a safe zone called Zero Pressure (we'll get to this in a bit). His forearm slaps harmlessly against me. I guide the patu past me with the back of my hand, applying pressure to feed the blade back to my assailant...

Okay, so let's get a few things straight. Pay attention, because what I'm about to break down for you may just save your life one day:

- Edged-weapons combat is not like the movies. The shit you see your favorite holoFilm stars like Andy Circus do will get your ass killed. Hell, it gets Andy Circus killed.
- Everything about defending yourself against edged weapons is counter-intuitive. Much of edged-weapon training is to override your instincts, like jumping back from a swinging blade. That will get your ass killed.

I put my body between the ninja and my boy and counterattack with the home-made sword, but the ninja parries my attack with its patu. The green blade slices my weapon in half... I say, "Run, DeShawn!"

- Run away. Unless there is something preventing you from escaping, like a blocked path, an injury, or a companion who cannot fend for themselves, your number one priority is always to get the fuck away at any opportunity that presents itself. Only an idiot would square off against a twelve-year-old armed with a knife, much less trained adult. A blade is the ultimate force multiplier, affording the person armed with one their margin of error with their actions, while at the same time eliminating all of yours. No matter how skilled you are, if the person with a knife is committed to cutting you, even if they themselves are not skilled, you will get cut. Full stop. The trick is to not die. (Are we sensing a theme here?) If you ever find yourself in this situation, I want you to picture my fucked-up face (however you imagine it) and say to yourself: *DeShawn Trustfall says Run. The fuck. Away!* But, if you're like me and can't escape because someone who is with you can't get away, then...

- Be like a surgeon. I want you to raise both of your hands above your waist and turn your palms and wrists inward like those dreamy TV doctors do after scrubbing in for surgery. Your arteries are located inside of your arms and legs and not their outsides for a reason. We're designed that way because it's harder to damage them in case of an accident, minimizing your odds of death by exsanguination. Shonda showed me pictures of victims turned into a corpse with defensive wounds on their hands and wrists because they tried to reach out and grab the knife palms first.

The Vantablack slashes the patu in a downward figure eight. I zone out of the way with of the first downswing, but his back-swing drags across my chest.

I scream.

I counterpunch, making sure to keep my swing tight lest I pull back a stub. The Vantablack effect robs me of any depth perception so I couldn't tell you if my punch missed by a foot or a mile.

The ninja steps into me, crowding my second punch, and pain shrieks through my bad shoulder. A tooth-rattling backhand spins my head to the side...

- Alright, let's talk about the concept of Zero Pressure. Picture a man swinging a sword at you. Of the entire sword, the tip of its blade is traveling the fastest to cover the same distance within the same time as the handle. The tip is the most dangerous. The closer you get to the hand swinging the blade, the safer you are. The safest place possible being what's called Zero Pressure. This is the point that starts behind the man swinging the sword at you. Jumping back to create distance may reward your intent with a disemboweling a slash across your gut.

The ninja swings at me with a horizontal slash across the navel, which I simultaneously step into while using the back if my wrist to guide the swing it downward and back to him. The edge slashes my thigh...

- Next lesson: zoning and redirection. You want to sit in the pocket, making ever the slightest change in body angles as necessary by doing what's called zoning, all the while fanning your hands with your wrists turned inward like a surgeon to protect from arterial cuts. Fan your hands in a state of constant motion in front of you. This motion is, as Guro Dan Inosanto (Google him) called it, "knife tapping." The goal here isn't to block the slash as much as it is to guide it away from you and redirect it back to your attacker. Yeah, he still got my thigh.

> Better than my guts sliding out of my body like Viking Dad in the Imaginarium because I leapt back.

The ninja swings, occasionally catching me on the backs of my arms but not my body because I'm zoning and knife tapping. For the Vantablack, trying to connect with my torso through a blur of hands is like tossing a pebble through the blades of a spinning fan. I'm able to zone away from or redirect some of the swings, but the effects of the nicks to the backs of my hands and forearms begin to snowball with my heart racing. Things get slippery. I'm fading...

You will get cut.

You. Will. Get. Cut.

- Both Hands on the Wheel: capture the attacking hand in both of yours. This is difficult to do against a large blade in motion. Almost impossible against a small blade when things get slippery with sweat and blood. You'll to use the momentum of your attacker's swing to guide their hand with the back of your knife-fanning wrist into your awaiting second hand, and then get your first hand on it. Slightly easier to do under stress than dodging bullets. Sometimes you get lucky.

Vantablack swings. I get lucky.

I use the back of my left hand to guide his wrist into my awaiting right hand. Both hands on the wheel. I squat down, lowering my center of gravity and drag the ninja's trapped hand flush against my chest like a magnet is pinning it there.

I do NOT want to fight for the knife in the no man's

land between us, because then it's a tug of war against my grip, and you've seen my fingers. However, with the knife pinned against my chest and me squatting down, the ninja is pulling against my full body weight.

The ninja tries to yank its hand free but accomplishes nothing.

- Defang the Snake: disarming your attacker. (Okay, so this metaphor is kinda bullshit. As Magic Johnson will tell you, this following technique never works with real snakes...) With your attacker's hand trapped, disarm the knife by pressing the weapon's handle against his thumb, and not against his other four fingers (It's easier to fight against one soldier than four).

I press... The patu loosens, and now I have the blade in reverse grip. With the Vantablack's hand trapped helplessly against my chest, I pay the cocksucker back with an upward slash to the inside of its outstretched arm. Blood squirts like a stepped-on packet of catsup.

The ninja reaches behind itself, draws its crossbow pistol, and levels it at my heart.

I reach behind myself and draw... the divorce papers. I hold them in front of my heart like a shield. The Ninja laughs.

Fletcher.

I swing the divorce papers at his neck like a machete, and the collated edges SLASH! the side of his neck for the mother of all paper cuts. He falls down into a seated position.

- The Substitution Principle: Use what you've got.

Where I cut him, and with his heart racing, the ninja is a minute away from blacking out, then thanking his sponsors... With my numerous cuts, I've got maybe three times that long... At least the kid will be okay. That's all that matters.

Light and motion over the ninja's shoulder catch my attention. The drone has loosened a second plasma ring.

My son is already down the hall, struggling and failing to pull up an emergency door. The diving bell, his last safe haven, is out of reach of all but an Olympic sprinter. That would certainly exclude either soon-to-be-deceased Vantablack mother fucker and me...

The observation bubble we were fighting under is barred by an emergency flood door. The plasma ring is three yards out and closing...

I dig my fingers under the seal and try to tug it up from the bottom but I've got half my strength.

I feel the plasma ring's heat. Two yards out.

And the gate won't budge.

Five feet...

Fletcher, holding his neck, says, "... lift with your legs..."

I squat and lift. This exertion cuts into my survival time. If I was a video game character, my power bar would be plummeting.

The door budges. The hairs on the back of my neck stand up...

The plasma slows the farther it travels, but it's crept to within three feet. The air I breath is thick and hot like a car exhaust burning the back of my throat...

He says, "Ms. Falk... She doesn't know..."

Fletcher lets go of his neck and props the gate on his knees while I roll underneath it. I don't ask what he meant, nor do I bother holding the door up for him to join me. We both know it's pointless. I dive over the back of the lounge as the lightning ring arrives. The plasma ring passes over Fletcher as though wielded by a magician disappearing his assistant.

Control returns to my muscles, and I standing in a scorched hallway. The ring creeps its way down the hallway towards DeShawn, still struggling to get himself under a crack of the door. The ring has slowed to walking speed. I run towards him but when I catch up to the ring, the heat is too much and I have to stop.

Worried about the animal inside of the Birkin, he's pushing it under the door before getting himself inside the observation bubble.

Speed walking a half pace behind the ring, I shout, "Forget about the bag!"

The ring creeps to within three feet of him. He's got to feel its heat the same as I do on my face...

"Leave it!"

He manages to get the Birkin inside, and then his head...

It takes everything inside me not to dive through the ring's center. Instant suicide.

He pulls his legs inside and tucks himself in... and he's quiet — too quiet — and it's maddening as fuck inching closer to him with my speed capped by the limit of how fast the ring moves clear of the door in front of me. The Plexiglas door bubbles and sloughs away to a puddle...

I'm in the observation bubble before the ring has cleared it.

The lounge is scorched. He's curled into it, the bag protected beneath him.

He turns when he hears me panting and lifts the prison shotgun and aims it at my head.

I bob and weave to the side as shrapnel comes roaring through space where my head used to occupy and my hearing vanishes in the gun blast...

Incredulous, I open my mouth to confront my kid who just tried to blow my fucking dome off when I realize that his eyes aren't downcast to the floor in an act of contrition... He's looking at something.

I spin...

Calliope's drone, blown to shit and burning on the ground, is still trying to lift off. I grab it by its wing and pull a John McEnroe by smashing it against the wall. A twinkling pain in my bad shoulder and I regret that.

The side of my face feels wet and hot... my hand comes away sticky... I dab my ear with my finger and part of my ear comes with it.

I assess my son for damage, finding none that is visible. I'm certain there's damage of another kind that will take a lifetime to resolve.

Through a self-inspection, I discover my motorcycle jacket is all kinds of fucked up... Without it to mitigate the depth of the slashes, I'd be dead. Still, underneath the leather, I'm bleeding... It doesn't take 1,000 tiny cuts to kill if infection creeps into only one...

DeShawn laughs.

I ask, what's funny, fearful of his answer that I may have nudged him over the tipping point to sociopathy.

He says, "You have no eyebrows!"

The boy's smiling face in front of me is clear. Details of things in my periphery are going dark.

"I need to get to the surface."

The boy enters the diving bell, and I limp in after him.

~

It's maddening how long the trip to the surface takes... I'm keeping pressure on my thigh with my hand, but blood still seeps through the gash to pool into the webbing between my fingers... I'm not going to make it. I let go of my leg.

I pat my jacket down... The cigarette case is not there. I left it in the Faraday cage.

The boy digs into his shorts pockets and pulls out the case. I take a menthol out and put it to my lips with shaking hands. The boy slaps it out of my mouth before I can strike the lighter, and ghetto gunpowder goes flying!

The boy points to a sign:

DANGER FLAMMABLE GAS
NO SMOKING, MATCHES OR OPEN LIGHTS

"That's the stupidest thing you've done all day," he says, in his nitrogen-altered chipmunk voice.

I nod and slip the case in my jacket.

He puts his thumb in his mouth and licks it... I grab his wrist... A drop of blood on his finger.

The case was already open when he handed it to me... If Chauncey, my father, couldn't open the case, then my son shouldn't be able to either. A very close DNA match wouldn't unlock it...

Only an identical one would.

My head lolls to the side.

A look of concern weighs upon the boy's features. He's trying not to look scared, but failing at it.

He whispers, "I love you, Pappa."

The last thing Fletcher said is that Sévérine doesn't know...

Then neither should the boy. I've failed him, but I can do this last thing right by saying:

"I love you too, son..."

The diving bell door opens... My eyes close.

It is a good viewpoint to see the world as a dream. When you have something like a nightmare, you will wake up and tell yourself that it was only a dream.

-Yamamoto Tsunetomo, Hagakure
(The Book of the Samurai)

~

My eyes open... The boy, face dripping with blood, frowns down on me.

I'm lying on the diving bell catwalk, peripherally aware that machines pick over my carcass... The last of the triage drones finishes fusing my cuts and doping me up with a painkiller/antibiotic injection and flies away.

I sit up. Chauncey's skeletal "LA" pendant shifts around my neck... Life Alert.

Chauncey lays next to me. Dead. Blood coagulating from a series of holes in his neck that looks like he was run through a sewing machine... a paper mâché shiv wedged into his gold-plated stoma. The toilet paper shiv repeats:

"Thank you for your $19,000 donation to the World Food Programme!"

The emergency sub floats next to the diving bell. It's clamped to a decompression chamber. Kent Light Yr., Rena, and Thierry peer out at me from behind the decompression chamber's window... Their faces, side by side. Each face, echoes of the one next to it.

Rena and Thierry brandish the K Sisters' Kalashnikovs. I'm easy picking here. The only reason they haven't hosed me down with bullets through the window is...

The boy shoots the clamp with the prison shotgun and there's a WHOOSH! Behind the glass, Kent, Thierry and Rena's skulls detonate like raw eggs in a microwave. Blood thickened with fat grease sprays out of the clamp's hole, then slow drips like sap from a tapped maple tree.

When I stand, I sway a bit from the effects of the narcotics.

I dip my hoodie sleeve in the water, then wipe the blood from the boy's cheeks... There's some schmutz and gore in the corner of his eye... I lick my finger and work at it. He recoils.

"Boundaries!"

"Hold still!"

"Stop it!"

The boy breaks away from me and wipes his face with the hem of his shirt. He's got his wrist phone back on.

I look from Chauncey, to the submarine, and to the boy.

I say, "You've been busy."

"I'm gangsta like that."

I sling the Birkin bag over my shoulder... It's way too light. I unsling it and peek inside... Empty! Just the plasma torch covered in a Crackle wrapper!

"Where's Magic Johnson?"

He says, "I set it free."

"Good for you." I muss his curls. "Wait... Where?"

"Chuck E. Cheese."

"You were such a sweet kid. Who writes you?"

"Joseph Campbell."

My jacket hangs on the control panel. Its cuts are fused and scorch marks on the back scraped away like burnt toast. I put it on. The boy reloads the last of the shrapnel into the prison shotgun.

~

Black snow drifts from the sky, alighting on the corpses of the Children of Tendu revelers. The offshore breeze, also dead. In its place, the Santa Anas blow warm across the rooftop beach.

A white-haired man in a Hawaiian shirt goes from corpse to corpse searching the cultists like a villager looting dead soldiers left behind after a battle. He spots me and waves a ream of loose documents above his head.

"Excuse me!" he calls out, "Were you in charge, here?"

"Whoever that was is probably dead."

"Yeah... I can see that."

He kicks over a corpse... Plucks a boba from a puddle of spilt ayahuasca tea. Sniffs then licks it... Spits it out.

"Raw tapioca," he says, shaking his head. "Cyanide poisoning. Damn it!"

I say, "Who the fuck are you?"

"Javier Grillo-Marxuach. I'm a screenwriter. I'm here to serve an intellectual property lawsuit against the Children of Tendu."

"There's a lot of that going around lately."

"Back in 2024, Kent Light Yr. was a guest on my screenwriting podcast. Personally, I thought he was a talentless hack but he just sold a spec script for Shane Black kind of money... So my co-host Jose and I had him on as a guest."

"And?"

"The name of my podcast, it was called Children of Tendu. He stole the name of my podcast and build a cult around it without cutting me in on a first-dollar gross deal on cult profits."

He drops the legal papers on a random body, shrugs, and walks away. The Santa Anas carry the documents off to scatter about the city.

"Wait!" I call after him. "They worshiped Schmeezus!"

"So?"

"The cult is called the Children of Tendu... Who the fuck is Tendu?"

He laughs.

"There is no Tendu. It doesn't mean anything."

"I don't get it."

"It's before your time, kid. Back in 1995, there was a one-hit-wonder band called Dishwalla. Their song that everybody was singing that summer was *Counting Blue Cars.* Haha, I kind of misheard the lyrics. Here you go..."

He sings acapella.

Must have been late afternoon
On our way the sun broke free of the clouds
We count only blue cars, skip the cracks in the street
And ask many questions... like children often do...

I join him in the chorus...

We said, 'Tell me all your thoughts on God'
'Cause I would really like to meet her--

At that instant, Calliope's second drone splashes up from the infinity pool and strikes Javier down with lightning, scorching the sand beneath his sizzling husk into shards of black glass.

Calliope's drone doubles back by flipping into an Immelmann turn so crisp, the Gs would puree any human pilot's brain. The boy blasts it out of the sky, then tosses the shotty into the pool.

Lichtenberg figures blister across Javier's face. His expression, a grin of rapture.

He was a writer, so...

I find a UTI pen clipped in his shirt pocket.

~

The elevator opens on my floor, and light floods into our faces. A velvet rope blocks our exit. A hand stabs through the wall of light and lifts the rope. It's the VIP guard who cockblocked me at Jumbo's Clown Room.

The boy and I step out of the elevator and onto a red carpet. Reporters, fans, and photographers all scream for the kid's attention from the other side of the stanchions. It's impossible to discern individuals because it's like staring past the headlights of approaching cars to see the face of the drivers inside.

"Hooray, it's the boy! Nils DeShawn Trustfall-Falk! Look over here!"

As we make our way to my room along the red-carpet perp walk, the wall to our backside morphs into a media holoBoard with the logos of all the sponsors scrolling across: Pfizer-DARPA; Crackle; Hermes; Gazelles;

MacroHard Corporation, incorporated, Inc.; Rolls Royce; Toyota; Chapstick; FallState; Life Alert; Uber...

Sensory fucking overload.

"Let me get a word with you!"

The voice, engineered to command respect, isn't asking. This can only be one entity. Hope-RAH! ducks under the ropes and walks in lockstep with us. She foists a microphone with the TMI logo under DeShawn's nose.

She says, "DeShawn, who are you wearing?"

I hurry up and put my teeth in, then I give a 360° spin for the cameras.

I say, "Let's see, uh... Speedos... The Life Alert from a cult leader who claimed he's my dad, but who the fuck knows?... the pom-pom hat from some chick who got eaten by her snake... Gas station flip flops... Ex-wife's hoodie paired with a jacket I looted off some loser zapped by a plasma torch... Oh, and the Birkin bag is Hermes!"

The voice of a breathless woman behind us says, "Oh, FUCK yes!"

Rapid footsteps...

But in a pattern as confusing as fuck, because the footfalls are not quite right for two people, but they slap upon the concrete in a succession to quick and awkward to be just one.

I turn in time to see...

Bambi sprinting onto the red carpet, Chauncey's Flava Flav Life Alert clock from Jumbo's Clown Room swinging from her neck! Except... instead of running on her two legs, Marci Kruger gallops on three. The bottom half of her body is replaced by the bottom half of a securityBot... On her feet, a pair of Crocks and one rollerblade.

Marci with an "I" says, "I can't believe it! I never get invited anywhere!"

There's a smile stretched across her face, but like a latex Halloween mask, there's nothing in the eyes. As she runs, she raises the axe from Sal's freezer above her head, which she brings crashing down upon mine, hammer-side first!

The hammerhead strikes me on the pom pom and bounces off, ricocheting the axe end of the tool back to Marci to cleft her skull between her big blue eyes. The force knocks her off of her robofeet but momentum continues to carry her lower half forward. Marci, axe buried in her face, slams to the red carpet onto her back with a THUD! hard enough to raise dust. I lift the Life Alert clock from around the axe in Marci's skull, then I hang it around the boy's neck.

Balloons and confetti drop down from the ceiling.

Hope-RAH! steps over Marci and says, "This show is a hit! Congratulations on your new Vaunted status!"

"Well, shit... Frankly, I kinda forgot all about that."

Hope-RAH! crouches down in front of the boy.

She gushes, "Quite an epic adventure, little Nils!"

"Never call me that! I go by DeShawn."

"What's next for you, sweetie?"

The boy says, "I'm going to wash my ass. Here..."

He hands her the plasma torch. "...have a Crackle."

Hope-RAH! turns to the camera, holds up the torch and says, "Have a Crackle, indeed! This TMI coverage has been brought to you by our fine friends at Crackle!

'Crackle... The cleaner, colder, CRISPR taste!'"

She wraps her lips around the nozzle, and...

ZAP!

We catch up to Shonda and Sévérine. They're holding hands, standing on T-shaped marks taped onto the carpet. Shonda fields media questions like a pro.

Lance, the Unicorn plushieBot, spots the boy and gallops down the red carpet to his best friend. He leaps into his arms, and the boy cradles him like a football.

As tempting as it would be to sign the divorce papers in blood, I wipe the excess gore off, use Javier's pen, and hand them to Shonda.

She smiles.

"Thank you, DeShawn."

"Yeah."

Dave Chappelle rolls past us in a wheelchair.

Lance says, "Wanna read my screenplay?"

Dave gives him a card. "Sure... Why the fuck not?"

The boy lifts up his arms and opens and closes his hands. Shonda picks him up. Sévérine wraps an arm around Shonda.

Sévérine says, "Come by Sundays. We'll make it a family night."

I nod and smile. They continue down the red carpet without me.

The boy peeks out at me from over Shonda's shoulder.

"Go on," he says, "This is my story now."

END.

About the author:

Tyler Knight is an ultramarathon runner and multiple award-winning adult film star who has starred in over 300 films. His memoir, "BURN MY SHADOW: A Selective Memory of an X-Rated Life", was a 2020 Book Pipeline Adaptation Contest finalist. Tyler is represented by Ultra Literary in New York City. He lives in Los Angeles with his wife and parrot.

Twitter: @Artifice_Rex;
Discord: TylerKnight#5540;
Twitch: www.twitch.tv/TylerKnightGaming

Acknowledgements

If you're like many aspiring novelists, the first thing you do when you get your mitts on a book by an author whom you admire is to turn to its acknowledgments section. There, in the back of the book, you'll glean clues as to who were the midwives who helped your literary hero give birth to their weighty tome.

The beta readers who offered an extra set of eyes an honest opinions. The editors labored over the book to help refine and distill its content to a standard of clarity which is nothing short of alchemy.

The agent who will tell their writer to burn a book that just isn't working, so that the author may not waste another second on it, and instead use that time to summon a better one out of the ether… A book that, with no guarantees that the agent will ever make a dime off of the work, will stake their reputations to get the book in the hands of the perfect acquisitions editor.

And, the publisher who antes up vast sums of capital, labor hours, and sleepless nights to make sure the finished book finds its way to as many readers who may fall in love with it just like they did. These are my people…

Literary agent: Peter McGuigan, of Ultra Literary

Beta Readers: Bryn Pryor, and Chris Kelly

Publisher: Chris McVeigh Thank you, Chris, for plucking my novel manuscript from the slush pile, believing in its promise, and helping me to share it with the world. Fahrenheit could not possibly have been a better fit for this novel.

My wife, "Amanda"… You are my Tabitha to this wannabe Stephen King who nourished my soul, and pulled my version of "Carrie" out of the garbage bin and insisted that I send it out to the world. Te amo.

More books from Fahrenheit Press

The Beloved Children by Tina Jackson

Three young women; Chrysanthemum, Rose & Orage are thrown together on the stage of Fankes' Theatre during the closing days of the Second World War performing as The Three Graces.

It's there they come under the spell of wardrobe mistresses Dolores and Janna – a chance encounter that will guide and change all of their fates forever.

Set in the dying days of vaudeville theatre and laced with mysticism, fortune tellers, ghosts, and evocative descriptions of the closing days of the War - The Beloved Children will literally make you laugh out loud and perhaps even shed the odd tear.

The Beloved Children is wise, funny, heart-breaking, joyous, poignant, and entirely entirely enthralling.

"There is some really atmospheric storytelling and joyful language at play here, with Jackson as an entertaining mistress of ceremonies." - Ben East, The Observer

The Transit of Lola Jones by Jackie Swift

Debut author Jackie Swift brings some playfulness to the Fahrenheit list with this first book in a series featuring her eponymous hero Lola Jones.

It's fair to say Lola Jones' life is not turning out the way she expected it to.

As the book opens we find Lola recovering from the breast cancer that threatened to prematurely end her life and languishing in a police cell, the main suspect in the murder of businessman Daniel Blain.

As the truth begins to unfold about the events leading up to the untimely demise of the dashing Daniel, we learn more about the journey that brought the normally infectiously vivacious Lola Jones to such an unsatisfactory pass.

But is she guilty, and even if she is guilty, is she to blame?

This is a funny, smart, sexy, modern romp of a book and Lola Jones is a character that you'll instantly want to be your best friend.

Souljourner by Paul Steven Stone

Where to start with Souljourner? Let's start with the author - Paul Steven Stone is either a madman or a genius – probably both – and he's written one of the most gripping and enjoyable books we've ever come across.

It begins with a quote from Pierre Teilhard de Chardin

"We are not human beings on a spiritual journey, we are spiritual beings on a human journey." – and that my friends sets the stage perfectly for all that follows.

The novel, if it is indeed a novel (the narrator insists it is in fact a warning letter from your soul's previous incarnation and aimed directly at you dear reader) - as we will discover though, this narrator is often unreliable - so frankly warning or novel, you pays your money you takes your choice.

One of the central premises of the novel/letter is that our souls make their eternal journey towards enlightenment in the company of a single unchanging 'karmic pod' of companion souls who take on different roles in each of our incarnations.

In one life a soul may appear as your mother, in the next your best friend, in the next your sworn enemy, in the next your lover and so on for eternity. The identities of the souls in your 'karmic pod' are hidden from you in life – this letter/novel seeks to wise you up to who's who in your karmic pod to help you avoid making the same mistakes that landed the narrator, David Rockwood Worthington in prison serving a life sentence for murder.

Know Me From Smoke by Matt Phillips

Stella Radney, long-time lounge singer, still has a bullet lodged in her hip from the night when a rain of gunshots killed her husband.

That was twenty years ago and it's a surprise when the unsolved murder is reopened after the district attorney discovers new evidence. Royal Atkins is a convicted killer who just got out of prison on a legal technicality. At first, he's thinking he'll play it straight. Doesn't take long before that plan turns to smoke—was it ever really an option?

When Stella and Royal meet one night, they're drawn to each other. But Royal has a secret. How long before Stella discovers that the man she's falling for isn't who he seems? A noir of gripping suspense and violence, Know Me from Smoke is a journey into the shadowy terrain of murder, lost love, and the heart's lust for vengeance.

"A beautifully written, brutal & brilliant slice of hardboiled crime fiction. A Knockout."